2020

INJECTION

Ashley McCoury

ISBN 978-1-64670-840-6 (Paperback)
ISBN 978-1-64670-841-3 (Hardcover)
ISBN 978-1-64670-842-0 (Digital)

First Edition

Covenant Books, Inc.
11661 Hwy 707
Murrells Inlet, SC 29576
www.covenantbooks.com

STAGE 1:0

Seventeen years old today and my life is over. It hasn't been a great life, so I guess in all reality, it doesn't even matter. Today I will either be chosen to be a "carrier" of new life or I will be given the "injection." Either way, my life is over.

I stood before the large doors of the sanatorium with fear and anger welling up inside, which were emotions that were never spoken of, and I am not sure which outcome was worse. To be able to procreate was considered an honor, but the thought frightened me. The injection was inevitable; I would get it now because I didn't have the correct genes to bring forth a child or after I gave birth to the child. Like I said, "my" life is over.

I pushed open the doors to proceed into the white sterile hallways. My appointment had been set since my birth, always looming nearer and always weighing me down. A rather large registrar looked up from the paperwork on his desk with dead eyes and asked me, "Serial number?"

"2020," I replied quietly. I didn't look at him for long; dread was making it hard to push back the tears.

"Fill out these forms and press your hand into the pad on the wall for confirmation of serial number." His voice was without inflection or concern.

I looked up at the hand scanner on the wall and lifted my right hand to it. "Confirmed, 2020." I took the paperwork and sat down on the metal bench a few feet away. My hand shook slightly as I filled out the questionnaire.

"At what age did you have your first menstrual cycle?"

"Any pain during your menstrual cycle?"

"Have you remained untouched?"

On and on the questions went, each one more personal and cringeworthy. I knew to leave them unanswered or to lie would call for immediate displacement into the reformatory. No one ever came out of there. So each question was answered, and each question was horrible. I handed the paperwork back to the large lifeless registrar and sat back on the cold metal bench, waiting for my number to be called. I waited for what seemed like eternity until finally, a very large female medic called my number loudly.

Without a word, I stood and followed her quickly down the hallway. The lighting played games on the walls as we drew closer to the end of my life. We came to a small room; she took my blood and she told me to disrobe. I complied and stood cold and naked while she examined me.

Humiliation burned my cheeks. We were taught at a young age that the human body was nothing to be proud or ashamed of. It only worked or didn't work. That didn't stop my feelings of shame as the medic so thoroughly inspected me. I wasn't the typical female, my stature strong and slight, skin olive, hair a dark mass of waves with sea-green eyes. Average was best, and average was tall, slender, blond with blue eyes. People watched me in public as if I were freakish. Maybe I was. The exam took much longer than I would have liked, and I couldn't help the relief that came when I was allowed to place the white medical rob over my slight frame.

"The scientist will be in to speak with you soon," she said loudly.

I wondered if she was hard of hearing. Surely not; the medical community wouldn't allow a "less than" to work in this capacity. Once again, I waited. I knew when the door opened, my inquiries would be answered. The scientist opened the door rather softly. If I hadn't been watching, I wouldn't have even known.

"You are for the injection." No introduction, no explanation, just facts.

That is the way, I guess. I immediately felt both relief and horror. I would lose whatever "2020" was—the me that dreamed, sang songs when no one was around to rebuke it, drew pictures in the sand, laughed silently at the squirrels playing in the trees. My surrogate had given me a name: Alexandra. I didn't want to lose Alexandra.

Our guides at the establishment said numbers and uniforms made us all, male and female, equal a.k.a. the same, but I didn't want to be the same. I wanted to be me. The scientist was speaking again.

"You will return on the first day of your next menstrual cycle. We will perform the injection after you have been cleansed and incubated for five days," she said indifferently.

She left, and I dressed, hoping the chills would subside with the clothing back in place. I walked down the hallway, staring at the outlet sign above the exterior door. Maybe the sunlight had broken through and it would stop the chills. It didn't. Chills ran up and down my spine.

I should have been ready for this. I knew they wouldn't want me to be a "carrier." I was too different. I was too me. I didn't really even want to be a "carrier;" who wanted to be artificially inseminated, partnered with a male you had never met, and bear a child which you both had to raise until the age of five? Not me. Not Alexandra.

The injection was even more frightening, though. All my life, I had heard of the "primal times" before the injection when males ruled the earth and females were somewhat like subjects to them, before the injection was created to make us all "equal." Males received the injection at the age of twelve, and females at the age of seventeen, or they became "carriers," and then they got the injection. At the establishment, we are taught that the injection made our society great. It healed all mankind, it stopped all wars, and even stopped famine. What would I be once they took away all my emotions and everything that made me female? How did having no feelings make the world a better place?

Walking had turned into a slight jog, had turned into slow running, had turned into an all-out sprint. I'm not sure what I was trying to escape from; there was no escape. I rounded the corner of a building and slammed directly into a male who was carrying a folder full of paper.

STAGE 1:1

"What the?" he said breathlessly as the paper scattered around our entwined bodies. I landed hard on him, real hard.

"I'm so sorry," I cried. Crying was frowned upon. I tried to draw them back in, but the tears wouldn't cease.

"It's okay, really, I didn't want to deliver these anyway," he replied softly.

I couldn't meet his eyes. I heard his kind tone but knew indifference would lie in his eyes as it did with all humans after the injection. We pulled apart and slowly rose. I helped him gather his papers and placed them back in the folder and gave it to him. I looked up and saw empathy.

"Are you all right?" he asked gently. His wording and tone threw me off guard; no one asked questions like that.

"Um, yes, yes, I am adequate," I replied formally, trying to bring normalcy back into the exchange. The benevolence in his dark eyes was so uncommon and his concern even more so. Society was never angered (as they called it in primal times), but it wasn't overly concerned for others either. Young children were allowed to play and laugh and even fight somewhat, but after the age of twelve, that all ceased. The boys got their injections and the girls were prepared to be "carriers" or to receive their own injections.

"What are you running from?" he asked, looking back over my shoulder.

I felt chagrin. I was running from the inevitable—my future.

"Nothing, nothing." I replied shamefully.

"You sure are running fast from nothing," he said with a slight grin.

I couldn't help but watch him; he was obviously a grown male and had to have had the injection. Why was he smiling? A Unity officer interrupted my musings with, "Is there an issue here?" She asked with authority. With the presence of the officer, a blank veil came over the benevolent stranger's face. He was now common, vacant, and unfeeling like all the others. Maybe I had imagined the concern?

"Everything is fine, Officer," he stated stiffly.

I remained silent. I didn't want the officer to place me in confinement because of my emotions. It was "not a punishment" my guides had told me the first time I was placed in confinement; it was a time to gather one's self and quiet unruly emotions. I found it frightening and unbearable and vowed never to repeat the experience. My vow wasn't kept; my emotions showed so clearly on my face, but as I grew older, I became less frightened by confinement. I still hated the thought, though, and avoided it at all costs. My eyes locked with the stranger, and he seemed to read me like a book; a flash of understanding was there for a split second before the veil fell over once again.

"I am escorting this female to the establishment," said the stranger without care or feeling.

The officer took him at his word and turned to leave without a second thought. "She is leaving," he stated without need.

"Thank you," I said, not really knowing why I was thanking him but knew I had to.

"I'm 91285. From Establishment Area 7," he informed me. He was watching me differently than any man had ever watched me before, curious somehow. Freakish, always freakish, but men never stared, only the girls and only before the injections. "You are beautiful." he said softly.

I was at a loss for words. Males didn't say that; in fact, the word beautiful was primitive and unused. I had only read about the expression in the primal books. I finally looked, really looked at him. He was large, dark complexed, older than me and had kind green eyes, much like my own. If I knew exactly what beautiful was, I might have thought him to be such. I ignored his strange statement and instead asked him, "Why are you so far from your establishment?"

I wanted to speak with him but also did not want to have him so focused on me.

"How old are you?" he asked, ignoring me also.

"Seventeen. Today," I said, remembering why I was even there in the first place. I gathered all the strength I had not to allow my emotions to take hold at the thought.

"Now it makes sense," he replied with the slight grin I had spotted before.

"What makes sense?" I asked.

"The tears before. The fact that your face gives everything away. The fact that there is anything to give away at all," he said it as if it was a good thing and with a silent chuckle.

Laughter? What was happening? An adult smiling? Speaking with emotion? That was for children. "Will you be a 'carrier' or receive the injection?" he continued. If any other person had asked that question, it wouldn't have felt so personal, but with him, it went beyond wanting information; it went beyond me giving him facts in return.

I hesitated. "I will have the injection," I spoke with as much control as I could muster, which sounded hollow even to my own ears.

"Is that what you want?" he asked gently. I was so taken aback at the question that I felt as if I was dealing with a "less than." Maybe he broke out of confinement; maybe he was an escapee from the reformatory and was on the run from the Unity officers. His countenance was that of a child, not a full-grown man, not of one who had received the injection. No one would ever even think to ask me that question.

I could never verbalize how I felt about the injection; my thoughts, if voiced, would place me in the reformatory. Maybe this was some strange test that the guides set up for me because of my many visits to confinement. I shook my head in response, hoping this strange encounter would end; or did I? "I don't know what you mean." I behaved as if I didn't understand the question.

He saw right through my misdirection and continued on. "You were crying when you ran over me and you were frightened of the Unity officer." He stated it as if I was a child that wasn't understanding an easy concept.

"I want the betterment of mankind." I gave him the practiced answer. I was growing more suspicious with every word he spoke.

"I'm not going to dispatch the Unity officer if you give me your opinion," he said, reading the doubt on my face. Maybe the injection wouldn't be so bad; no one could read my face, and it would end the visits to confinement.

"I don't even know why you are here so far from your establishment. Why would I express an opinion? That is, an emotion, forbidden." I was trying to draw back to all I had been taught and stuff my raging emotions down.

"Fine, little girl, I'll escort you to the establishment and be on my way," he said with a twinkle in his eye.

I started to walk toward my dormitory, hoping he would give up and deliver whatever he needed to deliver and leave me to explore my thoughts about the imminent injection day. I was born in Establishment 3, one of the smaller establishments in the Sovereignty. Establishments were once known as schools or universities during the primal days. Now everything was based on the Establishment; the entire world seemed to focus on the enlightenment of the young generation. The Establishment was completely run by the Sovereignty; actually, everything was run by the Sovereignty. I loathed the Sovereignty, and the thought put unease in my heart.

Soon we were at my dormitory, and I turned to 91285. "This is my dwelling," I stated, pointing to the stairs that led to a dingy block building with a large poster of our current Sovereignty leader, Eleanor Palmer, hanging above my door.

"All right then, have a nice day," he said with one of his chuckles.

Have a nice day? The behavior was so out of the ordinary that I had no response before he sauntered away. "Very curious," I said to no one in particular. Once in my dormitory, I sat down quietly on the floor and tried to let go of any feelings of misgivings about the injection day. Maybe my cycle wouldn't come for an entire month. Maybe they would forget about me. I knew, though; I knew I only had three weeks before I would return and had to have all of "me" stripped from my vessel.

STAGE 1:2

I gathered myself and changed into new attire to attend the evening fare. All females had to be there earlier than males. We were allowed to be first in line every other day. This was our day; at least I had something to look forward to. The female population was exactly even to the male population, so the line was perfectly half and half. Not that it mattered, but I always noticed things like that.

I stood in my position for approximately five-and-a-half minutes before 0207 arrived. She was perpetually late to all things. She was one year and five months younger than me and full of life to those of us who hated the Sovereignty. To all else, she was nothing; just like everyone else, nothing. Her face was expressionless until she was hidden from cameras and the guides sitting at the tables against the walls, and then she broke out into a smile as bright as the sun. Normally the smile warmed me, but today it only made me remember that in one year and seven months, that smile would be no more, much like my own would be in less than three weeks.

"What's up, Chica?" she asked in her lighthearted manner. She loved to use ethnic terms. She loved reading. She loved learning about the primal times. She always said she was going to live life like she was going to be injected on the morrow.

I felt as if I was going to be injected on the morrow. *Might as well be*, I thought morosely.

"Did they knock you up or are you doomed to be one of the empties?" she asked, using the term she called those that had the injection.

"I'll be an empty soon," I replied humorously, trying to match her animation. It fell flat; it never quite reached her on a normal day anyway, and today was not normal. She said that in the primal days, humans celebrated on the days of their births; today was the worst day of my life, and I couldn't imagine wanting to celebrate it. Her smile only faltered for a split second before it was back in full force.

"Well, how long do I have with you before I lose the only person who laughs at my joshing?" she asked.

"Three weeks or so, the first day of my next menstrual cycle," I said.

"They should have made you a carrier. You would have looked funny waddling around with a kid in your belly," she laughed. It was all fun and games to her still or maybe she was hiding her fear behind jokes; either way, I didn't really want to stay on the subject.

"I met the strangest man today." I changed the object of discussion; 0207's meddlesome nature was on full alert. There was never ever "strange anyone;" everyone was exactly the same after the injection.

"Really?" she said inquisitively.

"He was a full-grown male, but he was very…expressive." I couldn't really put it into words. She seemed about to ask me more when the loudest noise I had ever heard came from the front of the building. Suddenly, all the windows along the front shattered; people were running for cover, and others were standing like myself in shock, wondering what had happened. Smoke started to pour in through the broken windows.

"What in blue blazes was that?" 0207 whispered to me.

"I'm not sure," I replied, walking closer to see where the smoke was coming from. Everything was quiet. It was very eerie; the stillness made my flesh tingle. The closer we came to the broken windows, the worse the smoke became. I heard what seemed to be fire cracking and bricks falling. One Unity officer and another and another and another ran by the empty windows as fast as I had ever seen anyone go; the children were the only ones who ran. 0207 was asking me something.

"What is happening?" she said breathlessly. This must have been grand to her. An adventure, she would call it.

"Head to the confinement area *immediately*," a loud voice said over the speakers.

I looked around and noticed the frightened children. The Empties seemed to be unfazed, but the children were cowering under tables.

"Let's head to confinement," I said, wanting this horrible day to be over. We turned around and headed toward the back outlet. As we walked, we gathered the young terror-stricken children around us.

"Come on, let's get you to the confinement area," I said.

"This way," said 0207, holding their hands and guiding them.

A word I had never had to use but I knew the meaning of from my primal books came to mind as we stepped outside: *Chaos*. Smoke, sirens, shouts, running feet, and crying children was what greeted us. 0207 and I froze, seeing that the way to the confinement area was blocked by a building that had fallen over; from what, I am not sure. A Unity officer came to our rescue and instructed, "Come this way." No emotion, just a command.

0207, the five children, and I followed after him. Taking in the total ruination, we kept close to the Unity officer. My own fear increased the more I took in. What was happening? Never in my seventeen years had I seen anything like this, the waste. It looked like pictures of primal day wars; destruction was everywhere. Emotions I had never before experienced danced around me, taunting me with new feelings of terror and shock. I felt odd; nothing, I repeat, nothing ever happened out of the ordinary. Every day was exactly like the day before. Wake up at 6:00 a.m., eat at the facility, report to classes, mid-day eating, report to more classes, then evening fare and lights out at 8:00 p.m. Once you reached eighteen, it only slightly changed. You then replaced class time with a vocation that you were assigned by the Sovereignty, which revolved around the establishment you were in.

We were following the Unity officer blindly when I noticed the noise was not as overwhelming and the smoke was clearing. I tried to see the large overpowering doors of the confinement area, but it seemed we weren't headed the right way.

"Where are you taking us?" I asked the officer.

He turned back to me, and I immediately recognized the male 91285 from earlier that day. "You are a Unity officer?" I said, astounded.

"No, but for your safety, I am dressed like one," he said with a chuckle. His eyes crinkled at the corners. He was much older than I first thought; I can't decipher age with all these expressions in the way. "Me a Unity officer, that's rich," he continued.

"Where are we going?" I asked. I looked to 0207 and the children. They were so quiet; I could hardly hear them breathing. *What must they think?* "Why aren't we headed to the confinement area?" I asked before he could answer my previous question.

"Well, to answer your first question, we are headed out of here before it gets worse. And to answer your second question, the confinement area is the worst place to be right now," he said with authority. He didn't answer the where, though, and I knew he purposely avoided it. "We better keep going before this thing gets really bad," he was saying as he began to jog in the opposite direction of the everything I knew.

"What thing? What is even going on?" I asked as we started to jog after him.

"I'll explain later, just keep up." He was carrying a small female on his shoulders now, but it didn't slow him down. We continued to follow. I'm not sure why. Maybe he was a part of the destruction of the Establishment. Maybe he was just a madman or maybe his kind smile was comforting, and that's why I didn't turn around and run away. Whatever he was, he was headed away from the danger, and honestly, that was the main reason I kept following.

We were out of the Establishment's boundary, and the trees were getting thicker and thicker. I had never been this far beyond the boundary. No one lived outside of the Establishment; you were allowed to leave the boundary but only until curfew. We travelled for what seemed like hours with not a word spoken before we came to a clearing, and I could see an immense door that came out of the ground. It reminded me of the confinement area. I hoped this wasn't our destination. It was.

He put the little girl down and walked up to the door and began turning knobs, pushing buttons, and pulling levers. A smaller door to the right popped open so quickly, I jumped back in surprise.

"This way," he said, urging us on with a hand motion.

The children seemed both frightened and curious. So did 0207, and I was more frightened than I cared to admit. As I drew closer to the door, my heart began pounding faster and faster. The times I visited the confinement area came to my mind, and my feet didn't want to move any closer to the door that was so much like the one in my nightmares.

The children and 0207 had disappeared into the door, and the male 91285 was watching me closely, waiting impatiently. "Come on," he said, "we need to get underground." My feet wouldn't budge. I wanted to move but I couldn't. "What's the hold up?" he asked, not understanding my dilemma.

"I c…can't," I stammered.

It seemed to dawn on him that I was frightened. He came toward me with his hand outstretched. "Here, take my hand. I won't leave you," he said with kindness. His hand was strong and calloused, warm; physical touch was so foreign to me, unnecessary really. I held on despite the newness of the sensation, and it calmed my raging fear. I took sluggish steps to the darkened door. Inside, it took several unnerving moments for my eyes to adjust to the dim light.

"I'm not in confinement," I kept telling myself over and over. Up ahead, I saw 0207 and the children surrounded by people I had never seen before. These new people were like aliens to me. Some of the males had hair as long as mine. The males and females had black markings covering their arms; tattoos, 0207 had told me once. *Outlandish* was the word that came to mind. In the Establishment, males and females were simple, nothing bright, hair always trimmed and tidy. Clothing was issued from the Sovereignty, all the same, male and female. These people were all so…different. Not only different from myself, 0207, and the children, but even different from one another. Not one was like the other.

"Colin, what have you brought to us?" asked a shaggy headed male in front of the group of the Outlandish.

"There was an attack on the Establishment like we suspected. I couldn't just leave them," replied 91285, squeezing my hand gently. Colin. The man had called him Colin.

"Well, we could have, but no, I guess you couldn't have," he said with a chuckle. "If only someone else would've blended in like you," he continued, shaking his head.

I couldn't help but squirm under their scrutiny; they seemed as curious about me as I was about them.

"I delivered the warning only hours before the attack, but I did try," Colin said dryly.

"And the other?" the shaggy headed man asked.

"Done," replied Colin.

I was interested to know what they weren't saying but was too afraid to ask.

The children looked frightened; I didn't know how to console myself much less them. I tried to remember the five short years I had with my sponsoring forbears in the privacy of our home. The female surrogate would always speak to me of bravery, kindness, of looking into people's hearts, seeing beyond the surface, and her male partner had her sent to the reformatory for it. I wanted so badly to help 0207 and the children but I didn't know how.

A female with long dark hair came forward and said, "You all can follow me, and I will find you a place to rest. I'm sure you are exhausted after that ordeal." She spoke with great kindness. I realized I was still clinging to Colin's hand. I reluctantly released him. My eyes met his, and he gave me a wink. Never having seen a grown male wink, it made me smile. We all followed the dark-haired woman down a long hallway to another large door. She typed into the keypad, and it opened with a whoosh.

"My name is Sabra," she was saying. "What are your names?" she asked. The children one by one started softly stating their numbers; finally, 0207 gave her number, and it was left to me. I almost wanted to say Alexandra, but I didn't.

"2020," I stated without emotion.

"Well, you all need real names. You should pick ones," she said.

We entered a hallway with extremely tall ceilings and all different kinds murals cover the walls and ceilings. We all were amazed at the different pictures surrounding us; it was like nothing I had ever seen. The children were whispering to each other their awe and bewilderment, and 0207 turned back to me and said, "What in the world?" She was almost breathless. This had to be the best thing for her to see; she treasured art above all things, and the only time we saw art was in the primal books.

We came to a large door covered with intricate carvings and ornate wrought iron handles and hinges. Sabra opened it up into a welcoming room filled with wooden chairs and tables. Each table had a vase filled with beautiful flowers. Along the walls were large comfortable looking couches, and in-between each couch, there were doors that opened up into bedrooms that were just as welcoming.

We paired the children up and sent them to a room to share. 0207 and I were sent into one such room that had large sunflowers painted on the walls and ceilings. All we could do was look around us in awe.

"Try to rest up before dinnertime," Sabra was telling us.

"Do you all have rooms in here?" I asked her, wanting to know where Colin would be. He was the only familiar face amongst this Outlandish crowd.

"No, we all have our own areas down the main corridor. This area is for new delegates." She spoke as if new people coming to their underground "lair" was common. "I will leave you both to rest. If you need anything, there is an intercom in the common area," she said as she walked away.

"What have we gotten ourselves into?" asked 0207 the second Sabra was out of earshot.

"I'm not sure," I replied at a loss.

"I can't believe there are people living outside of the Establishment boundaries, and they even seem to have avoided the injection," 0207 said. "Either that or they are immune," she finished.

"Maybe. These people are nothing like the Empties. Their clothes, hair, and even the markings on their bodies are so…unique," I replied. I felt so out of place even saying the words. I saw 0207's weary face and realized how exhausted I was also. I wanted so badly to lie down in the comfortable looking bed, but I knew I needed to check on the children first.

We went into each room and made sure they were settled and resting. Some had already fallen asleep while others asked us a million questions we didn't know the answers to. When we reached the sunflower bedroom, we both couldn't help but go back and forth with what had gone on that day. I realized, for the first time, my worry of the injection hadn't entered my mind in hours. My main worry now was, were these people the ones responsible for the destruction of Establishment 3?

STAGE 1:3

I woke hours later with a start; a red light was flashing, and an alarm was sounding.

"What is that?" I asked 0207 as she peered out our door.

"I don't know. No one is in the common area," she said, speaking loudly to be heard over the alarm. "Should we have called Sabra on the intercom?" she asked.

"Yes," I replied. I ran to the intercom on the opposite wall and said, "What is going on? Anyone there? Please answer me. What is happening?"

No answer. The alarm stopped. The door that left the common area into the large hallway burst open. It was Colin and a slightly younger man.

"What is wrong?" I asked, trying to keep the worry from my voice.

"The Sovereignty is on the lookout for the people responsible for the destruction of Establishment 3 today. Their scouts were within the two-mile radius and set off our alarm. We have to go into concealment mode and lockdown without communication until they pass. It might be a while, and I didn't want you all to be alone in here," he said. Lockdown sounded very similar to confinement. At least I wouldn't be completely alone.

"Are they looking for you?" 0207 asked the question that had snuck into my mind over and over.

"Did I bomb Establishment 3? No," he said with a shake of his head. He didn't seem to hesitate, but how was I to tell if he was lying? I had never seen an adult lie. No one lied. There was no need. They all received the injection, and emotions are what caused humans to lie either out of fear or anger, and the injection took those away. The younger male seemed to find it humorous and let out a slight laugh.

"Who did?" I asked. True, I hated the Sovereignty; but the people, the children, I couldn't condemn them to die along with the government that took and was going to take so much from me. They didn't deserve death and pain, even if they were Empties.

"Well, there is another group we have been watching for quite some time now, and they seem to be gaining in strength and numbers at an alarming rate. We call them Seditionist. They call themselves Surviorist. They are nothing other than bitter young kids causing mayhem," said the younger male I had never seen before.

"I'm Merek," he said to us.

The children had gathered around 0207 and me, holding on where they could. This must have been so frightening to them; I know I wasn't all warm and cuddly inside either. The younger male, Merek, was very imposing. He was massively built with arms larger than my legs and dark hair that fell to his shoulders. His body was covered in leather, and knives were placed in several different locations along his leg; not only that, but he had hair growing out of his face! He seemed almost like an untamed animal. His eyes were a piercing green and taking us all in.

"You will be safe here. The Sovereignty can't find us once we go into concealment mode," he continued without a worry, it seemed. I didn't know who I was more afraid of—the Sovereignty or these new people.

"Shouldn't you send us back?" asked the small male 22507 who was maybe nine or ten years of age.

"Do you want to go back?" asked Colin gently.

"Why would anyone in their right mind want to return to the Establishment?" interjected Merek.

I wanted to defend the small boy but remained silent. In case I decided to try to leave these people, they wouldn't watch me as closely.

"I understand, little man, it's all you've ever known. I'll tell you, though, that right now, this is the safest place from the Seditionist. They aren't done with their destruction," said Colin. He seemed to know quite a lot of the Seditionist plans. I wanted to ask how he knew these things and get more details, but again, I also didn't want to know so much that they wouldn't let me go when this bloodshed was over.

"How did you all avoid the injections?" 0207 asked. I am sure that it had been burning in her mind since we arrived.

"We didn't exactly avoid it. It wasn't offered to us," said Merek ironically.

His answer only confused me more.

"Why wasn't it offered?" asked 0207, obviously having found her voice.

"That is story for another time," said Colin, dismissing her inquiry. He went to a cabinet along the back wall and opened it up to reveal very colorful fruits, nuts, and vegetables. He motioned us all to sit at the tables, and I helped him pass out dried apricots, apples, almonds, and cheese. I sat down beside 22507 and began to eat. I realized then that it had been hours since my fare time had been stopped short by the Seditionist, and I was ravenous. The children were also devouring the food before them at an alarming rate.

Merek sat in the chair between 0207 and me. He filled the small chair to overflowing and blocked my view of my companion. 0207 leaned forward and gave me a look of annoyance. I tried not to smile at her irritation. We ate quietly. That was the way of the Establishment, no unnecessary words; the two males seemed uncomfortable.

A few times, one would ask a question and then try to start "small talk," as 0207 had once told me it was called, but none of us knew how to do frivolous things like that. We finished eating in silence, and I had time to consider my own thoughts. My main questions all seemed to be unanswered, such as "Who are these people? How were they not injected? Who are the Seditionists? And why were they destroying Establishment Area 3?"

"How long will we be in lockdown?" I asked, thinking that a safe question.

"Not sure. Could be an hour more, could be a few days," replied Merek. I didn't feel comfortable speaking with Merek. He was overwhelming compared to any man my own age. Colin was also very… masculine, unlike any man I had been around in the Establishment.

"Do we have to stay in this area?" asked 0207.

"Unless there is an emergency, yes," said Colin.

"What is an emergency?" asked 22507 from my side. Not many emergencies happened in the Establishment, so I understood his confusion.

"You know, like someone getting hurt or us running out of food, that kind of thing," replied Merek with a hint of annoyance, I think. 22507 seemed satisfied with the answer, got up, and went to the table where the children were talking softly amongst themselves. Merek patted my hand in comfort as he walked away; strange. It was kind but strange.

"I know this all must seem insane, and it kind of is, but just know we won't harm any of you," Colin told us. I wanted to believe him, but with everything that was going on around us, I didn't know what to believe. "Merek and I will stay with you all until the lock-down is lifted," he continued.

"How many people were hurt in the attacks on the Establishment?" asked 0207.

"We only know rough details right now, but the death toll is up to 198 last we heard," said Merek.

I felt sick, and by the look on her face, so did 0207. The population of Establishment Area 3 was only at 2,000. that was 9.9 percent of our population gone.

"What is the purpose of such slaughter?" I asked.

"Just plain revenge, I guess. Their purpose is unclear," Colin replied. The males began telling us of their underground bunker, explaining the security measures and the many different areas. They had what they called a "mess" hall where they gathered to eat. I guessed they had to be messy if they called it such. They had a lab for sickness and research. They also had a gym for physical exercise and training. They each had their own apartments for living that was separate from each other.

Merek and Colin didn't seem to agree on anything. They argued about the size of the oven in the mess hall; they argued about who's apartment was larger; they argued about how long they thought the lockdown would be. The strangest thing about their arguing was the smile they both had in place the entire time. I wasn't sure if they were upset with each other or happy. It was all so confusing.

"Were you to be injected or be a carrier?" Merek interrupted my musing with a question that seemed irrelevant now.

"I would have gotten the injection. I suppose if we return, I'll still get it," I replied with mixed feelings.

"Well, you all can't go back now anyway. You have seen our fortification. We can't let you return," said Merek.

We were prisoners. My eyes swung to 0207, and I knew her terrified expression reflected my own.

"What Merek is trying to say, and I wanted to explain this later after you had been here awhile, is that we can help you all to have a better life without the injection, and right now, here is the safest place you can be. All ten establishments were under attack today, not just Establishment 3. Even if you return, they may send you to the reformatory, thinking you to be traitors," Colin told us remorsefully.

So what options did we have as prisoner here or a prisoner at the Establishment? I dared not look at 0207 again, afraid to see the fear there.

STAGE 1:4

The lockdown continued well into the morning, or at least I thought it was morning; inside these walls, there was only artificial lighting and no clocks in the area where we were stationed. They told us to try to get rest, but I for one couldn't sleep knowing I was a prisoner within this hole in the ground. 0207 came into my room sometime before the children began to wake, and we discussed what we should do.

"Do you believe them?" she asked me.

"They have no reason to lie, I suppose. We can't break out of this place, and even if we could, I'm not sure how to get back to the Establishment or what's left of it. What do they gain by lying to us?" I asked her in return. I didn't think them to be lying, but I also felt as if they weren't exactly telling us everything either.

"I don't know what we should do." 0207 voiced my own uncertainty.

"I am also at a loss. I am not sure we have any true options anyway," I told her.

"Maybe it won't be so bad. They seem so emotional, and you can see everything on their faces. Besides, the Sovereignty has never been my favorite nor your own," she said.

"I know that, but at least we were safe," I returned.

"*Were*. *Were* being the key word. You saw what I saw right?" she asked me. "There was destruction and death all around us when we fled, remember? We saw with our own eyes that the Establishment is no longer safe."

"That is true," I said, knowing she was right. Colin may very well have saved our lives. Leaving was a moot point; we were here, and as far as I could decipher, this was the best option right now. "We should place close attention, and if there is anything that indicates they may hurt us or the children, we have to find a way to go back no matter the destruction." I spoke very softly, knowing very well someone could be listening in.

STAGE 1:5

We cleaned up as well as we could in clothes that had many miles and a few days' worth of wear on them. The lockdown was lifted, and Colin assured us that everything was safe again and we could now go to meet Justin properly. Who Justin was and why I wanted to meet him was a mystery.

I walked behind Merek, Colin, and 0207; funny how numbers for identification always bothered me after reading the primal day books, but now it was even more out of place here in this strange place where laughter rang and people argued. I glanced back to check on the children safe in Sabra's hands; or at least I hoped so. I felt as if this Justin would determine my fate, not so unlike my visit to the Sanatorium to learn my fate from the scientist.

We traveled down the enormous hallway that probably connected everyone's apartments; the massive hallway seemed to have no end. We passed so many colorful people—large, small, dark, white, tan, short hair, long hair, no hair; it was incredible! And it all reminded me of being in a dream. I couldn't see 0207's face, but I knew she had to have a look of wonderment and awe.

We came to a large wooden door with an inscription over it in a language I didn't comprehend. After a loud knock, we were escorted into the inner room. It was overbearing with its dark walls, oversized wooden desk, bookcases overflowing with books, and plants that needed water or just care in general. The shaggy headed man we had met when we first arrived sat behind a large desk.

"Oh, hello there, ladies," he said with a smile. "How has your stay been? Have Colin and Merek taken good care you all?" he asked.

"Our stay has been comfortable," I replied.

"Yes, it has been adequate," said 0207.

He seemed amused by our answers, but I wasn't sure why. "Good. Good. I am Justin, I run this place, so to speak." he said. "Normally, when we have newcomers brought into our little fold, we have them vetted," he continued in a thoughtful tone. "We are making an exception for you all under the circumstances. However, I'd like to get to know you both and also let you know a little about what we do here. I will start off with telling you a little about our goals here," he said as he motioned for us to sit and waved Merek and Colin to leave.

"Our purpose is to find a cure for the injection and start a new world where life is enjoyed. Art, music, and drama are back where people have free will to choose and are not just empty vessels that follow the Sovereignty blindly," he stated with a somewhat zealous air.

"Are we allowed to leave?" I asked with some annoyance, knowing full well the answer but wanting to point out the irony of his last statement.

"I'm sorry, no," he replied matter-of-factly. "You aren't a prisoner, but we can't allow you to return knowing as much as you do," he said. What I knew, I wasn't even sure.

"What about this free will you just spoke of? If you keep us here against ours, how are you any different than the sovereignty forcing us to take the injection?" I asked him, feeling angered at his lofty ideals that obviously held no weight.

He laughed, not rudely, but more a soft chuckle that said I knew nothing of what I spoke. "You are not wrong, little one, but in times of war and change, sacrifices must be made," he said, shaking his head. "You all must stay with us for your safety as much as ours."

"I guess we aren't left with much choice," said 0207 sarcastically. After the destruction of the Establishment, I should have been happy to be safely underground, but I just couldn't bring myself to trust them.

"How old are you both?" he asked, ignoring 0207 entirely.

"I am seventeen, overdue for my injection, and 0207 is fifteen. What will we do if we must stay here?" I asked. In our establishment, there was never an idle day, yet I couldn't imagine these Outlandish people would have much for us to do.

"You will rename yourselves and then you will begin learning about the truth," he stated.

I was curious about this so-called "truth" but felt I had already pushed him with my earlier questions.

"We have a school not too different than the establishment that you all will begin to attend at your respective age levels and learn our ways and prepare for your futures here."

"Your futures here" sounded so final and permanent.

"You will be allowed to choose your area of interest, as we all do here, once you have a better understanding of what we do." He dismissed us with no further questions.

STAGE 1:6

The next morning, I was ushered to a lecture room not so different from what I knew at the Establishment. It held many desks and shelves covered in books with one large desk centrally located for the guides to instruct us. There were only eight other inhabitants in the lecture room, and they each were unique and vibrant. I turned around to try to retrace my steps back to my shared dwelling with 0207, but Merek blocked my way with a frown.

"Making a run for it?" he asked, grinning somewhat.

"Um, no, I was not sure this was the correct lecture room," I lied. Lied; this place was already changing me into an emotional liar. I had hidden my feelings before but never out and out lied. I felt another foreign emotion—guilt. I caught his look of doubt and knew he didn't believe me anyway.

"It doesn't matter," he said, rolling his eyes. "You are in the correct lecture room, and today we are testing to see where we are most gifted to better be able to decide what field to go into for our futures," he finished.

"Okay, thank you," I replied, not really caring or knowing what my future held. It all seemed so uncertain after the attack on the Establishment. I sat down in a vacant desk, and Merek sat down right beside me. I'm not sure if he sat beside me to reassure me or make sure I didn't bolt out the door.

"Our instructor, Abia, should be here any second to get the exam started. Don't cheat, it's not graded," he informed me. I knew what cheating was, but there was never a need to cheat, at least not in the Establishment.

Abia walked in with her hair braided in a multitude of braids, a brightly colored blouse with a lot of skin showing, pants that flowed as she moved, and she was barefooted. Oh, could she move! It was so graceful and elegant. She seemed to glide across the room to her desk. I watched her in awe, and then she turned to me with a wonderful smile.

"Good morning, marvelous urchins," she said loudly. "We have new blood today. Please stand up and introduce yourself, young lady," she said sweetly.

I had a moment of panic. Should I introduce myself with the number that I was to the Establishment or the name my surrogate gave me?

"Hello, I am Alexandra. I just arrived before the lockdown and am now here to stay." That's all I knew to say; pointless chatter wasn't something I was familiar with.

"Like the new name," Merek whispered with a grin. I ignored his comment.

"Thank you! Perhaps you can stay after the exam and chat with me?" Abia said with a kind smile.

I wasn't sure what we would chat about, but I hated to refuse her, so I nodded my head in agreement. She began passing out the exam and pencils. Once I had it in my hand and looked it over, it almost seemed frivolous. The questions asked how I felt, what I enjoyed, and what I would do in this situation. I didn't know what to answer. I answered as best I could and handed it in to Abia.

She looked up and smiled. "Well, that was fast. I will let you know your results in the morning, and you can then decide what area to focus your studies on," she said.

"Am I free to leave?" I asked her.

"Why, yes, we will chat another day when class isn't in session," she said jovially.

I had only been in the lecture room for two hours before I was once again returning to my dwelling. I was glad to be able to be in the slightly more familiar once again. Everything was so different here, but I hated the life I was about to be dealt in the Establishment. My body shivered with just the thought of being injected or becoming a carrier. Although I wasn't sure of these people, I had hope that they would at the very least let me be me. I vowed to learn their ways and watch closely for a hidden agenda; I knew that at the present, my emotions were still not welcome and had to be hidden. My entire existence had been trying to do that very thing and failing, but this time, I had to succeed; it truly might be life or death.

STAGE 2:0

Weeks passed, and my exam results came back, saying I had potential to be a mathematician, which I didn't question, and I was to report to a large lab every day to learn to analyze data of clinical trials. The days seemed strange, and each one slightly different then the day before, but I fell into a sort of routine going to classes and trying to keep watch of the few children I brought with me. I watched the Outlandish interact. I listened to the Outlandish converse with one another, the way they dressed, and some with the intricate drawings painted on their bodies. They seemed to be exactly as they said: People wanting freedom from the injection and the Sovereignty.

0207 named herself Kasi, and she adapted well to our new environment, speaking freely as they did, laughing loudly and never hiding how she felt anymore. She trusted too easily, but then she had never had reason not to. Every time I wanted to trust these Outlandish people, I remembered my kind surrogate being hauled off by the Unity officers after her male partner reported her to the Sovereignty, and I couldn't bring myself to trust. I thought more and more of her as of late. She would have fit so well within this compound; I could imagine her with bright clothing and a smile that outshone most people. I wondered if she had somehow overcome the injection. I remember how she would calm me during thunderstorms, softly speaking my name over and over.

"Good morning, Alexandra," Colin said cheerfully. He was my instructor for lab analysis and seemed to try every day to make me laugh or smile. Those things weren't easily done for me. I wanted to believe these people, but it was difficult. Through the lectures every day, I couldn't help but watch Colin closely. He seemed so at ease as if the world above us wasn't going mad, as if he had no cares at all, not like the Empties without emotion but more…content.

I sat down at a table full of Outlandish close to the same age as me but didn't interact with their bantering. Times like these made me feel so out of place here. I then sat, wondering if staying in the Establishment wouldn't have been better, even with the injection. However, immediately I put away the notion, remembering the pure terror of losing myself to the injection. Several of the Outlandish would try to start up conversations with me, but my totally inept responses soon bored them, and they would go on to new conversations with each other.

"Today we are doing a little something different," Colin interrupted my thoughts. "Today we are going to review what brought us to this underground bunker in the first place. Does anyone remember from their earlier edification the cause of the Great Synthetic War?" he asked with one eyebrow raised. I knew the answer I would give if I was in the Establishment, but surely here, they would have another explanation than "human emotions," so I remained silent.

Three of the Outlandish raised their hands; the rest seemed to speak without permission, and Colin waved them to be quiet and called on a girl that looked to be a great warrior.

"Well, if you want to boil it down to the cause, it would be control. If you want to blame someone directly, you would blame Dr. Marian Crawford. She and her research team came up with the injections, and many believe the idea to start the war in order to make everyone take the injection. They had the bunkers built that we are now in and many more. These bunkers are protection against nuclear attacks and chemical warfare of any kind. They required all who wanted to be safe from the pending war receive the injection before they could find safety in these bunkers. Thus, gaining control of the undesired hormones that cause emotion and all those who lived through the Great Synthetic War," she finished, looking very proud of her herself.

I was taken aback. Yes, I knew of Dr. Marian Crawford, but in the Establishment, she was hailed a hero who saved lives and prevented future wars, not a manipulative megalomaniac or a corrupt scientist. A million questions ran through my mind, but I remained silent to see if they would reveal more of the story.

"Short and sweet version, but yes, that sums it up, thank you," said Colin. "Now do you all know the reason Dr. Marian felt she needed to gain control of hormones on such a level?" he asked.

I heard many responses being spoken from no one in particular in the classroom. "Bipolar disorder;" "Abusive father;" "Her mother took her own life."

Colin kind of shook his head with a smile and said, "All good answers. Can we have a little order? Alexandra? Do you know the history of Dr. Marian's personal life?" he asked me.

He didn't call on me often. I wondered if he was testing me somehow. "Only details about her creation of the injection. I never thought to research her personal life," I replied.

"Understandable. Here in the bunker, we like to know the why. We believe that people don't just act on a whim but instead have been conditioned to act from their past experiences. I know this isn't behaviorism class, but this applies to our understanding of why the injection was created in the first place and may help us also find a way to cure it," he finished, and every person in the class seemed to agree. I did too, but I didn't completely understand either.

The remaining time in the class was spent solving equations, running scenarios, and calculating data. I relaxed doing these things that I knew. I must have gotten lost in my work. I looked up, and I was the only pupil left. Colin was eyeing me from his oversized desk. He smiled when we made eye contact.

"You enjoy equations very much, don't you?" he asked me.

"Yes, they are like a puzzle to me," I replied.

"Good. How are you adjusting to life here?" he inquired. My gut response was to say fine, like we all do if asked anything about our feelings in the Establishment, which wasn't often, but I didn't want to be that way anymore. I would have to have a little trust if I wanted to adjust to this life. Colin did save my life after all; if I couldn't trust him a little, I might as well find a way to leave.

"It is strange." I didn't know what else to say; strange seemed to describe it so nicely.

"I'm sure it must be, and I hope I can help you to adjust easier. I have been tasked with bringing you all up-to-date on our life and goals here. I know you have been here for a little over five weeks now, but we didn't want to overwhelm you to start, so we will put you all in a slightly vigorous training program now. It will be to help fill any gaps you may have, such as self-defense, the truth about the primal times, and a few other things," he said.

"Can you tell me if there is any news about Establishment 3?" I asked. There had been no news about the attacks since the day we met Justin. I wasn't sure if they were keeping us in the dark or if they were also in the dark down here in this old bunker.

"Only bits and pieces. The Unity officers seemed to have captured the few Seditionist that were egotistical enough to stay in the establishments after the attacks, and they had them sent to the reformatory. The Sovereignty is conducting an investigation, hoping to find the leaders, but they won't find anything. The Seditionist are very good at concealment, which makes me wonder if they wanted some of their people to be sent to the reformatory," he mused.

I knew nothing of the Seditionist, so I had to take his word for it.

"I wish I could give you more information, but we have to remain underground and hidden until things cool down, so to speak. We haven't even been in contact with our emissaries within the Establishment since the attacks," he continued.

"Kasi and the younger children seem to be adjusting well to life here. What holds you back, Alexandra?" He changed the subject so quickly, I felt off-balance. "I have watched you closely with your people. You smile, laugh, you sing songs to the little ones, wipe tears away, and even have long conversations with them. Yet with us, you almost seem as if you did receive the injection. You hardly make eye contact, answer most questions with yes or no. I understand that you do not know what to think about us. However, I feel like we have proven that we are who we say we are."

He almost seemed to be pleading with me. I knew that I didn't trust easily, but you couldn't change seventeen years of mistrust in a matter of weeks.

"You aren't in the Establishment anymore. We want you to be able to be yourself here," he finished.

"I understand, and honestly, I am trying, but I am very much out of my element here," I tried to explain. His genuine kindness made me want to explain, even though I wasn't required to. He always unbalanced me with his strong emotions. "I don't know how to have emotions with anyone older than I am," I added lamely. Children were safe. Children didn't judge or report you to the Unity officers.

"There is no reformatory here. There is no confinement here. If someone does something truly offensive, we take it to the council of elders, and they vote and decide what's to be done. Usually a fine or at the worst displacement. We don't try to control you or force you to believe what we believe, but I would like to get to know you. You have done extremely well on all your data analysis, and I want to give you more important work. However, I can't until I know I can trust you," he said. "Tell me about yourself," he inquired.

What to say? I knew I could spout off facts about my life, but I also knew that wasn't what he was asking. "I never believed the injection was a good thing. From a very young age, I saw that it only stripped away the bad along with the good, leaving nothing but emptiness," I confessed. "I believe what you all are trying to achieve here may be a noble thing, but trusting comes very hard for me," I ended.

"Why is that?" he asked.

I didn't want to answer him but felt I did owe him some honesty for saving my life. "My surrogate was betrayed before my eyes, sent to the reformatory for…showing me affection." I simplified it, yes, but I didn't want to go into a lengthy explanation and speak of things that should have long since left my mind.

"I see," he replied. And I could tell by his expression he truly did see. "I grew up in the Establishment. I was eleven years old when I was kidnapped from my dormitory and eventually ended up here. It was the best thing that ever happened to me. Life here is crazy, unorganized, and slightly intense, but it is really living, which is so much better than anything I ever had in the Establishment," he said, smiling.

I was starting to understand that, but the total chaos sometimes knocked me off kilter. I returned his smile and admitted, "I see that and I will try to be less like an Empty."

His eyebrows rose. "An Empty?" he asked.

"That is what 0207…I mean, Kasi and I call the residents of the Establishment after they receive the injection," I told him.

He laughed. "That is perfect!" he said with a wide grin. The conversation came to a close, so I picked up my books and placed them in the leather satchel Merek had brought me a week before and started to head to the door.

"Be ready. Tomorrow, training begins," Colin said as I waved goodbye. I nodded, even though I had no idea how to "be ready," and headed to my room.

STAGE 2:1

Training began with a veracity I had never experienced before—knives, guns, swords, sticks, arms and legs became learned weapons. Every day, we ran a different obstacle course followed by weight training, weapons class, and we still were asked to attend our regular courses. Every night, I made sure the children were asleep in their beds, and I then proceeded to make for my own bed. The nights seemed like a blink of an eye, and the days seemed to never end.

Merek was one of our many instructors, definitely one of the more impressive ones. He was an expert marksman, could wrestle anyone who dared challenge him, threw knives into targets that seemed ridiculously far away, and he was the fastest at the obstacle course by far.

Day twenty-nine of training, things began to come together for me. I could run the obstacle course faster than anyone in training, I was undefeated in my weight class for wrestling, and my marksmanship was breaking records for a trainee; not Merek's records, but still…

"Today, we try something new," Merek said to the trainees. "Today we fight without armor and with whatever you can find in the obstacle course. The rules are simple. You must be the only one to cross the finish line. In order to fight against the rising oppression of the Sovereignty and now the Seditionist, we must above all know how to defeat our enemy in every way. I will pair up the fighting combatants, and we shall begin," he finished.

This was very different; everything prior had been very structured and monitored. This seemed very out of the ordinary from the past twenty-nine days of training. Merek was writing the competitors' names on the blackboard. I was third to go with someone named Don. I didn't converse much with my fellow trainees, so I didn't even know how big he was or his weaknesses.

"You are not allowed to watch the competition. Please exit the training facility until we call your name," Merek informed us.

"Strange that we can't even watch," said Kasi as we left the training facility and waited outside.

Kasi didn't seem impressed with the training. It wasn't that she was incapable but more that her interests were elsewhere. She enjoyed her art and primal studies so much that it was almost all she ever talked about, except Merek; she did talk about Merek quite a bit. I usually changed the subject, because speaking about the opposite sex was so very confusing. In the Establishment, the only relationship you could have with the opposite sex was if you were a surrogate, and then it was only in a partnership type of situation. In the bunker, I did notice that the men seemed to favor the women, opened doors, helped them with heavy things, and even let them go first in line. In training, we all trained the same, but men treated the women with thoughtfulness outside of training. They also called themselves "couples" here in the bunker, holding hands, living together, and I even saw some "kissing" in a dark corridor once.

Kasi had begun devouring every "romance" novel she could lay her hands on, novels we didn't even know existed until we came here. Each novel had some "love story" and adventure inside, and she raved about them, always speaking of the primal times and how love and passion were such a beautiful thing. I didn't dwell long on those things. My days were too full, and my nights were spent trying to recover from them.

I enjoyed training so much more then I could've imagined. The exertion, the skill required to hit moving targets, and the pure adrenaline rush with every new challenge made me feel more alive than anything ever had. I still enjoyed my calculations classes, but training brought me to life. I discovered that not only did I enjoy it, but I was truly good at it also. I felt so much stronger and less like an Empty somehow.

We waited what seemed like forever before the next group was called. I saw the first combatants exit bruised and bloody, everyone hovering around them, asking questions, but they seemed unable or unwilling to answer and walked away in defeat.

Once my name was called, I felt the familiar rush of adrenaline and headed back into the training facility. Merek met me at the entrance to the obstacle course standing beside a wiry young man close to my own age, Don.

"This is a test of endurance, intelligence, and ingenuity. Neither of you may leave until one is unable to cross the finish line and the other does. Along the obstacle course are many hidden weapons and challenges that you have never experienced so far in training. Remember, only one can finish."

His instructions weren't instructions at all, it seemed, as if anything was permissible, and that was very out of the ordinary. I was completely confused by this drill up to this point. Everything had been not to destroy people that had the injection but defend ourselves against them and find the cure for it.

I stepped into the obstacle course and waited for the drill to begin. There were multiple starting points in the course, and I couldn't see my combatant Don anywhere. I had to get a weapon, proceed to the finish line, and disable Don. *Why* kept running through my head. This isn't what the Outlandish claimed to be; they claimed to desire a cure and not destruction. Fear welled up. What if they weren't what they claimed? What if they were the group that caused the attacks on the establishments? I couldn't become like the Establishment, but I couldn't become like the group that attacked them either. There had to be a better way.

All these thoughts were running through my head when I heard the loud ring of the bell signaling that our strange competition had begun. The lights were very dim, and there was a high frequency ringing that hurt my head from its intensity. I looked around, trying to locate something that could defend me against Don. I began by checking all around for a weapon before I proceeded to the wall that I had to climb. Nothing. I scaled the wall as quickly as I had ever done, hoping Don didn't come up behind me and drag me down. Once I was safely over, I scanned the room I had dropped into and realized I was alone. This room was a kind of cell that you had to find a way out of. My first time, I took thirty minutes before I escaped on the brink of terror. Small spaces reminded me of confinement, but after over two weeks of fighting my fear, I went straight away to the locks on the door, hoping to get out before Don came and we were confined in this small space together.

The locks were all changed and new from the last time I had been inside the cell, but I didn't let the terror take over. I concentrated on the escape route while listening for any sound that would indicate Don was near. I could hardly tell with the high-pitched frequency that was buzzing in my ears. The locks may have been new, and I may not have had any tools, but I pulled a pin that was holding back my overly waving hair and began to work on my escape. My hands shook with adrenaline, but I pushed my breath in and out, calming my nerves to remain steady. This had to work. I did not want to confront my competitor without a weapon. I didn't want to confront him at all, really.

The sounds of footsteps alerted me to his presence, and I worked furiously to get out and lock him in before he scaled the wall behind me. The door popped open in silence, and I rushed to close it behind me, listening for the satisfactory click of the lock. This room before me I had never experienced; there seemed to be no exit and junk thrown about in disarray. It smelled of week-old trash that made me want to gag. I needed to search through the garbage before me and find an escape and hopefully a weapon.

I took a deep breath and began digging through trash, trash, trash, stood up to take a deep breath, trash, trash, trash. Don was working loudly on the locked door behind me. I rushed as fast as I could without missing anything. Finally, after what seemed like hours, I found a wire, a hammerhead, and a thin pipe. I didn't want to waste any more time searching for a weapon and looked around for an exit instead. Nothing.

I started by running my hands along the edges of the floor and then went up the creases of the wall to no avail. I inspected the ceiling, hoping to find my escape there; nothing stood out. Then from the corner of my eye, I saw a flash of light where the ceiling met the east wall. A crack! I quickly piled the trash together to create a mound tall enough for me to reach the ceiling. With the back of the hammer head, I started prying at the crack, rushing to escape before Don did, and one of us had to be incapacitated.

This didn't seem right, fighting against Don; even if he represented the Empties, I wouldn't be trying to kill him. I would be trying to cure him. I pried open the ceiling, kicked down my mound of trash, and climbed through the small opening, closing it behind me. Don was still working on the locks. I could hear him fumbling around at the door and hoped he wouldn't notice the ceiling crack when he did escape the cell.

Coming up into the next room, I was blinded by light and water reflecting even more light. I had come up in through a hole which brought me onto an island surrounded by blinding water, I immediately began to perspire, my clothes sticking to me in odd places; this heat was almost unbearable. I couldn't decide if I should jump in and swim around, looking for escape, or if I should wait and see if the room changed with the rolling waves.

I looked around, hoping to see something other than white walls and water that would indicate an exit, but I knew it wouldn't be that easy. If only I had more time, I could wait, but I knew Don had to be close behind, so I jumped in, ignoring my misgivings. The water was as warm as bath water and only made my uncomfortable state worse. I ignored it and began swimming to the wall in front of me. I heard Don long before I reached the wall and knew he had caught up to me, and I had to decide what to do about good ole Don.

I kept swimming, not looking back, and hoping he was a slow swimmer. I held my breath and went under the surface of the water so that I could swim even faster. Once under, the world seemed to tilt, and I knew something had changed. I popped back up to see things dropping from the ceiling high above. Large dangerous things if they were to hit me, I dove back under, hoping the water would protect me. I opened my eyes, and the saltwater stung. That's when I saw him—Don in the water with a red haze around his head. Something hit him, and he was limp as a doll.

The choice seemed to have been made for me. I had won, I thought ruefully, and kept swimming. I reached the wall and felt for a ledge. I looked back in the direction of poor Don and saw that the island had completely immersed with water; surely, they were watching and would rescue him, but I wasn't sure, so I knew I couldn't leave him. I dove down, searching for him. There was Don. I grabbed him under the arms, pushed off the bottom, resurfaced, and noticed the large objects had stopped falling. I pulled him over to the wall, bobbing up and down, trying to find an exit. My breathing was in quick bursts. I was losing strength and stamina quickly. I had to find the exit if I was going to keep us both alive. To leave him would save me, but I just couldn't bring myself to let go.

My foot hit something like a latch. I had to place Don somewhere while I dove down and inspected the lock. With my free hand, I grabbed the wire I had acquired from the trash room, felt the wall, and realized above the water level the wall texture changed. With all the strength I had left, I slammed the wire into the wall. It barely made a dent. I was losing my grip on Don. I reached down again with my free hand and grabbed the hammerhead on my belt, slamming it into the wall. A small crack in the wall appeared. I couldn't help my feeling of hope at that tiny crack!

Placing the hammerhead back on my belt, I took out the wire, hooked it through Don's sturdy belt, moved his belt up under his shoulders, and tightened it. Attaching the wire to the now harness, I hooked the wire into the small crack in the wall, knowing it wouldn't hold him for long but might give me the time to inspect the latch under the water. Diving down, I reached the latch and pulled with all the strength I had left; nothing. My lungs ached as I swam closer and investigated it. The latch had to be turned before it would release.

Grabbing the latch again, I turned it clockwise first, and again nothing; I reversed the motion and felt the latch give. With burning in my chest, I yanked the latch, and it opened. The pressure from the water made opening it near impossible, but I must have had a rush of adrenaline, because it lifted free, and the water rushed into the opening in the floor.

Soon I was standing on the floor, taking deep breaths as the water drained around me and Don. I trudged along through the knee-high water at a slow pace, feeling the effects of my energy spent.

Don was hanging from the wall where I had left him. I could tell he was about to slip from the makeshift harness and I tried to speed up, but my legs felt like weights slowing me down. I saw him slip and go under the water. That gave me the added urgency to speed up and retrieve him. He was only under the water for a few seconds before I pulled him back up and dragged him to the opening in the floor. The water was pouring through at a steady pace, so I waited. The weight of Don became heavier and heavier as the water receded. Once the water was low enough, I laid Don face up on the floor and rested for a few precious seconds while the water finished going through the whole in the floor.

With the water through, I started down the exit carefully. The ladder led down only a short amount, and I was standing on a type of grate with the water below. I went back up to get Don and dragged us over to the opening; my slight frame could barely hold him up long enough to get him down the ladder, but somehow, I managed it. Safe on the grate, I remembered this part of the course and knew I was getting close to the end. Only a few more minor things, and I could call this finished.

I knew Don was safe enough that I could leave him, but I just couldn't bring myself to abandon him. So I pulled him over the grated floor to the scaffolding that led up to a new room. I had been here before; it was dark and full of flying rats or, as Merek called them, bats. It wasn't too difficult to escape. I just had to find a wall and follow it around to the exit, but getting there with the bats flying in my hair and landing on my skin was slightly horrifying, and the hardest part was not making a sound while all this was happening. If I made any noise, the lights would go on, and I lose, which I guess didn't matter because by dragging Don along, I was losing anyway.

I found the wall, and the bats found me. They streaked and flew into my face; it took all the willpower I had not to react. One, two, three…up to about twenty steps, dragging Don before I stopped and inhaled weakened breaths, knowing I couldn't stop; I wasn't done yet.

I reached the exit and went through two more rooms that were slightly a blur because of my exhausted state, but I must have already been through them because I automatically knew how to escape, and all of a sudden, I was at the finish line; poor Don was still unconscious. Merek was there to greet me, but I couldn't meet his eyes, knowing he expected me to do well, and I had failed.

"Well, you did it! I hoped you would!" he said with pride. That's when I looked up and saw he was smiling. I was so confused. I had failed. Why was he so happy? "You passed the test," he continued.

"What do you mean?" I asked through ragged breathing.

"The object of this exercise is to see who will go against orders and save their fellow man," he said with a wide grin, lifting Don from my grasp. "Only a few pass the test. In fact, I failed miserably last year and had to take a course on 'human significance' taught by the touchy feely Abia. You won't have to endure such boredom since you passed." he said with a slight chuckle.

Anger welled up that they would try to deceive us into betraying one another but also relief that they were still who they said they were. "Don't be angry, Alex, it is just a little test to see who you truly are," Merek said, reading the emotions on my face.

Medics came and whisked Don away from Merek, and he began walking beside me to my dwelling. I wanted to be alone but wasn't sure how to express to Merek just how distressed I truly was.

"I could have let him drown," I informed Merek sharply. Tears of frustration began to slip unwittingly from my eyes; my hands were shaking slightly. I couldn't help the look of disdain that I knew was on my face.

"We wouldn't have let him die," Merek replied with concern. "Calm down. It's over, you did good." He placed a reassuring hand on my back. "All truth from here on out," he said with kindness.

I wasn't used to physical touch from anyone, except the children. The sensations running rampant were uncharted and frightening. So many opposing emotions and no way to know what they could possibly mean. He was speaking again. "Alexandra, you did wonderfully, and now we know that you will preserve human life above all else. It took a six-week course for me to get it, and I even grew up here." He let out a laugh of self-deprecation.

"I'm not sure why I couldn't leave him," I said simply, hoping he would remove his hand and my warring mental state would cease. He didn't. In fact, he seemed even more concerned for me.

"It is because you are a selfless woman." I saw the admiration he had for me and wondered if this was how the whole "romance" thing that Kasi was always dreaming of started. I increased my pace, not wanting him to further compliment me and us continue to venture into the unknown. He seemed to take the hint and began speaking of my next steps in training and what courses I still needed to catch up since I came so "late in the game," whatever that meant.

He walked with me all the way to my door and gave me a curt goodbye before returning to help finish with the other trainees. Back to business; that I could handle. Once I closed the door behind me, I fell onto my bed and I allowed myself to cry over what I might have done. My last thought before emotional and physical exhaustion overtook me was about poor Don, and I hoped he was recovering nicely.

I slept fitfully through the night, and when my alarm woke me, I still felt the unpleasant emotions of the day before and wished I could forget it had ever happened. I entered the mess hall and headed to my usual table, only to be stopped by someone shouting my name.

"Alexandra!" I heard over the low morning voices.

I turned to see Don catching up to me. He looked worn-out and had a bandage on his head.

"Good morning," I greeted him in the Outlandish way.

"I wanted to thank you for saving me," he said with a slight blush to his cheeks. "So anyway, thanks for not letting me drown." He chuckled. I smiled. I liked Don; his smile was awkward yet inviting.

"You're welcome. Want to sit at my table?" I invited him.

"Sure, why not? I might as well get to know my savior," he said, shaking his head with a laugh.

Don sat down with the children, Kasi, and I, making us laugh at the strange food, the many different clothing choices of the others in the mess hall, and really anything that came to his head, I think. It was soon time to head to training, but I was enjoying myself so much I hated to leave.

"I'll walk with you to training," Don said as he neatly stacked all the dishes on our table for the mess hall attendant to retrieve. Kasi and the children headed to their classes as I waited on Don to finish straightening up the table.

"Don't we take rotations in mess hall duty?" I asked Don as we left the table.

"Yeah, but I hate to clean up a huge mess, so I try to make it easier for the ones doing it," he replied. "It's just better if everyone helps out, ya know?" he asked me.

"That makes sense. I guess I just always rush from one place to the next and don't give it much thought," I said thoughtfully.

"Well, sometimes slowing down and watching those around us makes a huge difference. Like you saving me. Did you know that only 5 percent of trainees pass that horrible test? That most people don't want to hurt their fellow trainees, but they follow orders above all else? I hope I would have stopped and helped you, but there is no way to know for sure," he said. "I'm a decent warrior. However, I'm a better psychologist. I am bound for the rehabilitation of the people in the Establishment if we ever find a cure," he informed me.

"So you will analyze them? Once they are cured, that is?" I asked him.

"Not really. More help them to adjust, understand, and learn that emotions don't have to control you. They can be an asset and give you intuition into situations. Our emotions make us unique," he said with zeal.

"I am still adjusting to life here. It's difficult to allow myself to express emotions, and I have been here for three months now," I said with a laugh.

"I think you're catching on. I heard about your confrontation with Merek after the test," he said with a funny grin.

"Who told you that?" I asked, knowing that Don himself had been unconscious and no one else was around. Besides, I didn't confront Merek. I just wanted to wring his neck for a few minutes.

"I have friends in the observation room. They said if looks could kill, Merek would be dead five times over." He was laughing out loud now. I couldn't help but chuckle myself.

Once we arrived at training, I tried to focus on being the best, but Don was close beside me to interrupt my concentration with a well-timed joke. For someone that studied behavior, he sure didn't take much seriously.

* * * * *

A few days later, I was to attend a course on what Merek called the "True Primal Times;" not exactly sure what the difference was between what we learned in the Establishment and what they taught here, but my curiosity was raised.

"Alexandra, there you are. How has training been going?" Colin asked from somewhere behind me.

I turned and saw him standing on a balcony high above me. *Must be his dwelling,* I mused. "I have enjoyed it very much," I replied truthfully. Connecting my words with a smiling face was still difficult, though, so I wasn't sure he believed me.

"That's good. I would like to speak to you privately after your classes today. Can you come by my office before dinner?" he asked.

"Yes, of course, I'll be there." I waved goodbye and continued my way, wondering what he could possibly need to speak to me privately about.

When I arrived for the "True Primal Times" course, it was only myself, Kasi, and the children in attendance, which suited me fine. We waited for our instructor to arrive by telling "jokes;" the children recently discovered them from the Outlandish children, and we all chuckled quietly. Soon Justin walked in, which surprised me because I hadn't seen him since he told us we couldn't leave here three months before.

"Good morning," he said cheerfully. "We will begin today by you all answering a few questions. First, why do you believe the injection was created?"

22507 or Kit as he called himself now raised his hand without hesitation. "To stop all conflict," he answered when Justin nodded for him to speak.

"That is not entirely true, but yes, that is what you have been taught," he said thoughtfully. "The intentions of the female scientist were pure at the beginning. However, as we are told, power corrupts," he continued vaguely. He seemed to pause and think for a few tense seconds. I'm not sure why, but I felt impending doom lay in his next words. "Our world was very mixed up. Wars were fought over oil. The media constantly stirred up strife among the people with their propaganda that most people swallowed hook, line, and sinker—"

He was interrupted by 1019, or Ellie as we now called her. "What is 'media?'" she asked in her kind eight-year-old voice. I wanted to know what "hook, line, and sinker" meant, but he spoke again.

"Yes, of course. The media was like a group of people that reported what was happening in the world to the general public. They were supposed to report on the happenings in the world unbiasedly, but they became more about how many people were watching and soon became just an opinionated form of entertainment," he answered and continued. "People didn't agree on *anything*. The nation was rot with discourse. People not only didn't agree, but also, they didn't know their own identities. They judged each other and themselves by their skin color, gender, age, weight, beauty, religion, political view, and even the clothing they wore." He paused again to let it sink in, I think. I couldn't imagine this world so different from the Establishment. We all wore the same things, most people blended into the background, and no one really cared, about...well, anything. In the Establishment, life was lived for the completion of tasks set before you by the Sovereignty, nothing more, nothing less.

He was speaking again. "Dr. Marian Crawford began research to develop the injection in the year 2020. She was determined to make all people 'equal' to stop the hatred, strife, and anger that she saw day in and day out. Her intentions were good, but her opinion about what caused the state of inequality was biased. She believed from her past experience with the male population that the predominant hormones that made up the male psyche were what caused most if not all conflict," he said.

This I had heard before, not that biased part, but the rest was not new information.

"Dr. Marian decided things needed to change and quickly. She made some very interesting alliances with people of questionable morals. These people had power and money." He was once again interrupted.

"Money?" asked Kasi.

"Money was what they used as a currency, much like the Sovereignty gives you Exchange cards in the Establishments. Once Dr. Marian had the funding, she began to build bunkers. The bunker we now inhabit was one of the very first to be built and a prototype for the future bunkers."

"How many bunkers were built?" I asked.

"Close to a hundred, but we aren't sure because some were built in secret for the affluent population, and rumor has it they were very lavish," he said. "Second question: Do you believe that the injection is necessary?" he asked with raised eyebrows.

The room remained silent for several strained seconds. I knew why no one spoke up. Our entire lives, we had been taught that the injection was a form of "salvation," so to speak, although I had never really believed that. However, I didn't want to voice an opinion. Opinions weren't something we were accustomed to.

"I don't think it is," Kasi said with conviction.

"Why?" he asked probing her on.

"Well, without emotion, there is no self-expression, art, music, drama, and not even love," Kasi said with all the emotion she could muster. Some of the children snickered behind their hands and some just smiled a shy smile.

"Very true, Kasi, but most important, there is no individual thought. Without emotions, people don't have any reason to question their leaders, because honestly, they just don't care enough to. They become puppets to their leaders and have no purpose except that of those in charge," he said. "Dr. Marian had 'solved' one set of problems but had created an entirely new set by making humans into sheep, so to speak. When she took away the individuality of our race, we became blind followers to those in charge," he finished.

"How have you all here in the bunker avoided the injection?" I asked the question that had been on my mind from the day I met Colin.

"Very simply. We ran," he stated flatly.

His answer was vague and slightly irritating, because I knew there had to be more to the story with so many people—439 was my count so far—being present in the bunkers. I chose not to pursue it anymore and find answers another way. I halfway tuned him out, trying to think about anything that might help me in my quest to find answers that he wasn't willing to give me when I heard him say, "Dr. Marian had a hand in starting the biological warfare that was a catalyst to our demise. Remember the allies with questionable morals I spoke of? Well, they wanted massive genocide and to be the only remaining race. These deadly allies began destroying cities that opposed them and were extremely thorough in their destruction of most major metropolises with a chemical agent created by Dr. Marian.

"Unfortunately for them, they were misled by Dr. Marian that the bunkers were only being built for their own kind. She had created the chemical agent, and only the injection could cure it. She required anyone wanting sanctuary from the biological warfare to receive the injection, and so began our world. She was hailed a hero, but in reality, she had a hand in the war in the first place."

This was inconceivable in my mind; how could she help people to kill so many and then dangle refuge over their heads with the requirement of the injection?

"However, her deteriorating moral standards didn't stop there. She did not require those she wanted to help rule this new society with her to take the injection, all female, and only those she knew believed in her cause. She built a world totally in her control, and if any opposed her ideals, they weren't allowed into the bunkers and soon died."

The room remained silent for many agonizing minutes. He was letting it sink in, the truth of our deluded existence. The fan overhead seemed to be running in slow motion—whoosh, whoosh, whoosh—and it screamed loud in our stunned silence.

"The female leaders of the Sovereignty are chosen at a very young age and still remain untouched by the injection to this day. For example, Eleanor Palmer never received the injection." He dropped the last truth, and it landed like a lead weight on my shoulders; they stripped us of *everything* for total control. Our leaders didn't receive the injection? Eleanor Palmer was living a lie, leading the Sovereignty, claiming the injection was for the betterment of mankind but refusing to be injected herself? This seemed the cruelest act of all.

I couldn't listen anymore I just kept hearing my guides from the Establishment speak of the great honor of saving society through receiving the injection, how *all* had to receive it if we wanted life to remain peaceful and equal. It wasn't equal; it was the furthest thing from equal. We truly were meant to be nothing but sheep to act out their needs and total submission.

Around me, everyone was leaving. We were dismissed for the day, yet I couldn't quite will myself to stand up and head to training. The physical excursion would probably clear my head, but getting there was the problem. I never truly believed in the necessity of the injection, but I never really doubted their reasoning for it.

"Alexandra?" Kasi said at the door, waiting on me.

"She won't be far behind," Justin answered for me. He was watching me closely. I felt exposed somehow and raw. "Will you be okay?" he asked.

I knew I would, but I felt two raging emotions screaming to drown out the other—one that everything I had ever been taught was a falsehood, and the other that I was justified in not wanting the injection. I knew I would allow the second to win, because I had no time to worry about the first.

"Yes," I replied and stood up with false bravado to head to training, knowing that would numb my thoughts too.

STAGE 2:2

I rushed through the winding hallways to arrive at the training facility, but the door was locked, and no one was inside. I looked up above the door at the timekeeper to realize in my clouded state of mind I had forgotten it was about to be time for the evening fare, and I had totally forgotten Colin had wanted to speak with me. I turned around quickly to head to his office. It was amongst the calculation labs and not too far away to still make it. As I rushed up to his door, I nearly collided with him as he was exiting.

"This seems to be a pattern with us," he laughed.

Slightly winded from my race over, I smiled and nodded my head in agreement. Teasing was something the Outlandish did often, and I was starting to get the hang of it. "Here, let's go inside," he said. I walked into the office and immediately noticed it was nothing like the rest of the Outlandish. I felt like I was back in the Establishment with their muted colors and simple decor, which was no decor. I felt welcomed by that, and it was unnerving.

"I want you to be a part of a special group of individuals researching how to cure the injection," he stated with no introduction at all. I wasn't surprised. Nothing could surprise me at this point, but I wasn't sure I wanted to day in and out be reminded of the falsehood of the injection either. "I know this isn't something that will be easy-going against all you have been taught your entire life, but you have a real gift with numbers and science, and honestly, we need you."

I remembered my earlier conviction to feel justified by my repulsion to the injection. This was it; this was my reprisal. He was talking again, explaining to me that I would understand more clearly the dangers of the injection as we tried to cure it when I stopped him with, "Yes, I will do it." I spoke with conviction and confidence that I didn't even know I had.

"That was much easier than I thought." He sounded surprised. "Well, then, you have to finish your training and lectures. Once all that is complete, you will head out with our group to the science bunker." He smiled at me as if I had gained his approval, as if he was proud of me in some way; at least, that's what I imagined his smile expressed.

We both quickly turned our heads to the sound of shouts and hollers. I couldn't tell if it was with joy, anger, or fright. My heart raced with dread.

"Why don't you stay in my office, and I'll see what the commotion is about?" he said with concern.

My gut reaction was to stay and cower in fear, but I knew this was the road I had chosen, and I couldn't hide any longer. I had to face any fear that may come.

"I'll go," I told him with false courage. *Maybe it isn't false. Maybe just forced,* I thought. I began walking before I finished speaking. Colin joined me at a fast clip, and we headed to the loud noise. As we drew near the crowd, I could see Merek's broad shoulders being slapped over and over with shouts sent up by the people standing around him. I looked at Colin, wondering if he was as confused as I was by the behavior. But no; he had a smile on his face that said everything was normal. *I may never understand these Outlandish people.*

"It was a success I take it?" Colin shouted above the roar.

"It was indeed!" Merek said with a large grin.

I became even more confused by their words. *What was a success?* I noticed that several people seemed lost and confused. Their faces were pale and drawn; some looked ill. I realized they couldn't be Outlandish. Their clothing was grey with numbers on their shirt pockets. I turned to Colin.

"Who are these people?" I asked. Before he could form words to answer me, I saw her. She was older and looked as if she hadn't been fed proper food in years. Her hair was slightly grey, the corners of her eyes had wrinkles that I don't remember, but there was no mistaking my surrogate. I never thought I would see her again in this lifetime.

When I was young, it was as if she knew we would be permanently separated. She always spoke of our afterlife being spent together with joy.

Colin was speaking to me, but his words weren't penetrating the daze I found myself in. She looked at me. Her eyes didn't show recognition, but she seemed to glance back at me every few seconds as if wondering where she knew me from. I tried without success to stop staring, but I couldn't help my curiosity. How? How did she escape the reformatory?

"Are you okay?" Colin whispered with concern.

I couldn't answer before I heard, "There you are, Alex!" Merek was loud in a demanding way. "Come celebrate with us. We are heading to the mess hall and no training today, only celebration," he said enthusiastically.

I still wasn't quite certain what the celebration was about, but I couldn't work up the courage to ask, so I followed after Merek, leaving behind Colin. I was glad for the distraction. Listening to those around me, I pieced together that Merek had led a small group of the Outlandish to free some important people in the reformatory. Why was my surrogate deemed important? I wasn't sure. Merek was boasting about the simplicity of the rescue, saying that the Sovereignty was shorthanded from the attacks and entirely too distracted to properly keep guard of the reformatory. I cringed at the shorthanded comment, knowing people had died, and I felt pity, even if they were Empties.

I noticed Sabra, the caregiver we first met when we entered the bunker, whisk the escaped prisoners away, including my surrogate, to care for their ailments. I wondered what I should do. Give it time see if she recognized me? Or just tell her, "Hey, I'm the child that you were forced to abandon. Remember me? 2020? Alexandra?" I thought to myself ruefully.

I kept pace with Merek, knowing he would notice if I fell behind. Ever since I passed that horrible test, as I will always call it, he seemed to have taken a special interest in everything I did. I wasn't sure how to take it.

"So Alex, did you even notice I was gone?" he asked with a grin. I didn't, but then I hadn't been in training the last two days. "Don't answer that," he laughed at his own joke and continued to the mess hall. Merek's emotions were extreme, even for the Outlandish, from total joy to complete anger at the very mention of the Sovereignty. His feelings were so much more apparent than the others who seemed to seek a solution or cure, not seek revenge.

We arrived at the mess hall, and it seemed as if word had spread of the successful mission, and everyone had gathered to celebrate. Music was loud, food was lavish, and people were dancing. I felt so out of place standing beside a jovial Merek as he spoke to all the people congratulating him as they passed us. I caught a glimpse of Colin moving toward us and felt slight relief; not far behind him was Don, and then Kasi dancing to the hypnotic music as she approached.

"You did it, Merek!" Colin said with genuine pride in his friend. "First mission you lead, and it was a blazing success." He slapped him on the back.

"No better a man could have completed this mission," Don said in his funny way.

"Congrats!" Kasi said shyly, using Outlandish slang that slightly irked me. She tried too hard to fit in.

"Thanks, little Kasi," replied Merek.

I saw Kasi turn her head slightly to hide the pink blush that rose with Merek's endearment. Colin and Merek began talking of the plans they had for these escapees, and I listened intently, hoping to find a clue as to why they broke my surrogate free.

"They were clinical lab rats for years. It may take them some time to heal and be of any help to our cause," Colin said. looking somber.

"Yes, yes, yes, but *they will be a help*," Merek said with excitement.

"Of course they will. These few were considered geniuses before they decided not to follow the Sovereignty and were locked away for it. At least the Sovereignty was conceited enough to believe they would always control them and didn't give them the injection."

"I thought only the female government officials didn't receive the injection?" I asked.

"That is true, but on rare occasions when the Sovereignty identifies people of great brilliance, they have discovered giving them the injection tends to diminish their intelligence. So they keep them around untouched by the injection and carefully monitored. If they make a mistake or step out of line, they are immediately sent to Reformatory, where they are studied indefinitely," Colin explained.

I wanted to ask if they knew who they had saved, if they knew they were bringing up a ghost from my past, but I refrained.

"What is wrong?" Kasi whispered over my shoulder. I shook my head, hoping to silently communicate that we could talk later. Kasi wasn't great at silent communication. "Alexandra, are you okay?" she said a little louder this time as if I was hard of hearing. At this, the people standing in close proximity turned their eyes on me.

"It's nothing, nothing," I said, hoping to quench their concern.

Merek and Colin didn't seem to believe me in the least, but the rest went on with their conversations. Merek stepped forward and gently grabbed my arm, leading me away from an even more concerned look from Don, Kasi, and Colin. He led me to a private corner away from the crowd where no one would notice us. My heart was racing. I didn't want to voice why I was so shocked. I didn't even know how to begin.

"Now, tell me, Alex," he said roughly, but I knew it was out of his distress for me.

"Merek, I…I think one of the women you brought back is my…surrogate." I knew he wouldn't let me avoid his question, so I forced the words out.

"What? Really? Your surrogate was in the reformatory? Why?" he asked in surprise.

"When I was very young, she was sent there by her male partner for showing me affection. She always whispered she loved me before bedtime. She told me I was beautiful every day and told me that above all, I must never forget I am loved. One day, she was tucking me into bed, and he walked in. He saw her holding me, and without a change of his expression, he summoned the Unity officers, and she was taken away. I was five years old at the time and was assigned a new home and then sent to the Establishment." I tried not to sound too emotionally involved, but my words were wavering.

"Alex, I didn't know. I would have warned you if I had," he said with his eyes pleading me to believe him. I did. Merek wasn't one to mask his emotions or try to pretend. "Justin. Justin made the list on who was top priority," he said with annoyance. I wondered then why Justin chose her and wondered if she was truly an asset or he was trying to convince me to join their "worthy cause," which I already had; there was no need for him to force me.

"I think I'd like to return to my dwelling," I said.

"Are you angry with me?" Merek asked me sincerely.

"No. You had no way of knowing. It's just a shock is all," I replied. Seeing this gentle side of Merek was always uncomfortable. I knew he enjoyed training me, and he really seemed to enjoy challenging me to become a better combatant, but gentleness was not something I had experienced from him, except for the time I passed that horrible test. Nothing had ever come from that encounter, though.

I turned to head to my dwelling, but he stopped me with, "Please don't leave the celebration. If you go back to your room, you know you will be even more miserable. I'll help you find out exactly why she was rescued and anything else you want to know first thing in the morning." He seemed to be pleading.

I knew going to my room wouldn't stop the thoughts running through my head; maybe a celebration would. "First thing in the morning?" I asked.

"Yes, first thing!" he replied with conviction. We returned to the celebration with concerned looks from Don, Colin, and Kasi, but everyone else was too busy enjoying themselves in high fashion, dancing, singing, and laughing. I wanted to join in but honestly wasn't even sure how. Trying to mimic them felt hypocritical and would only fall flat. Merek handed me a drink, and I slowly sipped on its bittersweet flavor, trying not to dwell on the upcoming encounter with my surrogate. Don, Colin, and Kasi joined us. I knew they wanted an explanation, but I forced a small smile, hoping they would let it slide until we weren't in the middle of a crowded room.

We all spoke for a few minutes. Kasi was whisked away to the dance floor by Don, Colin and Merek were teasing one another back and forth, then the music changed from a happy jingle to this sorrowful ballad that tugged at me. Unintentionally, I began to sway back and forth to the music. The drink seemed to have gone straight to my head. I had never in my life danced where others could see me. I remember dancing in the kitchen with my surrogate as she was humming a sad song. I missed that. I saw from the corner of my eye Colin elbow Merek and nod his head toward me. In my foggy mind, I wondered what they were communicating to each other. I smiled with all I had as Merek came closer, reaching for my hand.

"Dance with me," he said, returning my smile.

"Oh, I couldn't possibly. I don't know how," I returned, my smile faltering.

"Just relax and follow my lead. Trust me," he said and led me to the dance floor. My brain screamed to run because I knew I would look the fool, but my body betrayed me, and I followed him willingly. He drew me close to him, and I inhaled his pleasant scent and wondered if he just always smelled good or if he had time to shower once he returned from the rescue.

"You smell nice." The words passed my lips, but I didn't remember wanting them to.

He laughed. "I believe you have never had an intoxicant before," he said with a wide grin.

I had only had the one cup, but I did feel…different, less reserved somehow. He slowly spun me around, and I couldn't help but feel the soft sad rhythm of the ballad reaching deep inside my being. I almost felt like I was in a trance or floating on a cloud maybe. He drew me closer and closer as the song continued, and I let him. A feeling bubbled up from my stomach of unease…or maybe it was excitement? Whatever it was, I felt peculiar and confused all at the same time. He was humming the tune in my ear as the song ended too soon for me to discern my emotions.

"It's over," he said softly.

I slowly pulled away, not knowing what to say. He didn't release my hand very willingly, and it felt nice. We walked back to the table laden with delicious foods and heaped it onto the large platters they gave us. I didn't think I was hungry until the enticing aroma hit me.

We sat down near Colin who was speaking very enthusiastically to the beautiful Abia; they seemed to know one another very well. I longed to have the ease with which they spoke to one another—smiling, sharing, and laughing came so easily.

Watching them brought me back to the reality of just what an intruder I was. I ate my food in silence, just observing those around me when a lively song started playing, and Colin very cordially asked me to join him. I nodded my agreement, and he swept me onto the floor. The song was so cheerful and upbeat. I couldn't help but laugh when Colin exaggerated each move, trying to drawl out a smile from me. This dance was so different, so safe and peaceful. I realized I was most comfortable with Colin. He was my safe place, a warm fire on a cold day, or my protector; and yet he was also pushing me to protect myself. Colin was a kind man and friend.

"What are you thinking about so intensely?"

Colin's words broke my musings. The intoxicant must have worn off after eating, because I didn't just blurt out that I was thinking of him and the comfort he brought me. "A little bit of everything, I suppose," I replied vaguely.

"Oh, really," he said with unbelief. "And earlier, you left the room in a panic for no reason at all, I'm sure," he added sarcastically. Sarcasm was something I had grown accustomed to here at the compound, it was very confusing at first, but now at the very least, I knew when someone was saying something ironic and didn't truly believe the words they spoke. The dance music turned to something slow and dreamy. Colin didn't release me but instead gently twirled me around and back to him. When we came face-to-face, his eyebrows were raised in question, and I knew he would wait on me to answer him truthfully.

"My surrogate was one of the escaped prisoners that Merek freed today," I told him. I waited for him to react or to at the least have understanding for my array of changing emotions, but he seemed to just be pondering the situation. "Well?" I asked, not really knowing what I wanted to hear but needing him to say something, anything.

"It makes sense. Justin wants your undivided devotion," he said thoughtfully.

"He saved her to force me to cooperate with him?" I asked him indignantly.

"Maybe more to win you over to the cause," he replied. "As a kind of gift. I have never heard of her as being anything special, but you…you have so much to offer us. Your brain mainly."

He said trying to lighten my mood, I'm sure. I couldn't decide if her freedom was a gift or leverage. I may have trusted Colin and Merek somewhat, but Justin…I was still very hesitant about him. I wanted the cure as much or more than these people here, but the way he was going about it wasn't ideal in my mind.

"Why would the Sovereignty allow her to remain free from the injection if she wasn't brilliant or special?" I asked him, keeping my misgivings about Justin to myself.

"I'm not sure. There could be more to this story than we know. A mystery indeed," he said. We danced in silence for a few peaceful moments. I wanted to ask him a million questions, but I also didn't know what to ask.

"Merek said he will find out from Justin why she was saved first thing in the morning," I said, filling the silence.

Colin nodded, and the silence returned. He didn't seem to want to talk right now. He made me feel childish for my worry. I rested my head on his shoulder, finding the peace and security that he always gave me in his presence. Maybe the intoxicant hadn't completely left my system.

We slowly moved back and forth to the gentle music for what felt like an eternity. When it stopped, it was a rude awakening. We returned to the table where I noticed Merek was watching us intently, and I wasn't sure what his facial expression said, but I knew it wasn't elated like it was earlier. Colin didn't seem to notice at all and began talking to Abia about the classes for next week and pretty much everything. Colin and Abia went onto the dance floor and began dancing a lively jig. They danced so well that I felt I must have looked the fool trying to dance with Colin before. He was a very skillful dancer.

"They have always been very close," Merek said from behind me. He was also watching Colin and Abia. They outshone all the other dancers and didn't even seem to notice nor care that people were watching their talent so closely.

"They dance so well together," I replied.

"They both came from the same Establishment. Most of the people from Establishment 7 aren't given the injection right away but are taught to be leaders and enjoy some of the primal time arts. Obviously, the males are given the injection, but Colin was rescued before that happened." Merek gave me more information about Colin in a few sentences than I had learned the entire time I had been here. I was even more intrigued.

The night continued with much music, laughter, and merriment. I felt like I was on the outside looking in. I desired so very much to be in the thick of all the enjoyment, but it seemed fake to try to pretend. So I watched closely, smiled when it was appropriate, and didn't contribute to their conversations, only giving answers to any question they sent my way. Kasi fit in so well, but I didn't and couldn't seem to no matter what.

The night came to an end, and Merek escorted Kasi and I back to our dwelling. At the door, he hesitated and seemed to change his mind about whatever he wanted to say because Kasi was at my elbow, looking at him with doe eyes. "Doe eyes" was an expression used for someone that looked at another with longing or so Kasi informed me from all her romance novel reading. I turned in immediately, even though I dreaded what I may face in the morning. Sleep did not come quickly.

STAGE 2:3

The morning came earlier than expected, mainly because I couldn't sleep, so after tossing and turning for what seemed an eternity, I gave up and got dressed for the day. The morning fare wasn't for a few more hours, so I headed to the main meeting area, hoping that someone would be awake and give me some answers. The walk was silent; everyone must have been sleeping off the night before.

On my way, I passed the medical ward. I wanted to peer in and see if my surrogate was there, but I refrained and instead hastened my steps to reach the meeting area. Justin's office was directly beside it, and the light was shining, so I walked up and knocked with all the frustration and confusion I felt. It opened almost immediately.

"Do come in and join the party," Justin said as I entered. Merek and Colin were there. Colin looked calm as always while Merek was looking agitated as always. "I suppose you are here for the same reason?" Justin asked.

"If the reason is to know why you rescued her, then yes," I replied.

"Well, everyone, take a seat. I'll explain," he said with resignation. When none of us sat, he shook his head and continued, "I assure you it wasn't some ploy to control you, Alexandra. We need her almost as much as we need you."

"I can understand that, but why not tell us that before we left for the mission in the first place?" Merek asked in his coarse way. "All this was very surprising. Why not warn Alex?" he continued.

"Yes, Justin, you could have warned the girl," Colin said having an instant calming effect to the conversation. His words expressed his annoyance, but something about his tone soothed Merek and myself.

"Why is she so valuable to you and to the Establishment? Why did they keep her locked up without giving her the injection for so long?" I asked, rushing through so I wouldn't be interrupted.

Justin raised his hand as if to silence me, which made me want to scream. I refrained myself, waiting for him to explain. "She has a rare blood type, extremely rare. The injection can be given to her, and for a while, it works, but…it eventually wears off."

We were stunned to silence. The injection didn't fully work on her?

"In fact, there are only four recorded cases in the last eighty years or so. We don't know yet the patterns that it follows in a bloodline, but it does follow a bloodline, possibly skipping a generation and such. We haven't been able to study it until now, so we are slightly in the dark. In fact, until the attacks, we thought it may have been a rumor. You see, her blood and your blood may be the key to unlocking the cure," he finished with raising excitement. "We believe your blood and her blood is triggered by some biological change to resist the injection, and we need to discover what that something is," he said.

We looked at each other, none of us having much to say. I could see Colin's mind working a million miles a minute, probably making plans on how to find the cure now that he had this new information. Merek had excitement in his voice, when he asked, "You mean her blood may aid us in finding the cure, if not just give it to us outright? Why haven't we studied Alex's?"

"Her blood hasn't yet manifested itself to resist the injection. Whatever triggered her surrogate's blood hasn't happened to Alexandra or she doesn't resist it at all. We have much work to do to find out," he said.

"Why keep us in the dark?" Colin asked in his quiet but firm way.

"I didn't want to raise hopes without more information and without 0721, Alexandra's surrogate, here safely with us," he said.

"When do we begin?" I asked now that I understood there was no reason to sit idly by and wait for others to find the cure; we needed it as soon as possible.

"We are going to check 0721's health, then send her and you all to the science bunker. Hopefully as soon as possible," he replied.

We all seemed to have a shared mission, and so we left his office with a purpose and hope that there was a cure we could find. My next hurdle was facing my surrogate. I wasn't sure why I was so nervous, but I was.

"Do you want to go see her?" Colin asked me.

"I will, but I don't know what to say," I said honestly.

"Well, just tell her who you are. That's a great start," Colin said kindly.

"Hopefully she is willing to help us," Merek mused.

"I am sure she will after what they have put her through," Colin replied. "I can go with you if that will help," he offered.

"Thank you, Colin. I should probably go alone, though," I replied thankfully. He nodded his understanding and turned to go. I kept walking toward the medic's station, hoping the words to say instantly fell into my mind, but nothing was coming. I had reached the entrance to the medic's station when I heard footsteps behind me and turned to see Merek following at a distance.

"I already told Colin I need to do this alone," I told him, hoping he wouldn't argue. He would win. I didn't have much practice arguing.

"I will wait right outside the door. That way, you can do it *all* alone, but I am here if you need me," he replied in earnest. His thoughtfulness always caught me off guard, so I nodded in agreement and opened the door. A very cheerful, slightly overweight, redheaded female was sitting at the front desk.

"May I help you?" she asked with more excitement than I have ever said anything in my entire existence.

"Yes, I would like to speak with one of the escapees that was brought here last night," I told her, not wanting to give further explanation.

"Alrighty, which one dear?" she asked.

"0721," I said.

"I will page a medic, and they will take you back in just one moment. Have a seat," she said as her fingers were furiously typing away at her keyboard.

I took a seat and marveled at the difference from this "medic's station" and the Establishments "sanatorium." They both basically served the same purpose, yet the atmosphere was incredibly different. The sanatorium was painted in all greyscale, and there were benches along one wall. That was it. But the medic's station had a different mural on each wall, flowers on every surface, the chairs were overstuffed, and reading material was strategically placed in baskets throughout.

"Alexandra?"

I looked up to see Sabra calling my name at a door off to my right. I got up quicker than normal, and my steps to her weren't smooth by any measure. "This way," she said with a smile.

I followed her with a pounding heart. *Words, I need words.* She led me down a brightly colored hallway and opened the third door on our left to what I assumed was my surrogate's room. It was, and my heart pounded even faster.

"Here we are. If you need anything, I'll be in my office," Sabra told me, assuming I knew where her office was, but no matter. On the bed slept 0721, my surrogate, my birth mother as they called them here. I studied her face, looking for signs of the woman I knew and hoping to see the similarities between us. My nose and eyes were much like hers. I shared her olive skin and dark hair. The resemblance stopped there. Her mouth wasn't as wide as my own. She was much taller and more slender than me. I must have gotten the rest from the artificial inseminator.

I wasn't making a sound when her eyes fluttered open. At first, fear lay in her eyes, but once she looked around, she seemed to realize where she was, and it went away. She then looked at me with confusion.

"Are you a new medic?" she asked me. She was studying my face again, trying to place me, I'm sure.

"No," I replied simply.

"Do I know you from somewhere?" she asked.

"Yes," I replied, knowing I couldn't get much more out than that over the lump in my throat.

"Are you also from Establishment 3?" she inquired.

"Yes," I said.

"What is your number?" she asked. I could see she was processing the information, hoping to place me.

"Alexandra," I said, giving her the name she gave me.

Her face changed from total confusion to a bright light, from perplexation to realization. Tears began streaming down her face, but she was smiling through them. I didn't speak, I didn't know what to say.

"Alexandra! I never thought I would see you again!" she said through sobs.

I wanted to comfort her, because I always want to comfort people, but my feet wouldn't move, and I wouldn't have known how anyway. She was sitting up in her bed now, slightly rocking back and forth. "I can't tell you how many times I dreamt of seeing you again," she continued. "How did you come to this place? Are you well? Were you in the reformatory also? Are you okay?"

Her many questions brought me out of my silence, and I began telling her of my journey thus far. She nodded and shook her head at each new event and seemed worried for me at the appropriate moments. I shared with her my fears, my feelings of being out of place, my respect for and comfort with Colin, my reservations about Justin, and even my confusion about Merek. Somewhere in the middle of my long story, I had sat down in the chair beside her bed, and she held my hand. I kept thinking it should feel uncomfortable to be sitting here like that, but somehow, it felt right. We talked and we laughed and we even cried together. I wasn't sure why I had been so afraid to meet her; she was here, and somehow, all felt right. We sat like that for what felt like hours and we talked of many things, but we both avoided any discussion of her time in the reformatory. I think we were both too happy to dampen it with talk of such things.

STAGE 2:4

Everything was at peace for a few moments. Everything I had worried about felt far away and inconsequential. Everything was different for a split second in time. I slept that one peaceful night in the chair beside my "mother's" bed. I had begun referring to her in the same way as the Outlandish called their surrogates; we had talked until her eyes began closing without her permission. I had pity on her saying she was too exhausted to stay awake a moment longer. She was instantly asleep, and for a time, I watched her. We had spoken of many things, but out of my own fear, I didn't ask her of her time in the reformatory, and she didn't offer.

The next morning, I woke to Justin speaking to Mother in a hushed tone. My eyes were barely open, so he didn't notice and continued speaking.

"We have to find a cure, and you may be our answer. No matter what may have happened in the past, consider the people still in the Establishment and what a cure would mean for them," he said earnestly. What past he was talking about, I had no clue, but it must have been awful if Mother was considering not helping because of it. I continued breathing as steady as I could so as not to alert them.

"I will try," she replied calmly.

"You saved me, you know? I tried to free you once I had seen how bad off you were. The Unity officers came that very night. I wish I wouldn't have made such a horrible mistake with you. I broke away from them once we were scattered," he said, somewhat defeated. They knew each other. They had a past. How?

"I forgive you, Justin, I did a long time ago," she told him.

"Let me make it up to you," he said softly.

I had never felt comfortable around Justin. I never even really liked him, but I had pity for him in this moment. I must have made a facial expression or stopped breathing steady because Mother looked at me and said, "Good morning, little bird."

I smiled at the endearment I hadn't heard since a very young age. "Did you sleep well?" she asked.

With a yawn, I made a grand gesture of waking up, hoping they didn't catch on that I had overheard some of their conversation.

"I will speak with you both later," Justin said in a very formal tone.

As he left, I turned to watch and see what emotions would run past Mother's face. She smiled and said, "How much did you hear?"

"Only some," I answered vaguely, hoping she didn't continue her line of questioning.

"Enough to know that Justin and I knew each other before today, I'm sure," she said ruefully. "We grew up in the same Establishment. He was taken away by the Seditionist when we were eleven, still children, still easily influenced. They train the children that the only cure is to wipe the world clean of those who have been injected," she finished, sounding defeated.

"What happened between you?" I asked her.

"Many things, little bird, many things," she said.

I believed her. The medic came in and took her vitals. "You are improving rapidly," the medic said in a cheerful tone.

I was glad to hear it and hoped she would be able to head to the science bunker sooner rather than later. I was eager to find a cure, even if I wasn't sure how Justin would use it. When the medic left us alone, I asked Mother, "Will you go with us to the science bunker?"

"I suppose that there isn't much else I can do. I want to help, but we must be careful that the cure is used to help and not hinder," she stated with reservation in her tone.

STAGE 2:5

I spent the next few days getting to know my mother and preparing to leave. Not that I had anything to pack, more that I needed to be mentally prepared for whatever might lie above ground. I travelled back and forth between my dwelling, training, and the medic's station. The time seemed to slow down when I had something I so eagerly wanted to happen.

The day finally came that we were to leave for the science bunker, and the thought of breathing fresh air expelled all the fear. I was fitted in kind of camouflaged pants and a long-sleeved shirt with hiking boots that were heavy to walk in, and I was to carry an oversized backpack with rations, clothing, and medical supplies—the months of combat and fitness training had prepared me for the extra weight. We all met in the long hallway that led to the great unknown. Our party included myself, Mother, Merek, Don, Abia, Colin, and three Outlandish I had never spoken to before that day.

"I don't understand why I can't come," Kasi was asking Merek. She had complained continually to me the last few days about being left behind, and although I would miss her, after listening to that for the last few days, I was slightly ready to have a break. Even the thought made me feel guilty because I knew as well as Kasi that we may never see each other again.

"You have to receive a higher score in training before they will let you venture out of the bunkers," Merek replied calmly.

"I haven't failed my training. I have done pretty well, actually," Kasi said with a little less enthusiasm than her normal self. Everyone knew she wasn't interested in training; she couldn't even fool herself.

"If we are successful, they will send another party. Work hard, little one, and we shall see you soon," Merek told her kindly.

She seemed pleased by his endearment and so gave up the argument. "I will miss you all terribly!" she lamented in her most tragic tone of voice.

I couldn't help but smile at being sent off in the most "Kasi" fashion. I hugged her tight and whispered, "I love you, Kasi, and nothing will be as exciting without you to make it so." We laughed, knowing it to be true. After goodbyes to the children and the many Outlandish that had gathered, we were headed up and out.

When the doors swung open and I breathed the fresh air for the first time in months, a few silent tears fell as I continued up the steps and into the wonderful sunlight. My skin felt the amazing warmth, and I couldn't help but feel more alive than I had in months.

"This fresh air is much needed, I'd say," said Colin.

"Yes, studies have shown that sunlight and fresh air actually help elevate a person's mood," Don informed us. "Then again, so can chocolate, intoxicants, and a look from an attractive lady," he said wiggling his eyebrows at me.

I rolled my eyes with a laugh as Merek thumped him on the back of the head. "Pay attention now! Soon we will be out of our surveillance area and have to watch out for Seditionist and Unity officers," Merek told us. The warrior in him was determined to lead and protect us now; no time for games. "The Seditionist roam this area to raid and capture small groups of people, so be on the lookout."

I walked beside Mother, taking in all the beautiful colors of autumn equinox—yellow, orange, red, and even the vibrant green of the grass before the first freeze. When we had come to the bunker, I had been frightened and hadn't even seen the countryside. I had been intent on running, completely terrified.

"It is incredible, isn't it?" Mother asked.

"Yes," I breathed, "beautiful." I enjoyed this. The talking, the expressing emotions and sharing in the world's beauty—it was new and it was wonderful. The men were talking in low murmurs around us about the weather, the Seditionist, and animals that we might run into. Don was informing the group all about the wildlife, particularly bears.

"What do we do if we see a bear?" asked Abia.

“First, speak softly to identify yourself, help the bear to not be startled and know that you are human. Secondly, you must stay calm, because bears usually just want to be left alone, much like Merek,” he said with a wink. “We really shouldn’t eat while traveling or in our camp. That will definitely draw the bears in. We will need to move away slowly, sideways if possible. Come to think of it, interaction with Merek is much like a bear encounter,” he said, bringing the small group to light laughter at Merek’s expense.

Merek didn’t seem to mind much. He just rolled his eyes and continued to lead us on our way. There didn’t seem to be any clear path or road, but I could tell Merek had no doubts as to where he was leading us. The trees grew thicker as we progressed. Rocks, thorny vines, and the roots growing up from the ground slowed down Mother. I kept pace with her and helped her where I could. She wasn’t completely ready for this venture, but we all knew time was of the essence, and she didn’t object to leaving sooner rather than later.

“We will take a short break here,” Merek told us as we came upon a small opening of trees. “Get a drink and a small amount of protein to sustain you until nightfall.”

I helped mother get as comfortable as possible against a tree, and soon, she was resting her eyes. I took out our dried meat and flacon filled with mineral water and sought out Merek. He was standing alone, looking in the direction from which we came.

“What are you looking for?” I asked him. I almost hoped to startle him, but he didn’t even flinch.

“Making sure we aren’t being followed,” he replied without looking my way. “How is your mother faring?” He turned to look at me for that one.

“It is slow going, and she is wearing down rather quickly,” I told him, wishing I had better news for him.

“It’s a few days walk for a healthy person, so this may take us a week,” he said, somewhat dismal. “I won’t risk her health, even if we have to take a break every hour. As long as we stay far away from the roads and conceal our tracks, it shouldn’t matter how long we take,” he reassured me.

"I wish we wouldn't have had to travel," I stated uselessly, having heard all equipment we needed at the science bunker and did not have in our current dwelling. Merek listened without comment and gestured for me to drink. I did so without any comment. Colin joined us, and we decided to each take turns helping my mother along so that no one person would get worn out lifting her and guiding her along the way.

Soon everyone was sated, and we began again on our course. Colin took the first shift, assisting Mother on the trail. I walked close by just in case she needed me.

"I can't get over the intoxicating smells," Mother said to Colin smiling pleasantly.

"They are pretty wonderful, aren't they?" he replied. "I can't imagine going without nature for as long as you have. This all must be awe-inspiring. How many years have you been in the reformatory?" he asked.

I tried to slow my pace without them noticing so that I wouldn't miss her response.

"Over ten years, and yes, nature in all its splendor is breathtaking," she said without the sadness I thought for sure would be present.

"You seem quite over the experience. I mean, doesn't it bother you that you lost that much time?" he asked.

"Well, of course it bothers me, but I must believe there was a purpose, a reason I was there. Maybe I will never know in this lifetime, but I have to have faith." She spoke the words with a fervor that I didn't know she had. "Life can't just be a series of uncontrolled events that we are victims of. I can't believe that. Everything has to have a purpose," she finished confidently.

"You almost sound like you believe in the primitive religions," he said with a disbelieving shake to his head. "They weren't exactly proven or even feasible for that matter," he said added.

"No, I don't believe in religion. I don't believe in that at all," she replied. "Religion was a weapon that mankind used to condone all sorts of evils. Religion was made by man, for man," she said. "I do believe in love. I believe in him," she stated cryptically.

Colin must have seen her struggling in her step, because he focused on their walking, and the conversation was over. I wondered who "he" was? This man called "love" she spoke of. I let the thoughts wander as I took in all the forest, wildlife, and the beautiful blue sky above.

We stopped for the evening, setting up our individual tents many paces from where we intended to eat per Don's instruction. Once I had my tent and Mother's set up successfully, I began to gather extremely dry wood for a small fire, nothing that would smoke much, just enough to cook, and then it would be out before it could be spotted by any passersby. The three unknown Outlandish were Francis, Vita, and Drusilla.

The two women, Vita and Drusilla, were quiet and hardworking; they seemed to see what needed to be done long before anyone voiced the need. They were drawing water for the evening fare not far from our campsite, working without much but a few words passed between them.

Francis spent most of his time with Don, laughing and carrying on about unimportant things, but I had heard Merek praise Francis for his prowess, being a good combatant and having a warrior spirit, so I knew him to be a good man to have on this venture. We ate mainly in silence, except a few timely jokes from Don and some instructions from Merek about the way ahead. We had only the moon and stars to light the camp, but I could see Abia and Colin discussing something with such ease. I envied them their comfort and friendship. I always felt to be on the outside looking in, present but not included.

Don plopped down beside me. "What are you thinking about, Alex?" he asked without any reservations.

"Oh, nothing really," I replied, looking away from the comfortable pair.

"Uh-huh," he said with a smile, "Colin is the one who saved you right?" he asked. "He stayed with you all during the lockdown and has taken you under his wing, so to speak, correct?" he finished.

"Yes, he brought us to the bunker," I said, curious as to where he was going with his questions.

He interrupted me with, "He is a very handsome, intelligent, kind, and strong manly man. I mean Merek might not like the fact that you are looking at Colin with moon eyes, but I can see why you would."

"Moon eyes?" I asked.

"Oh, you know, like love, romance, desire, lust," he said impishly.

"I wouldn't know about any of those. I mean, I hardly laugh at your jokes, and you expect me to feel love, romance, desire, or lust?" I brushed it off.

"Love is not something you have to know about, Alex. It's not an acquired taste, like my jokes, and you will laugh at them eventually, I promise. Love is a natural emotion that we have for someone we care for, and sometimes it turns into a romantic type love," he said, laughing good-naturedly.

"He could be my surrogate. He is twice the age I am," I told him lamely.

"Love doesn't really go by age," he said.

"I don't know, but please don't tell anyone what you have said to me," I pleaded. I didn't know if he was right or wrong, but I had to know before anyone else.

"I wouldn't dare say a word. Merek would tear my head off and feed it to the bears," he said, shaking his head. I knew Merek enjoyed my company and took pride in how well I did under his training, but why he would be angry, I wasn't sure I wanted to know. Where Colin reassured, calmed me, and was my safe place, Merek was unknown, intimidating, and unnerving, someone that excited me but also frightened me at the same time. "Not a word will pass my lips," he said placing his pointer finger over his lips and giving me a wink.

I smiled at Don, knowing his love for humor would never outweigh his vow to me. "I'm glad Merek paired us together when they tested us," I told Don.

He raised his eyebrows and responded, "You're glad? I could be dead if I'd been paired with someone else. I'm alive because of you."

"They wouldn't have let you die," I told him. "I think they have safety precautions in place for things like that," I finished, not wanting him to feel he owed me for anything.

"You're probably right, but it gave me a good excuse to befriend the strange new girl, and that was exciting," he said affectionately.

I laughed at that. Strange was right in comparison to all the Outlandish, and even the Empties, really; I wasn't exactly a part of any particular group. I was like a bird without a flock, and that didn't seem to change no matter who I was with.

"It's getting late. Should we go to our tents?" I asked Don.

"We can sleep when we are dead," he said. "Look at the stars. Aren't they incredible?" He passed me the flacon he had been drinking from and gestured me to drink. I took a large gulp, thinking it to be water, and nearly threw up when I realized it was a very strong intoxicant. Don was laughing at me as I took another drink to prove I could, and it took everything in me not to choke. "Good job, Alex, I'll toughen you up yet," he said through his laughter.

"You two may want to quiet it down some," Merek said as he came up behind me.

"Alex was trying Francis' home brew," Don told him.

"That stuff is strong and can bring a grown man to his knees! Be careful, Alex," Merek said with concern.

"I only had two drinks, Merek, I'll be fine," I said with a sideways glance at Don who had an 'I told you so' face.

"You're teaching her all sorts of bad habits, aren't you, Don?" Merek asked with some annoyance.

"A little won't hurt," Don replied, untroubled by the comment.

"Out here, we need our wits about us, that's all," Merek informed us.

"Sit down and take a load off, Merek, you might enjoy yourself," Don replied sarcastically.

"Take a load off" was a somewhat confusing phrase to me. What load? Off of where? Merek wasn't holding anything that I could tell. Outlandish still spoke in riddles, and time didn't seem to help me understand most days. Merek sat, took out a small flacon of his own, and took a long drink. He sat close enough to me that I could smell the strong intoxicant.

"I am taking the first shift. Don, you will have to be on watch in four hours. Can you handle that?" Merek asked him.

"I'll be off then to take a quick nap," Don said as he stood and told us goodnight.

I was alone with Merek and, of course, I didn't know any words that would suitably break the silence. Merek handed me his flacon, and I took a sip, thinking it to be strong, but it tasted sweet and smooth compared to Don's strong brew provided by Francis.

"Can you take watch after Don?" Merek broke the silence for me, and I handed him back the flacon.

"Yes, of course," I said, thankful for an easy question.

"You did well today," Merek said.

"Well? We didn't do much, just walked and made camp," I replied.

"Yes, but can you imagine Kasi on this venture? She would either be exploring every rabbit trail or complaining she couldn't pick every flower along the way. And forget about her cooking a meal with so many new things to see. You saw what needed to be done and never complained. I'd say that was a good day," he said with a laugh.

I smiled, knowing he wasn't wrong. Kasi was easily distracted and didn't like to follow orders, even if they were important. "She is still very young and will grow up one day. Hopefully not too soon. I love her wild spirit." The intoxicant was making me feel more at ease, and I knew without it, I wouldn't have added that last part.

"She is a dreamer. It must have killed her to be in the Establishment and so bound by their rules," he said.

I knew he really didn't mean "killed," but whenever the Outlandish used that term, I always had to remind myself of their strange definitions and phrases.

"Yes, it was very difficult for her. We had signals to warn the others if we saw a Unity officer coming close enough to hear us, and she wouldn't use primal slang. I was never sent to confinement for slang, but they said that my body language spoke loudly," I told him.

"Yes, you can't hide much if someone cares to look," he said with intense regard. He passed me the flacon once again, and I knew I shouldn't drink much more or I wouldn't be afraid of Merek, and that was something I was terrified of happening. I took one small drink, enjoying the sweet flavor as the intoxicant went to my head.

"You're right. I know, because I spent many hours in that horrible place because of it," I told him.

"I'm sorry, Alexandra. You didn't deserve that," he said sincerely. "I can't imagine a life like that," he finished.

"It was a life lived in fear of turning eighteen, of being a carrier, of being sent to confinement, of the reformatory, of losing myself to the injection. I have never thanked him, but Colin has no idea how much I owe him." As I said the words, I realized I had never even voiced those thoughts to myself much less out loud. "I may not fit in here anymore than I did in the Establishment, but here, I'm free to choose or at least am free to feel." I was talking more to Merek than I had spoken to any Outlandish before.

"The thing about us here is no one fits, and that is how we want it. We are all unique, different, and don't have to be the same. You belong here with us, with me," he said, reaching for my hand. His large hand was rough and callused, but he held my hand as if it was something delicate and special. I knew my own hands to be larger than most women and, after the months of training, just as callused as his own, so his gentleness was unexpected. I didn't pull away. I blamed the intoxicant. Entirely.

"With you?" I asked.

"Yes, with me. Something about you draws me in like no other woman ever has. You are brave, kind, persevere against the odds, and have a quiet strength about you. Not to mention your beauty," he said. "I think we would push each other to be stronger, better people."

He was saying this as his thumb gently brushed back and forth across my knuckles. My stomach constricted with each caress. Was this desire? I didn't know, but it was so different than what I felt in Colin's presence.

"I know all this is new to you. I know love and desire aren't things that make much sense to you right now. Just think about it, think about me. Colin may have saved you, but he and Abia have always just been together, even if they don't act like it, and I doubt Colin sees you as owing him anything or even as a woman. Not like I do," he said with earnest.

I didn't know what to say, so I nodded my head, a yes in response to his plea. He gently pulled me closer to him and pressed his lips to my own. My stomach felt as if it had turned completely over and twisted itself inside out. The kiss was soft and slow. I felt at a loss to what my reaction should be, because the kiss was upsetting and unnerving. As he pulled away, all I could hear was the beating of my heart and my ragged breathing.

"Even if you don't understand it, I know you feel it. You're shaking, Alex," he said with a smile. "Just think about me. After we get through this, after the cure, once things settle a little, we could be united. Just think about it," he said as he got up and headed out to walk the perimeter. I knew sleep was impossible, but I headed to my tent anyway. My shift would come all too soon.

STAGE 2:6

The next day began much too early. I started the day off out of routine—breakfast, packing up the camp, helping Mother along the trail—and I was in a state of sleep deprivation the entire time that made my brain work at a slower pace. Thoughts of the night before were never far from my mind, and Mother seemed to notice my distress.

I was unsure if I should tell her what had transpired the night before, but I didn't have anyone else to talk to about it either.

"I am just confused," I replied vaguely.

"About what?" she asked.

"I spoke to Don and Merek last night, and they both have strong opinions about how I feel or should feel about people," I told her with bewilderment.

"How so?" she asked, trying to get me talking, I knew. So I let it pour out quietly as we walked a safe distance behind the rest of our party, all of it—Merek, Colin, and how I had no clue what I truly felt.

"Merek and Colin are both fine men," she told me. "I am no expert on romantic love or desire having spent most of my adult life in the reformatory, but I do remember a time when I felt what I thought to be desire and found true love." She took a long pause. "I was eighteen and had just recently been inseminated. My partner was an Empty, as you like to call them. I had ragging emotions and was extremely frightened about being a carrier, so I began plotting how to change my fate. I had heard stories of a group of people living outside of the Establishment, free of the injection, but I wasn't sure if they were true or not. So I planned my escape.

"It wasn't too difficult, but I had never been watched because I always followed the rules and had never been sent to confinement. They trusted me, you see. I had played the role of a mindless woman so well, they never thought I would give them a hard time or leave the Establishment." She stopped and looked around as if someone might be listening.

"So you escaped?" I asked with some surprise.

"Yes, I left and didn't know where to go or even who I would find, but I had supplies to last me for a few weeks and was glad for the free air that being outside of the Establishment awarded me. Justin found me on the very first day. I was so glad that my childhood friend wasn't dead. I was so happy to know that he was alive and well. We had been good friends, and immediately, it was as if no time had passed. I went with him to his new home. It was the camp of the Seditionist or, as they call themselves, Survivalist. It was a harsh place with only crud buildings and no real development at all. I was so glad to be free of the injection that I didn't think too far into the future. I hadn't found out yet that the insemination worked, so I was unaware that I was carrying you.

"I discovered very quickly that the men in the Seditionist camp held women in very low regard and acted as if women in general were to blame for all the world problems. This mentality was frightening, to say the least. The women were servants and did all the hard work while the men trained to fight, hunted and, in the evenings, drank themselves to oblivion.

I was from the Establishment, so they treated me even worse. Justin was the only kind one, making our connection grow even deeper. He took up for me often, but one time in particular, a man tried to beat me for dropping my plate, saying I had wasted food, and Justin stopped him by putting himself in harm's way. He was punished harshly for it. We became inseparable. I soon saw my life take a trail following him. I desired nothing but his company, to be close to him, to care for him, and him for me." She was speaking of her desire for a man that I knew she was kind to, but I never would have thought she once loved him; not romantically, at least.

"Once I knew I was carrying you, I was confused as to what I should do. Justin and I were making plans that didn't include a child. He spoke of being united and breaking away from the Survivorist, knowing I would never be truly accepted into his world. Justin was still in training, training that taught him to kill those whom had received the injection and all the leaders, take no survivors. Death to all people of the establishments.

"I finally had no choice but to tell Justin about you before I began to show. In that moment, I saw him change before my very eyes, and he handed me over to the leader of his camp, a man named Raymon Fuerte. Raymon was unwavering in his hatred of women, especially those from the Establishment, even if they weren't injected yet. I was imprisoned without any kind of trial, without any protest from Justin, and soon I became the outlet for Raymon's anger. He tortured me most days and did unspeakable things during the dark of night. I was so angry at Justin for rejecting me, for handing me over to be tormented. I wanted to die."

Her words pained me. My mother pregnant, scorned by her lover for me, completely rejected, beaten, and desiring death—it brought tears to my eyes. I had no words to speak.

"Everything changed for me one night after a notably bad beating. I thought I would lose you for sure. When I passed out from the pain, I had the most amazing dream. It was white everywhere. Everything was pure, was whole, complete. I couldn't make out people or even objects, but something spoke from the pureness, from the shining light. There wasn't exactly an audible voice. It was more like my own voice in my head, but it wasn't me. The voice was kind, concerned, loving, and the words poured over me like a cleansing shower.

"I had never felt so complete, whole, not lacking any need. Words like love, forgiveness, mercy, kindness, and hope. The voice told me that I was safe and that you were safe, that I must forgive them, they only hurt me from their own hurt, their own fear, that they knew not what they did. The voice called itself Ruach HaKodesh and told me to seek his voice, his word, and his true love. Agape love without borders or restrictions, a love that forgives at all times, keeps no record of wrongs, and a love that casts out all fear. I had never heard of such a love, but in my dream, I had felt it. I knew in that moment that I would forgive anyone and anything if it meant feeling this way always."

My mother had tears streaming down her face. She was smiling as if she were happy, so I knew they were good tears. We were far behind the party, and I could see that they had stopped for a break, so we sat together a good distance away so I could hear the rest of her story.

"The next day, I awoke without the usual anger that had become my only defense, and instead I saw the fear that ran rampant in the Seditionist. They thought the only way to protect themselves was to kill all who were different than them. I was still beaten by Raymon every night, but the voice would come back to pour love over me in my sleep. Agape love.

"Once I was allowed to go to the bathing area alone and saw Justin, he had never seen me since he left me with Raymon, I could tell by his expression he had no clue how bad my life had become. I must have been quite the sight to see—bruised, pregnant, looking like I hadn't eaten in days. He stopped abruptly, his face lost all color, and tears were in his eyes. He tried to speak but only choked up. I placed my hand on his arm, whispering that I had forgiven him, and I rushed away, not wanting him to get in trouble.

"I never saw him again, because that evening, Unity officers destroyed the camp and took me back to the Establishment. I thought they would send me to the reformatory once I was back, but they only questioned me about the camp, acting as if I was kidnapped. They then returned me to my partner and former dwelling.

"I attempted to live by their rules but couldn't help but overflow with the love I had been lavished with onto you and others. I was sent to the reformatory for it, as you well remember, but Ruach HaKodesh still speaks to me about agape love from time to time. That is the love that I know about. That is the only true love that really matters."

She finished. Her story was not an easy one to hear. Her pain was my own, and her hope was in something I couldn't grasp. "Who do you think this Ruach HaKodesh is?" I asked after a long pause where I was trying to absorb her story.

"He is love. He is Shaddai," she spoke with reverence.

"A god from the old religions?" I asked, only having read about religion in the primal books years ago and not remembering anything particularly good coming from them.

"No, he is love, he is the creator. Perhaps he was spoken of by religion, but they distorted and changed him to fit their needs." She spoke the words with such confidence. I dared not challenge her further. The party began traveling again, so we joined them. I had much to think about, so much more than Merek or Colin. I wanted to know of this love that cast out all fear. Fear was my consistent companion, and I hated him.

STAGE 2:7

On the fifth day, we were traveling near a suspected Seditionist fort, so we were extremely quiet and careful. I couldn't stand the smell of myself, so when we made camp by a spring-fed creek, I snuck away, telling only Mother, to bathe upstream from the encampment and in a somewhat private area surrounded by trees. I knew better than to completely strip my clothing just in case someone came along, but I felt safe enough to wash myself and my underclothing.

The water sent chills all over my olive skin, and I rubbed my arms up and down, trying to stay warm. Between the sand and the soap I used, it wasn't long before I felt refreshed and clean. I should have immediately gotten out of the water and hurried back to the camp. It only took so long to "gather wood," but the stillness and the complete serenity I felt in this place could not be left easily. I was floating aimlessly when I heard a branch crack not far from my peaceful pool. I jerked my body under the water with only my head slightly poking out. I knew better than to call out and remained silent, hoping it was a wild animal passing by. I held my breath, my heart racing for what seemed like an eternity before I heard the sound once again.

"Do you speak English?" an unknown voice asked from the place where the crack had come from. "You couldn't possibly be from the Establishment." The voice chuckled. "You are too wanton for that and too old to be untouched by the injection for that matter." It was then that I saw him emerge from the tree line. He was young, handsome, and sinewy with a dark complexion, tattoos marking up his exposed skin.

"I do. Who are you?" I asked, keeping my voice steady despite the fear welling up inside.

"Lieutenant Francisco Fuerte at your service," he stated dramatically. "And who might you be?" he asked in return.

"I am Alexandra," I replied, hoping that my absence was noticed and that soon my mother would send someone to check on me. *Foolish! Foolish!* I knew better than to lie and put myself in this danger.

"Well, Alexandra, you are now coming with me," he told me with no room for argument, but I couldn't not ask.

"Why? Have I broken some edict? What is my offense?" I asked with all the courage I could muster.

"Nothing but being in the wrong place at the wrong time, I'm afraid," he replied with a slight chuckle. "You can either get dressed or I'll drag you through the forest in your underthings. The choice is yours." He didn't seem to care if I opposed his command. He knew he had the upper hand. I proceeded to edge my way to the clothing lying on the ground, hoping Francisco wouldn't notice the knife and small hatchet by my pack. As my body came out of the water, my underclothes were clinging to me without forgiveness; I knew I shouldn't, but I felt ashamed and exposed.

He was looking at me as if I was something he wanted to devour, whether for lust or maybe he just desired to kill; I wasn't sure. I had to try to escape before he had his way with me, whatever his way happened to be.

"Where are you taking me? If you plan to kill me, go ahead. There is no need to go anywhere for that," I told him, stalling, hoping to see Merek through the trees.

"You misunderstand my intentions. I will not kill you, but after I bring you to my padre, you may wish for death," he replied nonchalantly.

Padre? I was so close to the hatchet now, but Francisco was edging ever closer to my pack. I wasn't sure how well of an opponent I would make to him. I had no choice, though. I surged for the hatchet and saw Francisco rush toward me almost immediately. My fingers curved around the smooth wooden handle as I felt the weight of Francisco hit me midback. I was knocked down to the ground but didn't let the loss of breath stop me from slamming the hatchet into his forearm. He let out a muffled cry. I knew I needed to shake free of him and run for all I had. He loosened his grip for a few moments, and I took full advantage, jumping up, running for the camp. I stopped when I heard a shot fired.

"Stop! I didn't want to use violence, but I will if necessary!" he said.

I turned to see him with his firearm pointed directly at my head. He took three rushed steps to me, pulled me to him, turned me around, holding me close to him with the injured forearm across my neck and gun at my temple now. It was then I noticed several unknown men in the trees to our left, watching with laughter in their eyes. Francisco wasn't alone.

"Alex, what is going on?" Colin asked from the direction of the camp. I knew they all must be there watching me, Merek, Don, and the others. "Release her!" Colin shouted.

"I don't believe I will," Francisco told my party with a shake of his head.

"If you don't, I will be forced to kill you slowly," Merek threatened. He was more frightening than ever with death in his eyes.

Francisco laughed. It wasn't a pleasant laugh; it sent chills down my spine.

"None are allowed to pass through my forest without paying a toll. She will suffice," Francisco informed them. Not a soul budged from their aggressive positions; instead, they seemed more alert than moments before. "My men will not kill you all if you let us go without incident," Francisco continued.

"Take me instead," Colin said.

I couldn't let that happen. Colin was needed to find the cure from Mother. I couldn't see her anywhere.

"No, no, I will be taking her." Francisco shook his head with his evil smile.

"What kind of man are you that you would use a woman for a shield?" Merek asked with disdain.

"A smart one," Francisco replied without hesitation.

"I am the leader, take me instead," Merek offered. He was putting down his own weapon and took steps toward us, hands up in surrender.

"*No!*" I shouted as Francisco tightened his grip at my throat so that I was unable to say more. Francisco's men rushed forward, grabbing Merek.

"I believe I will take you both," Francisco laughed as if he had told us a joke. I thrashed against his hold, not wanting my thoughtlessness to get Merek captured also. "Back away or we will kill them both!" Francisco shouted.

Colin waved the party back. Once they were out of sight, Francisco and his men led us away. Merek was bound, blindfolded, and gagged. They must not have believed me to be much of a threat because they dragged me along untethered. I had to free Merek somehow; we had to escape.

The journey to their camp was short, but they stopped often to ensure we weren't being followed. I tried to pay careful attention as we came in sight of their camp in order to know the best route for our escape. I remembered the way in which mother described the Seditionist fort and knew I was about to face the horrors my mother once had. I wish the loving voice she had spoken of would reassure me. However, I wasn't expecting anything but fear to scream at me.

As we passed through the large gates and they shut behind us, chills ran down my spine, they shoved us down to our knees beside one another, and I reached for Merek's bound hands, trying to reassure myself that I wasn't completely alone. His grip was strong and comforting. We hadn't spoken alone since the night he asked me to consider being united with him, but that seemed like a lifetime ago.

"Thank you. I'll find a way for us to escape," I whispered through my tears.

He could only nod his head and squeeze my hand in response.

Francisco was speaking to a shorter man that had the look of authority about him. I wondered what they would do with us. I dreaded what they would do with us. The pair walked over to Merek and me, looking us over with disdain.

"Meet mi padre, Raymon Fuerte," Francisco said with a wave of his hand in the shorter man's direction.

I instantly hated the man before me for the pain he had inflicted upon my mother for no other reason than that she was a woman. He was short yet powerfully built with menacing brown eyes that cut right through me. I never in my life desired someone's death like I did in that moment.

"This one may be of use." He pointed at Merek and spoke with a raspy voice that made my skin crawl. "We can send him through the program. He is young yet," Raymon said with no infliction or emotion.

"Padre, what should I do with the woman?" Francisco asked.

"Whatever you wish. I have no need for her at this time." Raymon dismissed me without a care.

"What shall I do with you?" Francisco whispered to me threateningly.

I wanted to scream in his face to let us go, but I knew it was pointless, so I refrained. Francisco jerked me away from Merek, my only comfort. I felt as if I was being ripped from my only lifeline, and panic blackened my vision. The entire venture, I hadn't screamed in hysteria, but I couldn't help the scream that tore through my vocal cords as Francisco dragged me away from Merek. My vision was pinpointed to Merek's reaction to my screams by him wrenching against his restraints and getting a blow to the head for it. I stopped screaming instantly and choked down my fear, not wanting Merek to be hurt anymore. The world finished blacking out, and I no longer felt anything.

STAGE 2:8

I woke to my hands being bound to a pole in the center of what looked to be one of the tents I had seen when we entered the fort. I was unsure how much time had passed. The fort was loud. I seemed to be alone, so I looked around for something, anything that would help my escape.

The far edge was obviously an area for meals, so I hoped to find a utensil that would loosen if not cut my ties. I stretched out my leg, hoping to knock over the baskets that were placed beside the plates and cups; surely a knife or fork was there. Extending my body and then my leg as far as I could, I couldn't quite reach the basket. Escape wasn't coming from the basket. Tugging on the ropes that bound me, I then started to think that if I could dig around the pole, maybe I could take the rope under the pole, freeing myself. Digging in earnest, I put all my hope in freeing myself. My ears were buzzing with the frenzy I was in.

"What is digging going to do for you?" Francisco asked from the opening in the tent. My hopes crashed at his voice. I refused to speak; words wouldn't change anything. "Not speaking anymore? That's just as well. I don't much enjoy overly wordy women. I do, however, love to talk. So let me explain how this new relationship will work. You are now mine. I own you. Escape is futile, and you may come to enjoy my company." He finished with a laugh that had no humor in it. I wouldn't enjoy anything from him, I was certain of that. "We will start with the marking." He said this as if I knew what a marking was, which I did not. He pulled out a small dagger from his belt and moved toward me. "You can either hold still or I'll drag you naked out to the center of the fort and allow everyone to watch as I mark you."

I believed him and didn't want that humiliation, so I remained quiet as he tore my blouse and pressed the dagger into my unmarked skin right below my collarbone. Surprisingly, the pain was dull as he carved deeply into my flesh what seemed to be his initials. I was numb with fright, that had to be it, because blood was pouring out, and even he seemed shocked that I didn't make a sound. "Strong woman," he mumbled to himself. "You will be cleansed for our ritual now," he informed me without explanation as he washed his hands of my blood.

Once again, I had no idea what he was speaking of or what a "cleansing" could be. He left the tent abruptly, and in came two women carrying a basket. They didn't speak to me, but their mutilated bodies spoke louder than any words. One had no ears, the other one was missing the tip of her nose, and despite my efforts, I cringed whenever she came close. They were replacing my clothing and burning my old clothing. I wanted to ask them who had caused them so much harm, but they probably wouldn't answer anyway.

"What is the cleansing ritual?" I asked instead.

"Prisoners are cleaned of all evil spirits," the noseless one answered in a strange accent. Prisoners, she had said. Perhaps Merek would be there. I needed to see that he wasn't harmed. The women stuffed me into a white dress that was so tight I could hardly breathe, and they cinched up the back even tighter so that my head began to swim.

"How will I be cleansed?" I asked, not sure I was ready for their answer.

"It is a three-part ritual through fire, water, and herbs," the earless one responded with a voice of one that doesn't speak often. The ritual sounded frightening, so I asked no more questions as they finished preparing me; however, I couldn't help the shivers that ran up and down my body as they did so.

All too soon, they were leading me from the tent to what seemed to be a platform surrounded by the residents of the fort. I took in many faces of the women as I was being led up the platform, and each face told me a story of neglect and abuse. I had never felt such horror before this day. Merek was there, beaten with a rope around his neck; blood had soaked through his clothing, and his eyes were swollen shut. My heart broke at the sight of him. Merek, with all his strength, was reduced to this for me, no less.

"Let the cleansing begin!" said a man in black robes to Merek's left.

I was placed beside Merek with a rope looped around my neck also. A man came up the platform, bearing a torch; the fire was the first step in this ritual. The robed figure took the fire from the man and began searing Merek's body with it, beginning with his chest and going down. Soon his clothing was in ashes at his feet. Merek was thrashing against the ropes that held him, only to go limp after the flame reached his knees. With nothing to hide Merek's many wounds, my pain for him only increased.

The robed figure came to me and slowly burned off the dress the two women had taken such time in preparing. The pain was such that I couldn't describe. It took the air from my lungs. I refused to pass out, hoping to see my way to escape. The clothing helped to lessen the pain. I wondered if the women had done something to the clothing to help me survive this ordeal. Merek came back to consciousness with a gasp.

"Merek, please don't die! I need you," I whispered knowing he couldn't hear me. We made eye contact, and I pleaded with him to live, not to leave me.

He nodded his head in what I took to be agreement. My dress was nothing but ashes at my feet now. I knew the minute Merek saw the marking Francisco had painful given me, because he once more thrashed against the ropes that bound him with a strength I wouldn't have thought him to have in the broken state he was in. Next, a barrel of what I assumed was water was brought to the platform, and Merek was placed into it head first by several men. I screamed and jerked on my own ties, knowing I was helpless to save him. I looked into the crowd hoping to find sympathy from anyone, and all I saw were the faces of men with the look of pure satisfaction and Francisco smiling as if he took pleasure in the sight.

Soon Merek's legs stopped twitching, and I knew he must be dead; my heart shattered at the thought. They took his limp body out and tossed him to the side without a thought, still bound and looking lifeless. The noose was taken from around my neck, and I was being led to the barrel with as much resistance as my weak body could handle. I kicked and bit and fought as they turned me upside down and dropped me into the barrel. My lungs were soon burning without oxygen, and I knew I would soon die or pass out. The last thought I had was a plea for help to Ruach HaKodesh. *You once saved my mother. Please, please save Merek. I dare not beg for myself, this was all my own doing.* I floated in darkness for only a short time before I was woken by the robed figure shoving something into my mouth.

"Swallow or die," he said with a voice that dripped with malice. The knife at my throat told me he was serious.

I swallowed the foul-tasting herbs and saw him nod to someone above me. The ritual of fire, water, and herbs was over. I had survived. I looked around, hoping to catch a glimpse of Merek, but he was nowhere to be seen. Francisco grabbed my bound hands and began to drag me. The crowd let up a cheer. Some men even offered a pat on Francisco's back and a harsh kick to my gut as we passed on our way back to the tent. I didn't want to dwell on my future in the secluded tent. I dared not imagine what Francisco had in store for me there.

When we were once again alone in his tent, he removed the ropes that had bound me and wrapped my bruised and bloodied body in a blanket.

"Sit," he commanded.

I was in some sort of shock and made no argument as I sat down on a pallet.

"I know you think me harsh, but you are mine now, and these are our ways. You had to be marked and cleansed in order to live among us. Some men mark their women by taking an ear or a finger. Be glad I only inscribed my name." He said this as if I should be happy that he only slightly mutilated me. I wanted to show him what I could do with the knife, if only he would let me. I knew that if I had to choose between escape and killing the man that had become my tormentor, the decision wouldn't be easy.

I suddenly felt the need to vomit the herbs; I had almost forgotten about them. Francisco must have known what my reaction would be and he handed me a bucket.

"Don't make a mess. The retching won't last long," he informed me, unconcerned. I heaved into the bucket until I had nothing left to heave. "There, you are finished. Nothing left of your old life, and now you are cleansed," he said with excitement.

"Merek. Did he survive?" I asked, breaking my silence.

"Don't concern yourself with him any longer. He is nothing to you," Francisco replied. He began removing his clothing. I felt my stomach drop, knowing his intentions and feeling revulsion at the thought. I ran to the meal area, grabbed a pan, and began fighting with all I had, which wasn't much in my weakened state. He easily dodged my blows and sent a fist right to my jaw. Everything was dark once again.

STAGE 2:9

Reality wasn't something I desired to deal with, yet I couldn't help but hear Francisco on the fringe of my awareness speaking to someone outside of the tent. I wanted to shut everything out if only for a few more moments. I had to find out if Merek was still alive. I had to escape and I had to kill Francisco. Not necessarily in that order, but it had to be done.

Shutting my eyes tightly didn't help. Avoiding awareness wasn't working, so I slowly started to move my body, discovering a few things in the process: 1. I was once again bound; 2. The inscription under my collar bone was crusted over and painful; 3. I had clothing on; and 4. Agony ran all over my body, especially my inner thighs. He had forced himself on me. My blackout didn't prevent me from fading in and out during the appalling nightmare. We had learned of procreation from the primal books. No one had ever spoken of the pain and degradation of the act if forced. Primal books explained that the inconsequential result was pleasure, but insemination had replaced the outdated practice, eliminating disease and unwanted pregnancies. I wanted to give in to the girl that was crying inside and break into a million pieces, but I had to survive if for no other reason than to save Merek and kill the man that had taken everything from me.

"I see you are awake. Now you will learn your daytime duties. If you work well, you will remain mine, but if I grow weary of your company, I'll give you to the highest bidder," he said, laughing.

I wouldn't do as he asked; for him, I would do what he asked to escape. I nodded my head in understanding. All the while, I burned with hatred. In that moment, I realized that my constant companion of fear was no longer present. He had been drowned out by the much louder malice, hate, and anger.

Francisco laid out what his expectations were of me during the day. Every task he mentioned was completed by him saying, “Refuse, and I’ll take pleasure in beating you.” I dismissed fear’s voice and latched on to anger, declaring I must escape and exact revenge once I was able.

“Just on the off chance you are planning on running, I have a new accessory for you to wear,” he told me as he placed shackles on my ankles. I knew this complicated my escape. However, I gave it no more thought than the fear that would overwhelm me if I didn’t fill myself up with thoughts of revenge.

Then began a sad existence that was my life. I tried, but no avail, to discover if Merek was living. Francisco didn’t allow me to leave the tent for any reason, and he hardly left for that matter. I fought him at each turn, for each new thing he commanded me to do, and was thoroughly beaten for it. Each night I scratched, clawed, and kicked as my body was violated repeatedly.

On the ninth day, I noticed Francisco was treating me differently. He watched every move I made, he spoke less, seemed not to command me anymore as much as asked me, was gentle in his dealings of me, and the violations stopped entirely. He did curious things, like as I pretended to sleep, which I was forced to sleep by his side hands and feet bound together, he would brush my hair from my eyes. He wrapped my shackles with animal hide in order to prevent the chaffing and once grabbed my hand, pressing his lips to them. I jerked my hand away, of course, but he was changing, and it wasn’t expected.

“Will you ever give in, my feisty goddess?”

I wanted to retch at the endearment, but I ignored him entirely, which only bothered him more. “Ignore me if you must, but one day, you will love me,” he said with some anger in his voice. I was surprised by his reaction. No matter how I fought him, he never roused to anger; he always seemed to be laughing at me. “Most women desire my attention,” he added, back to his arrogant self.

“I will never love you.” I replied with malice.

“You are very different from nearly all the women I have ever known,” he told me with admiration. “None have I known to fight quite like you. Most desire me or fear me." He finished with a shake of his head, almost as if he was speaking to himself. I couldn't think about being afraid. I had my fury to keep me surviving.

"I don't fear you. I loathe your existence," I spoke through clenched teeth.

He laughed at me as if I was no threat to him in anyway, and I wanted to take the life blood from his body at that very moment. I know Mother had experienced the same cruel fate as I had and found a peace I didn't understand, but for me, there was no dream, no voice of love, just a hatred that kept me breathing in and out, in and out.

"I find that you intrigue me. I have conquered your body, but I desire your mind and whatever keeps you fighting me. I desire you by my side when we conquer the Sovereignty," he spoke with determination. "The women in this fort have never been an acceptable companion for a warrior like me, but I believe you will be." He spoke as if I would change my mind and join his cause; the thought was repulsive.

Someone was calling him from the tent opening. He walked through the opening, and I heard raised voices and heated tones. I had to know what was happening, so I got as close as my shackles would allow and could just make out what was being said.

"Tu padre wants me to inquire if your infatuation with this woman will allow you to leave her presence for more than a few moments so that you can attend mealtime with him?" the new voice spoke with sarcasm.

"I'm as free as I've always been to attend mealtime," Francisco replied.

"Tu padre believes this woman to have entrapped you. He wants to discuss what shall be done. Women have no value or intelligence as you know and have been taught," said the unknown voice. I was hoping to hear of Merek, but they were just claiming I had a hold on Francisco. I wanted to close out the conversation, but new information, no matter how disturbing, could aid in my escape.

"The woman is mine, and I will decide what shall be done. Mi padre gave her to me to do as I wish. Would he take that back?" Francisco was close to yelling now, so I backed up to my former position, knowing the debate was over. He came stomping back into the tent, steaming from the accusations of his padre. I hadn't thought him staying in the tent was particularly strange. I thought only that he had wanted to make sure I didn't escape, but apparently, it meant more.

"I will be attending the evening meal with mi padre," he told me in a raised voice; the cool façade was no longer in place.

"You have never left me alone," I said, trying to agitate the already sore subject.

"I leave you when I want," he replied. "I won't be long, mi amor."

He spoke in a language I didn't understand and left me abruptly. His absence left me no outlet to spew my hatred. I made myself remain busy by mending the dress I had worn for the last eleven days. I couldn't reach the food that was intended for us to eat before the intruder manipulated Francisco into attending the evening mealtime, so I sat there hungry and waited. Francisco finally stumbled back into the tent sometime late into the night.

"You must be starved," he slurred the words.

I was but refused to respond. He began clumsily preparing me a plate of food. "Mi padre doesn't appreciate the time I spend in your presence. He claims I have neglected my duties, which I haven't, because right now, we are only planning our next attack, and I am only a figurehead. They claim I have authority. However, Padre makes the decisions. I am only to agree."

I listened closely, only in hopes of finding out what their plans could be. I didn't want to but knew in the inebriated state he was in that I should ask questions. I had to tread lightly.

"You didn't seem quite a leader when you captured me," I said it with malice, knowing he would suspect if I said it any other way.

"I am," he stated with irritation. "I would lead better than even Padre. I would conquer without all the death. We need people to see the truth, to become a part of us. I do not hate women as the rest of my people," he said, looking into my eyes with intention as he brought me a plate loaded up with food. He handed me the plate and began to loosen my shackles.

My shackles had become a part of me. They had not been removed since they were latched on eleven days ago. He began caressing my leg as I ate. I kicked him in the face the moment my legs were free. He fell backward, and I jumped up to make my escape. For being inebriated, he reacted much faster than I suspected, pouncing on me when I had nearly reached the opening in the tent.

"Will you ever give in?" he asked in annoyance. "They want me to sacrifice you to the gods. I refused, but maybe they are right." He was sitting on top of me and holding my hands behind my back now. I knew a simple maneuver would release me, so I caught my breath and waited for him to give me my opening. "You cause me more trouble than you are worth." I felt the pressure release for only a second. I twisted and used a scissor maneuver with my legs to knock him to the ground. He hit his head on the way down. Blood was everywhere. I didn't check to see if he was dead. I rushed to the opening to check for a guard. There were two, both sleeping.

"Wait," Francisco said from his slumped state. "If they catch you fleeing, they will kill you on sight." He was breathing heavily. It was in the moment that I noticed the back of the tent moving. I quickly placed the shackles on an immobile Francisco and grabbed his dagger from the chest in the corner of the tent where he always kept it. Pressing the dagger to his throat, I waited for whoever was coming through the tent wall. They wouldn't dare attack me with Francisco as my prisoner. With each tear in the tent, my heart increased in speed. The light was dim, but as the figures emerged, I recognized Colin and Don. My relief was instant.

"Colin? Don?" I whispered, not wanting to wake the guards outside the tent. Francisco was passed out once again, the injury to his head bleeding profusely. They rushed to me.

"You have a prisoner, I see," Don said as he embraced me. I couldn't help but flinch. Both Colin and Don looked at each other in surprise.

"We have to leave now before they change the guards and are more alert. We will take him with us in case we run into any trouble. He should be a good hostage," Colin said, hoisting Francisco's limp body over his shoulder. "Looks like you were about to escape without any help from us," Colin said with some amazement.

"Not many women could defeat this one," Don laughed, pointing to Francisco. We gagged Francisco in case he woke during our escape. "Do you know where Merek is being held?"

At the mention of Merek's name, my heart wanted to stop beating.

"I believe he is dead," I replied through my pain.

"*Dead?*" Colin asked. Both Don and Colin looked shocked.

"Last I saw him was at the cleansing. They burned and then drowned him. I too would be dead if the women hadn't put me in clothing that protected me," I told them. "I haven't been allowed outside of this tent since then. So I'm not certain," I finished.

"We knew you to be alive from a scout but no sight of Merek. He must be dead because we have been watching for several days trying to find an opening to rescue you both," Colin said, somewhat defeated. We were slowly venturing out of the tent, Don in the lead.

"We can't just leave without knowing for sure," I told them.

"We can't just wonder around the fort, hoping to bump into him either. We have a short window before these drunk guards are replaced with not so drunk guards that will be much harder to sneak past," Don informed me. "We saw they were celebrating and counted on them drinking too much. That's how we got here undetected," he finished with resolve. I knew he was right, but the thought of not knowing what happened to Merek was unbearable.

"We have him." Colin pointed to the limp Francisco. "He will confirm Merek's fate, and if he is still alive, we will rescue him too."

Colin gave me some hope. I nodded in agreement and followed their lead. As we walked past sleeping guards, I hardly allowed myself to breathe, not wanting to wake them. The distance to the outskirts of the fort was much shorter than I expected, and soon we were back into the forest near the stream where I had been captured, what seemed a lifetime ago. There to greet us was a group of Outlandish I didn't know but was thankful, nonetheless, to see. They had horses for us to ride and a small cart hooked up to a donkey. I had never ridden an animal, but to escape, I would ride a lion at this point.

"The cart was in case you were injured. You seem only slightly abused," Colin said, noticing my bruises and scrapes. I didn't tell him of all the wounds that he couldn't see, that I couldn't bear to voice. I didn't allow the thoughts to linger and instead helped them load Francisco into the cart and mount the horse behind Colin. Holding on for dear life, we were off in a flash, the cart bouncing around behind the donkey. I hoped Francisco broke a few bones on the journey. Now that he was completely at my mercy, I could hardly wait to end his life, but I knew we needed information about Merek and even the Seditionist fort itself. I had to bide my time and relish his coming demise. The riding lulled me into a sort of half sleep that I jerked out of a few times. Colin stopped the horse off to the side.

"Here, ride in front of me in case you fall to sleep," he said.

I obliged him, and soon we were off once again, headed to safety. I tried to stay awake, but the comfort I was now afforded in the refuge of Colin's arms had me in a dreamless sleep moments later.

STAGE 3:0

The sun was peaking up over the hills in the distance when I woke to Colin carrying me into a bunker, much like the one we had left only a few weeks before.

"I can walk now," I told Colin, needing space between us. He put me down without hesitation. I walked to the bunker doors. Mother was there waiting. She opened her arms, and I went into them without delay. I couldn't help the sobs that took hold of me. My nightmare was over but would always haunt me.

Mother was crying too. She knew; she understood the atrocities that had befallen me. I couldn't speak or subdue the tears. She didn't ask me to. She held me, she cried for me, and soon the relief of her presence slowed the tears to a trickle. The Outlandish took the bound and still unconscious Francisco into the bunker. I cringed at the sight of him, hoping they would torture information out of him. Following Mother, she led me to a private room where she was staying.

"You don't have to tell me anything, but when you are ready, I'm here. I understand," she said.

I would never voice the things that were done to me. I couldn't. In silence, she mended my wounds and dressed my cuts and scrapes, not saying a word about how they came about. Soon I was clean and mended, lying in her bed.

"Rest now. I will bring the evening fare once you wake." Her voice was shaky as she shut the door to leave me in peace and quiet. Peace and quiet was not something I would ever have again. I knew that. I attempted to rest. I did for what seemed like hours, but closing my eyes only brought on images I never wanted to see again—feelings, sounds, and tastes that made me want to retch. I ran to the latrine and barely made it in time before I threw up over and over until there was nothing left. That's where she found me. I'm sure I was a sight.

"Are you ill?" Mother asked, worry evident in her voice.

"I don't believe so," I replied, wishing she hadn't found me in such a state. I think she understood why I was ill because she left it at that.

"I brought something to help you sleep," she told me, holding out pills and a glass of water to take them. I took them without asking what they were, anything to help me sleep and not think. "Come back to the bed. They should work quickly," she urged me. I collapsed into the bed, and soon, oblivion overtook me.

STAGE 3:1

I slept for a few days aided by the pills Mother would provide each time I woke to eat. Waking was always harsh and unforgiving, so I desired the effects of the pills more than I cared to admit. I lost count of the days in my drugged state of mind until one day, Mother said the medics recommend that I be lucid for their exam. I wanted to run and hide at the thought of an exam but agreed nonetheless.

"They just want to make sure you are healing, and there are no long-term effects, little bird." Despite what she said, I knew there would be so many long-term effects of my imprisonment. I would never be the same. She looked at me as if she knew what I was thinking and gave me a sad smile.

"I'll go. I have slept enough, I'm sure," I told her, trying to ease the discomfort that my attitude had placed over us both.

"You can take as long as you need. You know that, right?" she asked me with concern. I knew she would let me sleep away the pain for a time, but how long I needed, I wasn't sure.

"Did Colin find out anything about Merek?" I asked, ignoring her question and feeling shame for not asking sooner. *Merek, how could I forget?* I blamed the pills and its addictive properties. Taking the pills wasn't an option anymore. I had to find Merek and then end Francisco.

"The prisoner only woke today. He has been in a coma. The medic wasn't sure he would make it," she told me.

"How many days have passed?" I asked, passing any mention of Francisco the prisoner.

"Only three days," she told me.

"We must find out about Merek and send a team to save him if he is still alive," I said in earnest.

"They will, I'm sure!" Mother replied quickly.

I dressed into my typical attire since coming to the Outlandish. The pants were a sturdy material, a plethora of pockets to hold anything I might need. The shirt was thicker than most clothing I wore while living in the Establishment, but it suited me now. The boots laced up my ankles and had a steel toe for protection. I wanted to feel secure and back to myself, but the clothing couldn't hide what happened; nothing could.

Mother hovered over me. I didn't mind, but there were no words to ease her mind or my own for that matter. So I didn't speak. I just followed Mother to the medic's office and hoped it wouldn't be too humiliating. Mother spoke to the medic for me. She answered all the questions she knew the answers to, and I ignored the rest. The medic didn't seem offended by my silence but instead was very delicate and thoughtful throughout the entire process—checking my reflexes, shining a piercing light into my eyes, ears, and nose, taking blood, and telling me I needed to eat more. That kindness was so in opposition to my experience in the Establishment. I wanted to cry again but denied myself the luxury.

"I will run a few blood tests, and we will know much more. You are healing nicely. However, you shouldn't take the sleeping medication unless absolutely necessary," the medic informed me but was looking pointedly at Mother as if to tell her to watch me closely.

I saw mother's nod to the medic and knew they shared concerned for my dependence on the sleeping meds, as did I. The thought of sleep without the aid of oblivion seemed frightening. I wasn't ready to dream. I never wanted to dream again.

"I will contact you the minute we have the blood test results back," the medic said, dismissing us. As we walked back to Mother's room in silence, a stray thought popped into my mind about archaic intercourse and what the results were—a baby. I came to a sudden stop at the thought. The medic was testing me for pregnancy. Fear was back in full force. I couldn't have a child from that monster. The thought was impossible and utterly disgusting. Surely my body wouldn't betray me in a such a manner as to accept his horrible seed.

"What's wrong?" Mother asked with distress.

I couldn't speak. My voice was stuck somewhere deep in my chest, gripped in terror.

"Are you in pain?" she inquired in urgency.

I shook my head in response. "I—" I choked on the words, and anger welled up at the thought of such a reminder growing inside my belly.

"Alexandra, what is it?" she asked, worry radiating from her entire demeanor.

"Am I with child?" I finally got the words passed the enormous lump in my throat. It was as if the words physically hurt Mother. She flinched in pain.

"We won't know for sure until the bloodwork comes back," Mother said quietly.

"This can't be happening," I whispered more to myself more than Mother, but she hugged me in an attempt to comfort me. I felt numb. I wanted to ask her for the sleep medication to drown out the reality I found myself in, but I knew at this point, she wouldn't allow me to take any. "Can't the medic do some procedure to end the pregnancy?" I asked Mother. Recollections from my primal studies brought to mind procedures that ended unwanted pregnancies.

"I don't believe the people here allow them. Primal history shows how barbaric they were. That is why they developed the monitored insemination in the Establishment. Here they use contraceptives," Mother told me.

"I wasn't given the option of contraceptives!" I said, raising my voice in anger. I regretted my outburst; Mother was only trying to help. I had seen the pictures from the primal books. I knew how awful they were, but I couldn't allow such an atrocity to exist. I had to end it. "Can't the medic just give me a pill to end it?" I asked her in a calmer voice. The shrill was still present and uncontrolled by me.

"We aren't sure you are pregnant yet. However, I will speak to the medic," she said, trying to control her own emotions. I could tell. I turned and left Mother behind. I had to take my fury out on someone, so I wandered around the bunker until I came across Don.

"Where are they keeping the prisoner?" I asked forcefully.

"No 'Hello, Don' or 'Thank you for rescuing me, Don?'" he said in his usual humorous manner.

I ignored him. "Tell me where they are keeping him," I demanded.

"Okay, okay. Follow me," he said, turning back the way he had come, taking me to the holding area. We walked with no words passing between us. I counted the hallways and doorways we passed, needing to calm myself with some distraction; altogether twenty-three. Once we arrived, I pushed past Don and burst through the door. Francisco was hanging from the rafters by a chain attached to his wrists, swaying back and forth. Colin was there and two men that I had never met before. They were questioning Francisco about Merek's status.

"Is he still alive?" the shortest man asked. "Give us some information, and we will let you down."

"Hmm, I rather enjoy the swinging. It's quite soothing." Francisco spoke with nonchalance. The men all seemed to notice me at the same time and looked at me in surprise, especially Francisco. Gut burning with rage, I advanced to Colin, pulling the knife from his scabbard and thrust it into Francisco's bicep. He screamed in agony.

"*Is he alive?*" I screamed.

Colin stood in shock for only a slow second before he grabbed and pulled me away from Francisco. I fought with all I had while screaming the question over and over. Colin carried me back to the door and put me down out of reach.

"Calm down, Alex, we can handle this," Colin tried to reassure me.

"No, we have to know *now*," I yelled.

Francisco wasn't smiling anymore but was instead writhing in pain.

"Tell us!" I demanded again.

Mother came into the room, and I heard her gasp from the doorway.

"Cisco?" she cried. I saw Francisco look up at her with astonishment and realized they knew one another.

"Isa?" Francisco asked breathless.

Of course she knew him. She had been his father's slave for months. He must have been six or seven years old when she was enslaved.

"I didn't know it was you," she told him in anguish.

I wanted to remove the knife from his bicep, just so I could slit his throat, but Colin was holding me fast to his side, almost as if he suspected I might attack at any moment. Mother was in tears again, crying for the monster or for me; I wasn't sure.

"*Tell us if he lives!*" I yelled in fury.

Francisco looked from Mother to me and seemed to make the connection. "When I left, he was alive. I doubt they will keep him that way long since you have taken me prisoner," Francisco informed us.

Spontaneously, two emotions raged in me; the first one was hope that Merek could still be breathing, and the second was elation that I could now end Francisco's life.

"Tell us where he is," Colin said from my side.

"What do I gain in return?" Francisco asked.

"This isn't a negotiation. Tell us, and we will make your death swift, and you won't feel a thing," Colin told him.

I made no such promises and planned to kill him slowly.

"I believe you will negotiate. This man was important, as am I," Francisco said with pride.

"You are no more important than a dying rat!" I replied. "Tell us how to find him!" I said, trying to break free of Colin's grasp.

"I will draw out a detailed map of where to find him, and once he is free, you will release me," he continued to negotiate.

I wanted to spit in his face but refrained for Merek's sake.

"You will draw out a detailed map, and we might let you live," Colin countered back.

I wouldn't let that happen but remained silent.

"Isa, can I trust these people?" Francisco asked my mother.

"Yes, Cisco, they have proven trustworthy," Mother replied.

The two men assisting Colin took Francisco down and escorted him out the back door. Heart still racing, I shook loose of Colin's hold and rushed to leave. Don met me outside of the interrogation room.

"Did he say anything about Merek?" Don asked with concern.

"He said that Merek was still alive when we left and will draw a map of where he can be found. Francisco indicated that the leaders may have killed Merek once they discovered that Francisco was kidnapped." I tried to warn Don we may yet have lost Merek.

"Surely they wouldn't have killed him, thinking we could do a prisoner exchange," Don said logically.

"Who knows how they think?" I replied.

Colin came out of the room and looked at me with worry.

"As soon as he gets the map ready, we must make plans and rescue Merek," I commanded with all the authority I didn't possess.

"You aren't ready for a mission like this. You must stay behind," Colin said gently.

"*I will not stay behind!*" I told him, trying to control the anger rising in my voice. How could he even think I would not be there to rescue Merek? I had no clue. "I need to be there," I pleaded.

"Alex, you have already been through so much. Please let us deal with this," Colin beseeched me.

"I can't stay behind. I have to save him," I told him, tears welling in my eyes. I didn't realize how much I needed Merek to be safe, how much my fate felt tied to his. I had only two purposes in my life—to save Merek and to kill Francisco. Once those were completed…well, I couldn't think past that.

"I will see what I can do," Colin told me.

Mother was coming through the exit door of the interrogation room, and I wanted to ask her so many things or yell or run—I never felt so confused before. Francisco had called her Isa. He seemed very familiar with her, also cordial, and the thought disgusted me.

"Can we talk, Alexandra?" Mother asked in a soft voice.

I nodded but didn't make any moves to follow her as she headed away from Colin and Don for privacy.

"Go with her, Alex." Don nudged me toward her.

I slowly followed not wanting to hear what she had to say.

"I knew him when he was a child," she told me once we weren't within earshot of the men. "I took care of him the few months I was staying in Raymon's tent."

"You mean while you were enslaved in Raymon's tent as I was in Francisco's?" I retorted sharply.

"Yes, little bird, while I was enslaved in Raymon's tent, just like you were." She paused and seemed to consider her next words. "Francisco has grown to be much like his father. I know the pain you are going through. Please don't shut me out." Her pleas were genuine and heartfelt, but I couldn't voice anything that had happened. Mother dealt with her pain by hearing some mystical voice telling her to forgive and love. I heard no such voice and only wanted retribution. Sharing how I felt wouldn't change that.

"All I can think about is saving Merek. Nothing else matters right now," I told Mother.

"We will find him. I truly believe that," she said in return.

I wasn't so sure. I wasn't sure of anything anymore.

STAGE 3:2

The crusade to save Merek began the next morning. I showed up at the tunnels leading to the surface before anyone else arrived. I hadn't slept, so most of the night was spent looking at the timekeeper on the wall, waiting for this moment. Colin had told me he would allow me to accompany them back to the fort but made me promise to wait with the horses while they searched for Merek using Francisco's map. I waited rather impatiently for the rest of the party to arrive in order for the rescue to begin. Don and Colin were the first to show up, looking as if they didn't sleep much more than I did.

"Did you sleep at all last night?" asked Don. Exhaustion must have been evident in my demeanor, but I didn't allow myself to be concerned with such trivial things. "You realize sleep is a necessity, right?" he continued with his interjections.

"I'll sleep when Merek is back safe with us," I lied, knowing I never wanted to sleep again.

"The map is very detailed. I believe we will find him," Colin reassured me.

Three more men arrived. Colin introduced me, but I didn't retain their information; it made no difference at this time. I was instructed to assist Don with readying the horses. We worked side by side with few words passing between us. Even Don was anxious to save Merek. The sun hadn't even peaked out over the trees when we set off astride our mounts. I rode alone, having no clue what to do, but Don said even a twit could ride the mount he put me on.

"Stay in the middle of the saddle. The horse will follow us," he instructed, none of his usual humor present. It wasn't long before we were at the edge of the fort. My heart was racing the closer we came. The men dismounted, not a noise made. I slowly made my way down the saddle, trying to be just as silent.

As they prepared to infiltrate the fort, I tied horses and made myself as useful as possible. Soon they were headed away, only giving me a nod in confirmation that I would remain behind with the horses. I waved them away and began pacing back and forth, holding my rifle ready and a hatchet hanging from my belt. I wouldn't be caught unawares again.

The time passed slowly. I heard bird songs, squirrels foraging for the nuts, and saw a lone deer drink from a stream that was only an arm's length away from me—the beauty of such things didn't penetrate my apprehension. I heard a blast from the fort and saw black smoke billowing up from the center, I suspected close to the area they held the cleansing. Worry was overwhelming. It was crushing me. They should have been back by now.

I watched the direction from which they would return and pleaded with whatever higher power was listening to let them make it out with Merek. Holding my breath, I waited. Starting to count the seconds, which turned into minutes, and then I saw them carrying a limp body between them. *Merek. It has to be Merek.*

I rushed to see for myself. It was Merek, and he was breathing! Relief washed over me like a refreshing waterfall. He was safe, alive, and we just needed to return before we were captured.

"The explosion was a distraction," Don whispered. We all carefully placed Merek into the cart, much like the one Francisco had ridden in only a few days before. "He was beaten badly, but he is the stronger than even me. He'll be fine," Don told me with a wink as I cocooned Merek's sleeping body in with pillows and blankets, not wanting him to receive any more injuries on the ride to the bunker.

"Can I ride with him?" I asked no one in particular.

"Yes, that should be fine," said one of the men whose name I couldn't recall. I looked over Merek's limp body, and shame flooded me. His poor state of being was entirely my fault. Both of his eyes were blackened, angry gashes on his face and exposed skin; he was tortured beyond what most men could survive. Climbing into the cart, I lifted Merek's head as gently as I could and maneuvered my legs under him in order to support him on the journey back.

The cart jerked forward, and we were off at a fast clip. I couldn't help but watch the obvious path we were leaving, hoping the Seditionist were too busy with the explosion to notice Merek's absence.

"You are safe now," I whispered in Merek's ear.

He moaned slightly, and then his eyes fluttered open. "Alex?" he asked in astonishment.

"Yes, Merek it's me," I said through my tears.

He reached up to my cheek and brushed the tears away, which of course only brought on more tears. He gave me a weak smile. "You visited me so many times in my dreams," he mused and closed his eyes once again.

I cradled his head, hoping to absorb every jolt. He didn't wake again, so I hoped that was a good sign.

The sun was up and blazing when we came within sight of the bunker's entrance. We were met by medics and a small crowd of unknown Outlandish. Medics immediately secured Merek's neck, laid him onto a gurney, and then strapped him to that. I quickly followed them into the bunker, not letting Merek out of my sight. I had to practically run to keep them in sight, and we rushed through doors and down hallways, finally coming to what looked like a surgical area. The swinging door closed behind them and I hastened my pace so as not to lose them.

"You'll have to wait outside. Only medical personnel beyond this point." A medic stopped me the minute I was through the doorway.

"I cannot leave him, please," I begged.

"Are you blood-related to the patient?" the medic asked.

"No, but I can't leave him," I said in earnest.

"You can watch from the observation deck. Go through those doors and up the stairs," she told me, turning to assist in saving Merek. I hurried to find the observation deck and watched as they began to restore him back to health. I was unsure what all was wrong with him, but tubes, needles, and stitches were flurrying through the surgical room. There were other people in the observation room with me, but I paid them no mind. I stood at attendance for several hours until they seemed to be satisfied that he would make it, and once they left him alone with only the beeping of the monitor, I found my way to his side. He was attached to all sorts of medical equipment, washed cleaned, his breathing was steady, so I place my hand over his heart to feel the stable beat, and it gave me comfort. Surely, he would live.

"You aren't supposed to be in here," someone said from behind me.

I turned to see Colin. "I can't leave him alone," I told him.

"I understand. Let me get a medic to get him into a room," Colin said, leaving through the door directly across from the observation deck. I was once again alone with Merek.

"Please be okay," I pleaded with his unconscious body. "You have to be okay." I added authority to my voice and commanded him.

The medic came in followed by Colin and led us to a patient room.

"I can stay with him awhile, Alexandra. You need to rest," Colin told me.

"No, no, I will stay," I insisted. "I will let you know if he wakes," I said, dismissing him.

"Your mother is looking for you," Colin told me, ignoring my dismissal.

"Tell her I am fine and I am staying here with Merek," I replied cordially. How Mother didn't know exactly where I would be seemed moronic. Where else would I be?

"I'll be in the waiting area if he wakes or you need anything," Colin said, heading to the exit.

So I was finally alone with Merek; alone to feel the full weight of my actions and the repercussions not only for myself but also for the man lying in the bed beside me. The weight was almost unbearable, and I willed him to wake, just for reassurance of his well-being. He didn't wake up, so I held his hand and spoke to him of pleasant things, all the beauty in the forest we traveled through, the wonderful creatures I saw, and the pleasure of floating in the cool spring water, which brought me to darker subjects that refused to remain quiet;

things like the cleansing, being captured, and the fear that turned into hatred. I dared not speak of the darkest of things even to an unconscious person. To voice what happened felt as if it would give it more power over me somehow. So I glossed over things and told him over and over how sorry I was that he was in pain for me.

STAGE 3:3

Pain, darkness, chains, and an unwanted caress woke me with a start the next morning. I jerked away from a groggy Merek who was shocked at my painful reaction to him holding my hand. He was awake. I rushed back to the bedside and grabbed his hand.

"Merek, you're awake," I stated the obvious.

"I am." His voice had the unused sound of morning about it. "I knew I would see you again," he told me confidently.

"Are you in pain?" I asked him.

"Not too much," he replied with false bravado. With all the hours the medics had spent to save him, pain was inevitable. I couldn't help wanting to check every bandage, bruise, and stitch. I had to care for him. "Alex, did they hurt you?"

Merek's question threw me off-kilter. He didn't need to worry about me, but I hated to lie completely. "I'll be fine. Only a few bumps and bruises," I replied lightly, using primal slang to disguise my lie. I would never be fine.

His eyes narrowed at me as if he knew I wasn't sharing the entire truth, but he let it pass.

"How did they find me?"

Of course, Merek would ask a logical question that I didn't want to answer.

"We have a prisoner. He drew a map after much persuasion," I said, avoiding the use of that demon's name.

"How long were we captured?" Merek asked. "I kept track for a while, but when I wouldn't agree to their insane doctrines, they beat me, and I blacked out for some time."

I flinched at his words, hating that he endured such pain because of me. "Colin and Don helped me escape after eleven days. It took a few days to get the prisoner to draw the map in order to find you, so I would say fourteen days in total," I replied.

Merek was still holding my hand. He didn't seem to want to let go or lose sight of me anymore than I wanted to lose sight of him. Our shared suffering seemed to connect us somehow, although I knew I could never tell Merek the depth of my own affliction. We were now no longer two separate people traveling through life. I felt tethered to him in such a way that the force of it frightened me. He gave me a weak smile as if he knew how I was feeling; maybe it frightened him too.

"You should probably rest," I told him.

"I don't want to close my eyes. What if I when I wake up it's all a cruel joke and you aren't here?" he said, only half joking.

"I won't leave your side. I promise," I vowed, taking a more relaxed posture.

That seemed to appease him, and he closed his eyes once more. I watched him breathe for a time, and then Colin came into the room, followed by a medic.

"Has he woken at all?" the medic asked me.

"Yes, but only for a few moments," I replied.

"You should have gotten us," Colin said with concern.

I knew that Merek and Colin were close, but honestly, I had forgotten entirely to fetch him when Merek had awoken.

"I forgot to get you, I apologize," I said sincerely.

The medic went about checking equipment and vitals. Without a word, she left the room.

"How was he?" Colin asked, taking the only vacant chair on the opposite side of Merek's bed.

"He was lucid and said that the Seditionist tried to convert him to their doctrine. When he didn't comply, that's when they beat him to unconsciousness," I told Colin sadly. "This happened because of me. How will I ever make it up to him?"

"First of all, it could have happened to any of us. Just because you weren't doing what you had said you were doesn't mean the outcome would have been any different," he reassured me. "Secondly,

Merek would give his life for yours, so there is nothing to make up, and he would be insulted if you tried."

"I'm sure you're right. I just feel so responsible for his pain," I confessed.

"Well, get over it, you're not. The Seditionist are," Colin stated factually. "Once we have the cure in hand, we will deal with them." He finished, anger welling in his voice. He was right. I knew where to place the blame, the hate, the retribution—Francisco. "Can you tell me what happened while you were captured?" he asked me gently.

I looked away from Merek and made eye contact with Colin. His expression was tender distress, and my gut clenched at such concern.

"He was cruel, evil, vile. And I'd like to slit his throat," I stated, trying to keep the rage from my voice but failing if the look on Colin's face was any indication.

"We don't allow murder here in the Republic of Autarchy. Besides that, Francisco may yet provide crucial information about the Seditionist that could help us to stop them once we have the cure," Colin said.

I wasn't sure if he took my words for truth and he was just giving me information that he thought I needed to know or if he was warning me to stay my desire to kill Francisco. This might have complicated things, but I wouldn't be thwarted in my next mission.

"My only concern right now is Merek. All else will have to wait," I replied.

"If he wakes again, I need to speak with him. He may have information we can use," Colin said, standing to leave.

I hoped that Merek wouldn't wake for some time. He didn't need to be interrogated until he had more strength. "He needs to mend, not be questioned," I told Colin, surprising even myself with the tone of annoyance in my voice.

"I'll tread carefully, Alexandra. He won't be distressed by it, I promise," he vowed with sincerity and took his leave without a response from me.

"Are you awake?" I asked Merek, noticing he shuddered as the door closed behind Colin.

"I wish I could sleep," he moaned. "My head feels like it might explode," he added, reaching his hands to his temples and rubbing.

"Here, let me," I said, replacing his hands with my own. Strange how touching him was healing to me. It solidified that he was a living, breathing Merek, not a creation from my own guilt-ridden imagination. He watched me intently as I sat beside his bed, trying to ease his discomfort.

"You seem older, different somehow," he mused aloud. "What happened to you in their fort?" He asked the question I desired above all else to never answer. I hesitated for a long pause. I knew he deserved to know the truth. He had risked his life for my own. I didn't want him to know the horrid things that were done and also never wanted him to look at me as I now saw myself—broken, empty, used up with nothing left but a roaring flame of desire to avenge myself.

"Merek, I never thanked you for trying to give your life for my own, and I can never repay you or make it up to you, but please let me speak of my captivity to you when I'm ready," I said, knowing I couldn't avoid the question again, but maybe honesty would work.

"Is it so horrible that you can't tell me?" he asked, his voice saddened. I knew that Merek didn't know I had been given to Francisco, only that I too was imprisoned.

"Let me just be glad that we saved you, and we can deal with everything else later," I told him in all truth. I couldn't think past his restoration; revenge would have to wait.

STAGE 3:4

People came in and out of Merek's room to visit. They brought food, medic's checked his vitals, and Mother would sit with me, because I only left for short breaks to the latrine. He slept with the aid of drugs through most of it. On the second week of Merek's stay in the medic's station, Colin and Don came by for another visit with rounds of questions about the fort, sprinkled with good-humored joshing.

"I can't believe a big strong warrior like yourself wouldn't have the entire fort conquered by the time we got there. I mean, the fact that you needed our help to escape just shows me what a cream puff you really are," Don teased relentlessly. "Maybe you're just play acting in order to garner the pity of a certain beautiful young lady," Don continued, wagging his eyebrows across the room at me as I folded the sheets I had pretended to sleep on the night before.

Merek laughed in response, but he was looking at me as if he didn't want to lose sight of me. Colin was back to inquiring about the time Merek spent in the Seditionist fort and making plans about how they would go about dominating them. I hated to listen about their plans when they spoke of converting the Seditionist to their cause, so I made my way to the hallway.

"I am going to check in with the medic. They said you should be able to leave here soon," I said as I left them to make their plans. The men all looked up at me as I left, but none protested my absence. Merek gave a slight smile and nodded, Don winked, and Colin looked at me with grave concern.

I walked down the winding hallways, not really knowing where I was going, having no intention of speaking to the medic. Once we left the medic's station, I would have to face things I wasn't ready to do yet. Caring for Merek had kept my mind off my own hurt, except for the wee hours of the night when I would nod to sleep and wake in a fright that I was once again chained to that pole in the tent with Francisco. A few times, I would wake to tears running down my face, a cold sweat covering me from head to foot, and I would be shaking uncontrollably. Merek was wakened once by my torment, he gently pulled me close and wiped my tears away.

I thought after my experience, I wouldn't want a male's attention in any way, but Merek's touch was kind and unthreatening. I let him console me back to a fitful sleep. In the light of day, neither one of us spoke of my night terrors, but I saw the concern and questions in his eyes.

As I was almost clear of the medic area, the female medic that had examined me when I first arrived waved me down from her work area.

"Alexandra, I got your blood test results back," she said.

"Yes?" I asked with dread.

She looked around making sure no one was within earshot. "You are with child," she whispered, pity plainly in her eyes.

The new information slammed the breath from my lungs; my heart stopped and then started with such force, I'm sure the medic could see my chest expand painfully.

"Don't share this information with anyone, please," I pleaded in earnest once I could speak again.

"Of course not!" she replied.

I left without another word to her. My own body betrayed me. I was having a difficult time breathing, so I slowed my pace and leaned against the wall to steady myself. Everyone would soon know the extent of my tragedy, the extent of my shame…even Merek.

My wandering through the hallways led me to the holding cells. *Francisco must be in there*, I thought. How hard would it be to break in and end his existence? I didn't really care what they would do to me after, but I was afraid they might stop me from succeeding, and once they knew my intentions, it would not be simple to gain access to Francisco a second time.

Lost in my head, planning his demise, I was taken aback when Mother came through the door, leaving the holding cell.

"Alexandra?" she said as I tried to leave without detection. I turned back around and waited as she came to my side. "Have you slept at all?" she asked me.

"Were you visiting Francisco?" I asked her, ignoring her question and getting right to the point.

"Colin thought Cisco might divulge more information to me than anyone else," she replied calmly.

"And did you get any viable information from the prisoner?" I asked cuttingly. I could tell my tone of voice pained her, but I didn't care. My pain outweighed her own right now.

"He shared a few things that may help the cause, yes," she replied softly. "I am concerned for you, Alexandra. You haven't had proper sleep in days, you are losing weight from not eating, and you have hardly left Merek's room since he returned," she said, worry lacing each word. The burden I was carrying was heavy, and logic said that if shared, it would be lighter, but the shame and anger kept me silent. "Have you spoken to the medic?" she asked. I knew she would ask about my condition. However, I refused to answer the real question she was asking.

"Yes, I have," I answered her, not giving any more information than necessary. "How is the prisoner? Well, I hope," I asked sarcastically.

Mother ignored my question and ushered away from the holding area to an atrium filled with plant life. It was serene, quiet, with benches placed strategically throughout to provide privacy. I saw a few Outlandish people reading books or just sitting there, taking it all in as Mother led me to a private bench far from the other occupants. She sat down and motioned for me to sit beside her. I sat as far from her as I could. I needed space from her.

"I wish I could give you the freedom I have. I wish words could express the fullness I have felt after knowing Ruach HaKodesh but it isn't something mere words can explain. It has to be tasted and seen." She spoke with such passion as if this being was living, breathing, a person she knew intimately. "For a time while imprisoned, I was so fearful, angry, and desiring retribution that I didn't see how much I was falling into the pattern of the Seditionist." She spoke with a quiet calmness that though the words troubled me, I couldn't seem to stop her. "Everything they did was out of fear—fear of being taken advantage of, fear of the unknown, fear of defeat, fear of pain, fear of different people, fear that women would raise up and take over, and that fear turned into anger. They split away from the Establishment out of fear, but they became barbaric when they let that fear turned into anger."

It almost seemed as if she felt pity for that evil group of humans. "While Raymon would torture me, he would speak of how low I was, that I was only a weak woman. I couldn't defeat or enslave such a man as he and, in a sense, he was right. I couldn't overpower him physically, but once I knew Ruach HaKodesh, it no longer mattered. He could control what I did day in and day out, but he couldn't control how I felt, my spirit. I no longer feared him, and he noticed."

Her story raised gooseflesh on my arms. "The beatings became worse, and every night when I spoke to Ruach HaKodesh, he would renew my spirit to face the morning. I gave up my anger, resentment, and saw Raymon for what he truly was—a frightened man that desired only to protect himself the only way he knew how by hurting others as he had been hurt. I would speak of forgiveness to Raymon while little Cisco would be forced to watch Raymon beat me. He said that Cisco had to watch to learn how to treat women.

"Cisco would cry and, for his tears, be slapped across the tent. After a short time, Cisco no longer cried while Raymon beat me, but once Raymon would leave, Cisco would always help me tend my wounds. He was a small savior for me during those times. I believe Ruach HaKodesh sent him to save me so that you could live also. We may not have survived without his kindness."

She finished her story. Francisco may have helped my mother survive torment, but he had been my tormentor. There was no good in him. "Would you have me forgive Francisco? I have had no higher power speak to me of love and forgiveness," I told her angrily. Her story was impossible. Perhaps she had become like a "less than" with all the hits to her head; forgiveness for something so vile was impossible for any human.

"I would have you seek truth from Ruach HaKodesh," she said, unoffended by my terse response.

"How do I seek truth from something I don't even know truly exists?" I asked her, dumbfounded by her insistent reference to this unknown force that she claimed freed her.

"He will reveal himself to you when your heart is ready to receive. I know that to be true," Mother spoke with confidence.

If the "being" were true, why would he allow such atrocities in this world? Part of me wanted to argue with her, but how does one debate someone who may have lost their mind? I did what any reasonable person would do: I changed the subject.

"What are their plans for Francisco?" I asked. There were so many subjects I couldn't talk about, but this I needed to know. I had to know.

"I haven't heard. I received word that Justin is coming to this bunker soon. In fact, he should be here within the next few days. I am sure once he arrives, they will make decisions about how to handle Cisco," she replied.

"I need to get back to Merek. He will be wondering where I am," I lied, knowing full-well Merek was probably weary of my hovering and wanted me to rest as much as Mother did.

"Take care of yourself, little bird, you will find healing in time," she told me with all the love she had for me in her eyes. I nodded in response and stood to leave. "I wish I could show you my heart, and you'd see the healing I've been given," she said, somewhat defeated.

I left without another word, more confused and angrier than before I spoke with her.

I wanted to go back to Merek's room, but I was afraid that he might see the absolute panic I was now in. A child…I was going to have Francisco's child! I started to feel light-headed and queasy. I looked around the hallway to find a latrine. I didn't want to be sick where everyone could see. Up ahead, I saw one, so I rushed through a small group of Outlandish that were congregating ahead of me and made it just in time. I had eaten hardly anything since returning, so it wasn't long before my stomach was emptied, and I was washing my mouth out in front of a large mirror.

Mirrors were so strange. In the Establishment, we had mirrors, but the people there only used them to make sure they were clean and tidy, not for vain purposes like here. In the Outlandish bunkers, there were mirrors everywhere, latrines, sleeping quarters, hallways—even the room Merek was staying in had a large mirror above the bed. Women stared into them to paint their faces, men had them to style their facial hair and trim their beards, Outlandish cared so much about how they appeared to each other, and it was confusing to me still.

As I looked at myself in the latrine mirror, I hardly recognized the person staring back. My olive skin had a grey hue with yellow healing bruises speckled about. I pulled the collar of my shirt back to see Francisco's brand was an angry red color. My wavy hair was held on top of my head by a string, and my eyes looked hollow and dead. I hated what I saw, hated what I was carrying, and hated even more the person that did this all to me. No matter what the Republic had in mind for Francisco, my plans would come first.

STAGE 3:5

As I roamed the bunker's many different hallways, meeting rooms, and mess halls, the chatter and laughter grated on my blemished heart. Some tried to smile and introduce themselves, but more than ever, I had nothing to say. When I finally made it back to the medic station and Merek's room, I had composed myself as much as I could. Opening the door, I noticed Don and Colin had left, and my cot was prepared. I didn't realize how late I had stayed away.

"The medic came in and said I can leave tomorrow," Merek said restlessly the minute I came through the door. I knew this was coming, but I still didn't know what the day after tomorrow would hold, and it unnerved me.

"That will be good. How are you feeling?" I asked, putting aside my misgivings.

"Stronger, still sore in many places, but ready to be on my feet again and help in this new fight against the Seditionist."

I flinched at the mention of them. I couldn't help it, and Merek noticed. "I know they hurt you and I plan to make them all pay." If he only knew how bad they had hurt me, but "they" isn't correct. It was a he, Francisco, and I had access to him if only I could bypass the guards. I realized then that no one had told Merek I was enslaved by Francisco and kept as his pet. Merek thought that they had tried to convert me to the Seditionist cause like him. I felt relief that perhaps he would never know, but then I remembered everyone would know in only a few short months, because they would physically see my humiliation.

"I thought we were seeking the cure and trying to dispense it on a massive level?" I asked.

"We have been working on a cure for years. It isn't a fast process. We have patience, Alex, and we have your mother now. That should change everything. However, in the meantime, we must maintain order, and the main threat is the Seditionist. They have caused mass destruction in the Establishment, tortured us, and they won't stop there. I believe they are just getting started. They thought they could recruit us!" he said with a humorless laugh. "They have big plans, and hopefully with a little persuasion to Francisco, he will tell us of those plans," he finished.

"I'm sure you are right. They should be stopped if for no other reason than what they did to the establishments. Innocent people died, too many. I could have been counted as one of the dead if Colin hadn't helped me to escape," I said in clipped sentences. I didn't know how to plan for an attack on the Seditionist when the only one I wanted dead was within my grasp. Merek was watching me closely as if I said something that bothered him. "What is it?" I asked.

"It's almost like you are saying the right words, but you aren't even really here or something," he said, confused. We had been in each other's presence for months during training, and the last few days, I hardly left his side. The fact that he could read me so well was unnerving. I wondered if he could see the anger, hurt, and shame I was currently growing in my womb.

"I have been off since I came back. Everything feels upside down," I confessed, hoping he would let it be enough for now.

"You haven't left my side since I came to the medic station, yet you seem distant. Why?" he asked.

"I have never been good at opening up to people. The Establishment doesn't exactly encourage that," I tried to jest, but it fell flat; he wasn't amused.

"Alex, do you trust me?" he asked.

"Of course, why wouldn't I?" I asked in return.

"You have stayed by my side day in and out, but not one word of your time in the fort has been spoken of," he replied thoughtfully, and I realized as Kasi would say, "I walked right into that one."

"I…I just don't know what to say. It was horrible. I was beaten and marked and…I'll never be the same." I had tears on the verge of falling but kept them at bay by digging my finger nails into the palm of my hand with all the strength I could muster.

"When they took me away from the cleansing, I thought you were dead. I saw you passed out on the platform. You didn't make a move, and I couldn't tell if you were breathing." He paused for a long moment as if he had to carefully consider his next words. "Alex, nothing mattered to me more than your life. I wish I could explain…I am not good with words or telling people how I feel, what I feel for you. It…well, it scares me sometimes." He staggered through his speech, making my heart ache with the wanting and knowing I could never be with him how he desired me to be. I was forever marked with the stain of Francisco and soon the stain of vengeance.

"Nothing mattered more to me than your rescue. I could hardly take a steady breath knowing you were still there. You mean more to me than I thought possible." I had to tell him how I felt with full knowledge that he may change his mind about me when he knew what was growing in my womb. My words seemed to ease some worry in his eyes, and he nodded his head in agreement.

"We don't have to rush things, but please don't shut me out," he pleaded.

In that moment, I wanted so badly to share with him the utter horror I had gone through, the anger I now wore as a cloak around my shoulders, but fear once again held me back from speaking the words he thought he wanted from me, so I lied.

"I can't speak of things that were nothing but a haze to me." Truthfully, I remembered the things I went through with a clarity that disturbed me and left me with sleepless nights.

He looked at me as if he wasn't sure about the validity of the words but didn't raise an argument. The medic came in just before I was about to make up more lies about not remembering the tragic events that befell me. I hated having to lie to him, but the alternative was not a possibility right now.

"You can leave tomorrow after the morning rounds. In ten days, we will have a follow-up and remove your stitches," the medic told Merek cheerfully.

One more night; only one more night before we would have to be separated and living our own lives. His would lead him to defeat the Seditionist, while my path led me to a place of no return. I am not even sure what the Republic would do with me—banish, imprison, or possibly put me to death once I went against their orders and killed Francisco.

As the medic was leaving, I pulled my cot close to Merek's bed, not wanting distance between us, knowing soon my choices would soon tear us apart. We didn't speak when we were alone, but instead, he held my hand gently as if he too suspected our time together would come to an end with the rising of the sun.

STAGE 3:6

Morning came despite my desire for things to remain the same, and from the look on Merek's face, he too wasn't ready for our separation. With the rising of the sun came medics and visitors alike to keep any promises from being made between us, and I knew with my intentions for Francisco, promises would be futile, but part of me still longed to hear him say it.

"Well, now, maybe we all can get some work done and stop coddling you," Don told Merek with his usual grin.

"Yeah, I am sure my injuries have put a damper on you, Don. I bet you have been sick with worry," Merek replied in jest. They went back and forth the entire morning while the medic explained care and medication Merek still needed to be taking. Too soon, he was released, and I stood outside the room, knowing I had nowhere to go.

"I will need my own room now," I told Colin as Merek and Don walked ahead.

Colin looked at me in surprise but didn't ask whatever question he had. "You should talk to your mother first. She is expecting your return," he said.

"I will." I lied once again; lying was becoming a part of every conversation now. "I have to go," I told him. I needed to observe how Francisco was taken care of if I planned to be able to complete my mission of revenge undisturbed.

"We are having an assembly about our plans for the Seditionist, and also, we would like for you to begin working in the lab on the cure using the test results from your mother's blood," Colin said before I could turn to leave.

"I will be there. When is it?" I asked.

"1300 hours, in the meeting area. Do you know where that is?" he asked me.

I looked at the timekeeper. I only had a few short hours to observe Francisco's schedule.

"I am sure I can find it," I replied.

Don and Merek had slowed enough to notice I was parting ways with them.

"What do you have to do so urgently?" Don asked, obviously not caring if it was even any of his concern or not.

"I have to speak to the analyst about the results of my mother's blood tests. I am supposed to begin running numbers to help find the cure."

Colin looked at me as if he knew I was lying once again but didn't ask any questions.

"I will be at the meeting as soon as I know what they need me to do," I told them all.

They nodded their heads but seemed worried about me at the same time. I left before they could argue and headed to the holding area, hoping to get some information on the daily routine of Francisco's sentries. Having only a few hours before the meeting, I hoped to observe something, anything that would give me an opening from which to plan my mission. Coming upon the holding area, I acted as if I was lost and tried to open the door I knew led to Francisco. Immediately, a sentry came out.

"What can I do for you, ma'am?" the sentry asked politely.

"I am looking for the science lab," I said innocently. I needed to find out this man's schedule but wasn't sure how to start up a conversation leading to that. "I am new here and don't know my way around yet," I finished, hoping he would be the overly helpful type.

"I know who you are," he said smiling; here, much like the Outlandish bunker I had left, I was noticed and out of place. This time not as an Empty from the Sovereignty but instead as a captive from the Seditionist camp. I hated both titles. He seemed to take pity on me. Going back into his office that had a large window for him to watch the holding cell entry, he returned, holding a piece of paper.

"Here ya go," he said, handing me what looked like a map. "This should keep you from losing your way again."

I looked over the map and thanked him for his kindness. Although I was unable to find out his schedule, I realized the map would be helpful for me to complete my plan. I took the map and headed to the atrium for privacy. Safely tucked away in a brick alcove resting on a bench, I studied the map, hoping it would help me on my quest. Right away, I noticed that the back wall for the lab adjoined the back wall for the holding cells. Now I only needed to know the interior layout of the lab and which cell Francisco was in to complete the plan that was forming.

I got up and headed to the lab, knowing I could inquire about what they needed me to do to aid in finding the cure. I then wouldn't be lying to Colin, Merek, and Don, and would also see the layout for myself. Although the holding cells and the lab shared a wall, the entrances were what felt like miles apart. I needed to come up with an unstoppable strategy as long as no one found out before I could finish my task. I didn't put much thought into the after; in my mind, there was no after.

Upon arriving at the entrance to lab, I hesitated only for a few moments before walking in and introducing myself to one of the lab techs. "I am Alexandra. I am supposed to report here and aid in research," I stated plainly. The lab tech was a slightly overweight female who seemed excited about everything.

"Oh, you're the girl they just saved from the Seditionist camp. Was it terrible?" she asked with bated breath.

"Yes, it was. Do you have an area for me to work? Perhaps instructions on my duties?" I replied, trying to ignore my racing heart at the question.

"Yes, yes, the supervisor told me to have you work at the gold area, that one over there," she said, motioning over to the back wall. I couldn't believe my good fortune—right where I needed to be. "My name is Gabby. The name has always fit me very well," she said, laughing at herself. "We will set you up here, and once the supervisor comes back, he will give you your instructions. The assembly is being called in less than an hour, and everyone is expected to be there. That includes you, little lady. So come along, we can work on the cure once it is over."

I followed Gabby out of the lab without a good inspection of my new "gold" work area and couldn't wait to get back to see if I had enough privacy to complete my task uninterrupted. Gabby seemed eager to get to the meeting area for the assembly, so I kept her pace as we weaved in and out of passages through the bunker to end up at large doors with inscriptions over the doorway that were marked out slightly.

"Why is the inscription marked out?" I asked, curious what it said, not recognizing the language.

"It was written when the bunkers were built, and it reads *igne natura renovatur integra*, which is Latin and loosely translates 'through fire, nature is reborn whole.' They marked them out, refusing to agree with anything the Sovereignty inscribed on walls." She was rambling on about the history of the bunker with enthusiasm in her voice as we entered, and I scanned the crowd for Merek. I realized that Gabby's knowledge of the bunker made her very useful to me when completing my undertaking and began asking her questions.

"How long have you been in this bunker?" I asked innocently.

"My entire life, all twenty-eight years," she informed me proudly. Although she was ten years my senior, I felt as if I was the older one.

"You seem like you know a lot about the history of the bunker." I complimented her, hoping to coax information from her as I needed it.

"Oh, I do! I love knowing where things come from and their past lives, even buildings, not that they have a past life. If I thought buildings had past lives, I would be a less than, now wouldn't I?" she giggled to herself. "No, I enjoy knowing what happened and how things are made," she finished.

I spotted Merek, Don, and Colin sitting to the right of the platform. They seemed to be discussing something of grave importance.

"I see my team. I had better sit with them," I told Gabby. Although I knew I needed her familiarity with the bunker, it was difficult to be around her nonsense and giddiness.

"Yes, of course. I will meet you back at the lab after the assembly." She waved goodbye as she took her seat in the back of the meeting area.

Making my way to the platform, I dodged in and out of small groups of Outlandish loudly voicing their opinions on everything from the new plants that were being planted in the atrium to the battle against the Seditionist.

"Cutting it close, Alex," Don teased as I sat down beside him.

"The lab tech was very verbose," I told him. My eyes connected with Merek's, and he had a look of apprehension about him.

"Did you find everything all right?" Colin asked from Merek's side.

"Yes, the supervisor wasn't available, so I will meet with him after the assembly," I told him. He seemed to be weighing my words for truth. The assembly was called to order, and everyone else took their seats, and silence covered the meeting area. Two women and Justin walked out onto the platform, and applause ensued. I clapped along half-heartedly, not wanting to join in, but also not wanting to draw attention to myself. I noticed Mother was sitting on the platform with a small group of Outlandish I supposed to be more leaders.

"Good afternoon, we have gathered the assembly together to inform you all of our progress with the cure and also our plans to defeat the Seditionist," Justin said with authority into the amplifier for all to hear. More cheering answered him. "We now have a better chance of discovering the antibodies that fight injection. In our possession is Subject 2, and she has a natural immunity to the injection. There have only been two other recorded cases," he said with excitement.

Everyone seemed to feed off each other in their enthusiasm for ovation. I remained silent, an observer on the outer edges.

He continued, "We have many lab techs and scientists working around the timekeeper to discover how Subject 2's immunity works. There is also a new development with information regarding the Seditionist. We have captured Raymon Fuerte's son and right-hand man, Francisco."

He paused, letting the meaning of that sink in. I cringed at the mention of his name; my sight quickly switched to Merek who seemed to be watching me intently.

"He has already aided us in the rescue of Merek Wharrier from the Seditionist camp and has begun divulging information regarding their plans for more destruction of many of the establishments, including 3, 5, and 7. Although we do not agree with the ideas and doctrines created by the Sovereignty, we do not condone innocent lives being taken. We will do everything in our power to put an end to their needless destruction."

He finished so eloquently. I wondered if the Outlandish clapping so loudly knew about Justin's former life with the Seditionist. I wanted to get up and leave but knew that would draw unwanted attention, and that was something I didn't need right now. Other leaders came up, speaking about the progress of the cure and the plans to defeat the Seditionist. I only partly listened. Merek was looking at me again, and I could only feel the loss of what could have been between us, even if I never truly understood it. There were moments I felt it, I think.

Not soon enough, the gathering was over, and we were free to leave.

"Well, they told the people what they needed to hear, I guess," Don said, somewhat annoyed. "They gave no concretes, no grand plan, no objectives even…just a quick we are going to defeat them…. yay," he continued.

"You know they won't share the plan with those outside of the militant personnel," Merek responded with a look like Don should have already known that.

"Oh, I know, I just don't get why they brought us here to tell us nothing," Don said, shaking his head. "Complete waste of time," he added under his breath. I was glad I wasn't the only one feeling that way.

"Don, you are called to the council tonight. All the information we need will be disclosed then," Colin reassured him.

"They requested I attend?" Don asked with excitement.

"No, I requested you attend, and Colin seconded it," Merek said. He saw me edging away. "Alex, I didn't think you would be ready to attend, but if you think you are, I can request it," he said hopefully.

I knew he wanted me to join. He wanted me to be okay and be able to continue on with my life, but he didn't know the whole truth, and even though it was my own fault, part of me wished he knew. "I think I will be too overwhelmed with calculations for the cure to be of much help, but maybe next time." I knew there would be no next time. I had to act quickly to end Francisco, and after that, I would more than likely be banished from this place.

"Yes, of course," he said in agreement, but the furrowed brows spoke louder. I wanted to ease his mind, but my anger wouldn't be appeased by anything less than Francisco's life for the one he had stolen from me and the life he had impregnated upon me.

"I have to go meet up with the supervisor," I told them in farewell.

"I'll walk you to the labs," Merek offered.

"No, don't worry yourself. I have to walk with Gabby back. She is probably waiting," I told him; they must have all known her, because they looked at each other with wary grins. I turned and left abruptly, not wanting to have to evade any more inquiries. The meeting area had all but emptied out, but up ahead, Gabby was waiting while talking to the maintenance attendant. Of course, he didn't seem interested, and she didn't seem to care.

"Did you know that sweeping the floors versus using a suction device causes the bacteria in the dust particles to fly in the air and possibly cause illness? You should really use a suction device," Gabby informed him. To this, he just kept on sweeping as if she hadn't said a word.

"Gabby, are you ready to head back?" I asked her before she could inform the poor man about other things he didn't care about.

"Why, yes, Alex!" she said enthusiastically. I was coming to realize she said most things that way. "The gathering was very exciting, didn't you think so?" she asked. I began to speak, and she immediately started talking again. "Justin is so charismatic and extremely handsome. Well, not as handsome as the gentlemen you were sitting with. I haven't seen Merek in years, but he has always been a striking male specimen. Colin too. I mean, those deep green eyes, but the one that surprises me is *Don*. Last time he was in our bunker, he was a gangly little boy making uncouth jokes. He has matured into quite an attractive fellow." She continued on without much input from me until we reached the lab.

I went straight away to gold area, my new workstation; the desk was stacked high with what looked to be statistics and possibly experiment data. A few weeks ago, that would have intrigued me, but I was single-minded in my mission. The supervisor came over, kind of a stiff woman that reminded me of the Establishment's guides. She explained my duties and left no extra words; just to the point and done. While the lab was full of people, I began running numbers to discourage any unwanted conversation that might arise.

Running numbers, collecting data, and looking at equations all day did not deter me from my goals. I planned and tried to gather as much information as I could so that I couldn't fail.

STAGE 3:7

After three weeks of not much progress, with my nights spent avoiding Merek and my mother, I was almost ready to do something drastic and force my way in to finish Francisco. It was an evening much like the rest with Gabby being the last to leave. I think she lingered, hoping to walk me out, but I had no intentions of going anywhere for now.

My days always seemed the same—wake up before Mother after a night spent tossing and turning, head to the lab with a pit stop in the lavatory to empty my stomach from the sickness that gripped me, the shame I had to hide from the world, and then spend the day working in the lab. I only ate when absolutely necessary and focused on the work in front of me. At night, to fight off the fiends, I planned my revenge.

"You sure stay busy for a newbie. We usually all leave here around 1800. Want to walk with me?" she asked.

"I only have a few more things to do so I won't lose my place," I replied.

"I can wait. We already missed the evening fare. I am going to the canteen after this, though, I can't go all night without food," she laughed sourly.

"The bunkers are very interesting, but unfortunately, I am so easily lost," I told her, trying to get her talking. If I did, I knew she would disclose pertinent information about the holding cells.

"They are interesting!" she replied. "The layout, the attention to detail, the secret passageways connecting everything," she finished with an air of conspiracy.

My ears perked up with the mention of the passageways. "You mean no one knows about the passageways?" I asked, trying not to sound too interested.

"Oh, no, many people know about them, they are just never used. Probably have rodents and spiders living there since no one uses them," she said, shivering with the talk of the rodents. "They were used to spirit people away unnoticed right after the bunker's formation. The Sovereignty didn't want to ensue panic, so while the injections began working, anyone that rebelled was whisked away and sent to the holding cells unknown to the rest of the population. It was quite ingenious and barbaric at the same," she said in awe.

"So the passageways lead to the holding cells unguarded?" I asked. I couldn't help the excitement in my voice. Unmonitored access to the holding cells, just the thing to get me in and be unstoppable.

"I wouldn't exactly say unguarded. The cameras monitor them regularly, but the guards are pretty lacking on monitoring the monitors," she said, laughing at herself.

"These hallways must be pretty frightening if they are unused and full of rodents, but the undisturbed history must be a thing to see," I told her, hinting at my desire to know how to access them.

"The children sometimes dared each other to use them to show their courage. I never did. I was always timid, and small animals scare the willies out of me. I don't know why anyone would want to go into them," she said with incredulity.

I wanted to press her for more information but also didn't want her to grow suspicious of my intentions, so I let her just keep on talking as I continued to finish up my work.

"The entrances are so ingenious. They literally could be any bookcase you pass in the media center or full-length mirror in the canteens. Some statues that are carved in the wall of the atrium are actually an entrance too! I think the only people who truly know every entrance are the militant personnel and me," she informed me, laughing. "I love to study things, and I have every passageway memorized from my studies," she told me proudly.

"That is incredible, Gabby. Did you study a map or blueprint or what?" I inquired, coaxing as many pieces of information from her that I could.

"I can show you the blueprints. They are old and blue and so wonderful," she said, very happy to have such an avid listener. I knew she was intelligent, but the way she spoke made me question it.

"That would be great!" I said, truly excited to have stumbled upon such a perfect way to reach Francisco. I finished up the data I was working with and tidied my workstation as Gabby continued to talk nonstop.

"Shall we go look over those old and wonderful blueprints?" I asked, interrupting her monologue about the possible species of spiders crawling through the passageways.

"Yes, let's do it. I must stop by the canteen and get something from old Fred, the chef, *I am starving*," she said with exaggerated flare.

"Fred the chef?" I asked.

"Oh, he hates being called that. He wants me to call him Frederick, but I refuse to call him that. He is my little brother," she said, laughing.

I never thought of siblings. I had never known a real family.

I followed her through the hallways to the canteen, and Fred the chef was the only one present. He blushed horribly when Gabby introduced us, but I could tell he didn't mind the name too much.

"What can we eat?" Gabby asked him in desperation.

Fred didn't say a word but instead brought out a cover dish and lifted the lid with finesse. It was a half-eaten cake, but the cake was beautiful, even if it was only half of a cake. Decorated with flowers, stems, and intricate designs, I marveled at his handiwork. "My little brother is the best chef/baker/cake decorator in this bunker, probably all the bunkers, and for sure the Establishment," she told me proudly.

With the first bite, I had to agree with her assessment of her brother's talents. Food had never been something to enjoy until I came to the bunkers. It was always just bland and nutritious in the Establishment, but here, they treated it like an art form, something to be enjoyed and savored. The cake was delicious and melted on my tongue. I had never tasted something that made me want to groan in delight until that moment. I didn't groan, but I wanted to.

Fred was a man of few words and many smiles. He watched us as we ate, taking pleasure in our pleasure. Under normal circumstances, I would have felt uncomfortable under such scrutiny, but I was too busy eating the cake to care. We both had several helpings, and for the first time since I met Gabby, she was silent, intent on finishing her portion.

Once we were both sated, we bade her brother goodbye, and we headed to her chamber to hopefully find the blueprints. The relationship that was developing with Gabby was one that I didn't have to work at. She talked, and I listened. Well, I listened when it suited me, but needless to say, she didn't inquire about me or my experience, and that made things easier. Arriving at her chamber, she fumbled with the keys until she found the correct one, and the door swung open.

"Home sweet home," she said.

I wasn't sure what she meant, so I just nodded in response.

"I have books, blueprints, old newspapers, magazines, and really anything from the primal times that interests me," she told me enthusiastically. We walked into an entryway that was pleasant and very feminine. Beautiful fresh flowers in a large vase sat on the side table to greet us. She took off her outer coat and hung it from a hook opposite the table and led me into the main sitting area. I was surprised how well-kept and attractive the area was. She didn't seem to slow down enough to think about things like décor. She was telling all about the process of decorating her chamber as she led me to a closed door.

"Don't judge. I have a small problem with throwing things away," she said with a self-deprecating giggle. She opened the door, and I immediately knew why she warned me. The room was packed full from the floor to the ceiling with old things; things I had only read about in the primal books such as magazines. I picked one up and saw a half-naked woman looking at me strangely from the cover. The title read *Sports Illustrated*. I flipped through the pages and shook my head at the absurdity and uselessness of such a publication. *What purpose could it possibly serve?* I thought skeptically. Gabby seemed to have some sort of obsession with the primal times. *Kasi would love her*, I thought.

"Where did you get all of this?" I asked, amazed.

"Well, most of it is duplicate stuff that the media center was going to reutilize into something else, but I saved it from imminent destruction," she informed me. I watched as Gabby began rummaging through a rather wide stack of paper. The stack swayed back and forth as she roughly took out papers and restacked them somewhere else. She seemed to know what she was doing, so I watched in silence. "This stack is all about the bunkers, deeds, old rules and regulations and, you guessed it, the blueprints," she said as she pulled out a tube from behind the stack. She smiled in triumph. She led me back into her living area and closed the door behind me, hiding once again her den of cluttered shame. It was hard for me to understand sarcasm; still, I don't think she really cared if I judged her or not about it. In fact, she almost seemed proud about the cluttered room.

"This blueprint shows all the entrances to the passageways and everything. It's quite interesting, really," she spoke jovially. She had laid it out on a table in front of a chair that seated more than two people. I sat down beside her and looked it over. At first, I couldn't tell what was what, then Gabby started to point out things I knew. "This is the medic's station. Over here is the atrium, and this is our lab area. See these dotted lines? They are the passageways while the full lines represent the common rooms."

That's when I saw it: An entrance right beside my lab area, and it led only a short way to the holding cells, even if it was monitored. If I could somehow make a distraction for only a few moments, I could get to the holding cells undetected. I began asking questions that I hardly cared about the answer to work my way up to important ones.

"The atrium has many entrances to the passageway, I see. They twist and turn a lot," I said, acting as calm as I could. Gabby went into a long speech about how the atrium needed more entrances because of the layout and the fact that people couldn't be monitored in every corner. "The holding cells seem pretty unique and secure," I said, pointing at the area on the blueprints.

"Aren't they, though? I mean, only one of the cells is in working order right now, but still, they have it so you never even have to go in the with the captives if you don't want to. It is all set up for clean out, food, and even showers so that no one is required to maintain them daily. Frees up the personnel required in that area," she finished.

"Wow, only one cell. That seems strange, why aren't they all in working order?" I asked.

"We don't have many captives here, and maintaining such a hi-tech cell was very labor intensive once they began to malfunction. The Republic decided to only keep one in working order," she said, pointing out the only one that worked.

I had what I needed, but I didn't want to rush away and cause her to wonder about my intentions, so we stayed that way, looking over the blueprints for almost an hour before she grew tired of the subject.

"I had better retire. I am sleepy." She spoke through her yawn.

I was quite spent myself but knew that sleep wasn't going to happen for me. *How long can one go avoiding sleep?* I wondered.

"How far is your chamber?" she asked, looking concerned for the late hour.

"Not too far," I lied, not wanting her to offer me a bed. Just in case I slept, I wouldn't want her to hear my night terrors. "I will see you at the lab tomorrow," I said, rushing out the door before she could protest.

"Goodnight!" she yelled as the door closed between us.

STAGE 3:8

I headed to the atrium, knowing I could have privacy there. The hallways were empty and eerie, and my mind couldn't help but be filled with thoughts of my time with Francisco. Long before I reached my destination, I began to shake with the rage I had to keep concealed from others for weeks.

"Alex!" A voice startled me from behind. I turned to find Merek walking toward me forcefully. "Your mother is extremely worried, where have you been?" he asked, concern weaving itself through each word.

"I was with Gabby," I told him in all honesty.

"Then where are you headed now?" he asked, reassured of my former whereabouts.

"To rest," I stated simply.

"Where are you going to rest? Your chamber with your Mother is that way," he said, pointing in the opposite direction.

"I can't sleep there. I was headed to the atrium." I was so worn thin that making up a plausible lie wasn't an option.

"Why are you crying?" he asked.

I hadn't even noticed the tears that were on my cheeks. "I do that sometimes," I replied vaguely.

He didn't press me for answers but instead matched my step as I turned to leave and continue to the atrium.

"Can I sit with you awhile?" he asked carefully. We had both been so busy, I didn't realize how much his presence calmed me.

"I suppose," I said in answer.

We walked in quiet harmony the rest of the way to the atrium, and I picked a spot on the grass to recline against a large stone, not wanting to dream but feeling the days with little to no sleep wearing me down. Merek sat down beside me and leaned against the same stone. There wasn't much distance between us, and his presence comforted me into a state of half-awake, half-asleep.

"I wish you'd let me help you." He said it so softly, I wasn't sure if he was speaking to me or just stating a fact. I was hardly able to hold my eyes open, and I felt him gently pull me close to him. For a second, my body tensed and then relaxed as he was speaking nonsense to me in tender tones, and soon the world slipped away and all was dark.

STAGE 3:9

I woke suddenly. My body was clinging to Merek's as if he was a lifeline. The atrium was silent. Then came the little girls' laughter, they were running through the atrium, chasing the butterflies and delighting in the beauty around them. Merek was wide awake, watching me intently. I felt shy knowing he had essentially been my pillow the night through, but the smile in his eyes said he didn't mind so much.

"You seemed to sleep soundly last night," he said in a groggy voice.

I liked being the one he spoke to before anyone else and I realized for the first time since I was captured, I had slept, and very soundly at that; not one fiend visited me in my slumber. I smiled in reply, sitting up with my legs crossed in front of me. I stretched my arms out above my head with an immense yawn. "You might want to tell your mother that you aren't staying with her anymore," Merek said cautiously.

I had avoided deep conversation with her since her speech in the atrium several weeks before. Being around her was too difficult, knowing what I had to do and what would come afterward.

"Isn't the Militant personnel headquarters close to her chamber?" I asked with an air of innocence. "Could you stop in and tell her I'll be staying closer to the lab so I can focus on my duties?" I could tell my request wasn't something he wanted to do, but I hoped he would help me to continue to evade her presence.

"You should really be the one to tell her," he said, placing his hand gently on my knee. I had to force myself not to jerk away, which was irrational after spending the night in his arms. I had two choices: Be honest to a degree, of course, and tell him I couldn't face her, or lie and act overwhelmed by my new duties as an excuse. My mind only took a few seconds before I realized I didn't and couldn't lie to him any more than absolutely necessary.

"I can't talk to her right now. She is very disappointed in me," I confessed. Although Mother had never said those words, I knew she had to be.

"Don't you think you should go talk to her about it?" Merek asked me with concern. This calm and kind new Merek was hard to understand. I knew he was trying very hard to draw me out and "fix me," but what he didn't know is I could never be "fixed."

"I can't just yet," I told him in all truthfulness. "She may or may not want to speak with me."

"I'll tell her," he conceded. "You can't sleep here again. I have a small chamber, why don't you stay with me? You'll have to avoid Don, but it is comfortable, which I can't say for your choice last night," he said, sitting up stiffly.

After a restful night beside him, I was slightly tempted to take his offer, but I knew if I continued to grow closer to him, I might not go through with my plans; better to be alone.

"I planned to stay in the lab. There are accommodations in the back," I told him, remembering an offhanded remark from one of Gabby's long monologues about the lab. The thought of sleeping in the lab sent chills down my spine. I would be only a wall away from Francisco. Better to stay awake and plan.

"I have to leave. Can I see you at the noontime meal?" he asked. Even knowing that I was walking on the edge of a cliff that if I fell off of it would change the course I was headed down, I couldn't deny him. I was unable lie to myself either and say that it was only for him. Since coming back, something connected us, and I couldn't sever it.

"Yes, I'll try. I am sure the lab supervisor will have quite a lot of work for me today, though," I warned him. Once I wasn't in his presence, I would think clearer.

"I could bring you food. You can't not eat," he countered with a grin.

"All right, I'll see you then," I replied, realizing he had beat me.

His grin widened. He leaned forward and planted a soft kiss on my forehead. It seemed so innocent, but the pit of my stomach ached with the gesture. He stood quickly and headed off to the Militant Headquarters. His stride was strong and sure, and I sat there watching him until he waved goodbye.

As I waved in response, a small crack in the walls I had built around my heart formed. It would not be easy to discard my future with Merek for revenge, but I knew it couldn't be helped.

Outlandish were busy rushing off to their duties as I exited the atrium. I headed toward the lab, ready to start down a path that would end my pain. I watched the people. They all seemed so unconcerned with life, so carefree and light; I envied their existence. Only a short distance to the lab was left as I passed the mess hall, and the smells hit me square in the face. My stomach felt immediately nauseous. I quickened my pace, veering off to the canteen, hoping to avoid humiliation by vomit. Slamming through the doors, I made it just in time before I retched. Having nothing much in my stomach, it didn't take long before I was heaving without anything coming up.

The evidence of my violation was growing, only to me now, but soon, everyone would see. I wondered then how Merek would treat me. I had to end Francisco before that happened. I washed my mouth out thoroughly, opening the satchel that Merek had given me a lifetime ago for the necessary toiletries to freshen up. I avoided looking into the mirror. I knew the sight was stark and hollow and not something I wanted to see. I quickly gathered my things into my pack. The dagger blade reflected the light, reassuring me of its presence, and I left the canteen. I came in sight of the lab when I heard a loud yell.

"*Alex!*"

I turned quickly, recognizing the voice as Kasi. I felt both pure joy and dread at the same time. She was running to me and slammed her body into mine with a fierce hug. "I have missed you so so much!" she said through happy tears. I couldn't help the tears that fell from my eyes either.

"When did you arrive?" I asked, completely caught off guard by her presence.

"I travelled with a caravan. We arrived yesterday. I stayed with your mother. We were both worried when you didn't come to the chamber *all night?*" She posed it more as a question than a statement. "Where did you stay?" she then asked outright.

"I was with my new lab partner most of the night," I told her, hoping that would suffice. "Your journey was safe?" I asked to change the subject quickly.

"Yes, we were escorted in these wagons. They were old motorized vehicles that no longer worked that were pulled by massive horses. It was incredible! Such an adventure! We passed through beautiful countryside, and oh, the animals, the flowers, the blue skies, and the complete wildness of it all!" she said dreamily. "Your mother said you were captured?" she asked, flying from point to point.

My mind had been so focused on finding a way to access Francisco unobserved, I never dreamed I would see Kasi, much less talk to her again. I did not want to have this discussion with her. "Yes, for eleven days," I told her, knowing that she wouldn't allow me to avoid anything she asked.

"That must have been terribly frightening," she said, looking at me a little too closely, prodding me for more information.

"It was," I stated simply. My terse response pained her. I could see it in her wide brown eyes. "Kasi, I have missed you so much. Let's talk of happy things. How are the children?" I asked, hoping to redeem myself.

She smiled as if to clear her mind and started in on how well the children were enjoying their new lives in the Republic. As she talked of all that had happened since I left, which was really just a series of funny misfortunes, I urged her to follow me into the lab area. Gabby was absent, which was a slight blessing. I wanted to begin working and knew if she and Kasi began talking, I would never get anything done.

"All the children miss you and were very unhappy with my departure, but I told them we will be together again soon, I am sure of it," she said with confidence.

I was not so sure. In fact, I wasn't the same young girl that left Kasi five weeks before. I would never be that girl again.

"I do miss them," I said with longing, full knowledge that plans would forever part me from them. We were both seated comfortably in the golden station as I began working. Kasi continued to tell me of her adventure to the science bunker. Soon, I couldn't help but share in her wonder, and I was telling her of the wonderful things we saw on our own journey to the science bunker.

"There was this beautiful hidden pool. It was so cool, and I floated in it like a sea creature." I stopped abruptly, realizing my story was heading down a dark and morbid path that I couldn't share with anyone, not even Kasi. Of course, Kasi noticed my abrupt halt, but I was saved by the sudden appearance of Merek.

Kasi ran and surprised Merek with a violent hug in greeting. He smiled awkwardly and hugged her back. I glanced at the timekeeper. It was already the noontime meal; I was surprised at how quickly time had passed.

"I brought food," he stated with a sideways grin.

"Good, I am starving," Kasi said, smiling up at him in adoration. A person would have to be blind not to see how much she idolized him. *Maybe once I am gone, Merek will welcome her esteem.* But right now, he just patted her head and winked at her good-naturedly.

"How was your journey, little one?" Merek asked her. I wasn't sure if Merek called her "little one" because her head only came to his chest or because she was ten years his junior; either way, it always irked Kasi when he did.

"Maybe I'm not so little. Maybe it's just you're so big," she said in response. I was surprised she didn't stomp her foot as she spoke; she said it with such cheekiness.

Merek chuckled and began handing me food from his satchel. In the process, my hands would brush his, and I felt as if an electric shock went right to my gut. He smiled at me as if he knew what I was feeling. I needed to stop the attraction that was budding. Soon I would have to leave him.

"I bet everything has been extremely boring without me," Kasi said over her mouth full of food. Merek and I couldn't help but laugh. I watched them both as we ate together and knew they would be happy together once I was out of the equation. Merek might only see her as a child now, but one day, she would grow up, and he would see the beautiful person she was becoming. I smiled to myself, knowing they wouldn't be alone for long.

"I have to head back," Merek told us.

"I am supposed to go help organize paperwork for Justin," Kasi said with annoyance. "I guess I have become his assistant." She rolled her eyes dramatically.

"I can show you where his office is set up," Merek offered. "We will see you later," Merek said, smiling at me.

Kasi hugged me tightly, and off they went.

The minute they were out of sight, I began. I drew a map of the passageways from memory and headed to the closest entrance. It was nothing more than an unsuspecting bookcase. I double-checked that no one was around and began feeling the edges of the entrance for a latch or something with which to open it. My fingers felt a gap, and I reached my hand in to feel a lever. Pulling down on the lever, the bookcase slowly drew back along the wall opening into the passageway that led to my redemption.

My heart began pounding with the knowledge that I was so close to my goal. I quickly shut it before anyone happened upon me. Tonight had to be the night; the longer I waited, the more reasons I would find to live among the Outlandish, and I couldn't allow myself to second-guess the destiny laid out before me.

STAGE 4:0

I went through the motions of analyzing data long into the evening, hoping to be left alone in the lab area. Gabby had popped her head in every few hours, and I pretended to be overwhelmed with work, so she soon lost interest and left.

My plan was simple—distract the guards and sneak into the holding cell through the passageway. As soon as the lab was empty, I gathered some supplies and headed to the atrium. The hallways were vacant as well, and I quickly made it to my destination. I began preparing my distraction, placing paper and chemicals around the wooden arbor that was placed in the very heart of the atrium. One side would be a slow going fire, and when it reached the chemicals, no one would be able to ignore the explosion, leaving me time to execute my objective.

I pulled the matches from my satchel, held them in my hand, and just stared at them for a few moments. Once this was lit, I would no longer be able to go back. The spark of the match burned bright as I held it up to the prepared kindling. The slow flame began to smoke as I turned to leave before anyone noticed the disturbance. I walked quickly back to the lab, hoping no one would come upon me.

The entrance to the passageway slid open with a loud screech. The sound seemed so much louder in the quiet of the lab. I pulled out my handwritten map and began edging my way to the only functioning holding cell. The passageway was dark, and I could hear the scurry of some rodents; even with my skin crawling, I didn't allow myself to hesitate. I knew from studying the blueprints I was near the holding cells. Then I heard it, an explosion, my explosion; quickening my steps, I knew I had a small amount of time in which to end my pain.

Reaching the entrance to the cell, I slowly opened it to find myself looking at several holding cells and a long hallway that led to the observation room where the guard would be stationed. I waited a few moments to come fully into the room, hoping the guard was off helping with the explosion, and closed the entrance to the passageway securely behind me. He must have already gone, because no alarm went up as I looked for Francisco. The first two cells were vacant.

Coming up on the third cell, my heart began thundering in my chest painfully. There he sat, alert on a cot, one hand shackled to the wall. He must have wondered if his father was attacking the bunker in an effort to save him.

"No one is here to save you," I said, breaking the eerie silence.

He turned to me quickly. I saw a flash of surprise in his eyes, and then it was masked by his insolence.

"Ah, mi amor, couldn't stay away?" he asked, smiling.

I returned his smile, knowing I had the upper hand, and soon he would no longer be smiling.

"I plan to end you," I told him. I watched to see if he would react to his imminent demise, but if he was afraid, it didn't show.

"But we would have made such a force that no one could defeat. You know you felt it too," he said, carefree.

I laughed at him and knew I could perhaps frighten him yet, remembering Mother had once said that in the Seditionist camp, women that could bear children were treated slightly better than others because of the high infertility rate among them.

"Too bad you shall die today, and tomorrow, so shall your child," I said as I placed my hand on the slight bulge of my womb. I saw it then, first surprised excitement followed by fear. I hadn't planned to say that, but the look of terror on his face was well worth it. Besides, how could I ever love the spawn of his seed?

"You would kill an innocent?" he asked with a tone to his voice I had never heard from him. He was ready to beg.

"I could never love the child made by force, so once I am through with you, I shall find a way for the rest," I said, taking out my hatchet from the satchel. He didn't seem to notice my weapon, but he pleaded.

"Kill me, but why must you hurt the baby?"

I hated that he called it a baby, but I ignored him and opened his cell by turning the key that controlled the panel of levers, advancing toward him to end his sad existence. "Please, mi amor, I will do anything! Don't harm the child!"

I was surprised by his pleading, but I was even more surprised that I believed him when he said he would do anything I asked if I spared the child.

"Will you take your own life?" I asked him, feeling the power of his life in my hands.

He hesitated only for a moment. "If you so wish," he said with resignation. "You must promise to let the child live. Isa would gladly care for a child, and you could be free of her then." He spoke as if he knew the thing growing inside of me was female, which surprised me again because of the Seditionist low opinion of the sex. For a slight pause in time, I wanted to take his offer, but I dismissed it. It was the power I held. I may or may not keep the child; he had no say in the matter.

"I don't believe I will," I replied, anger and rage boiling inside of me. I was just out of his arm's length, and even with his left hand bound to the wall, I knew he wouldn't be easy to kill. With my free hand, I took the knife from my belt. Now armed with all the weapons that I had, I hurled the hatchet directly into his right foot, pinning him in place.

He let out a bellow of agony, and that's when I attacked, releasing all the rage that had boiled inside of me for the last month. Francisco didn't fight back but only tried to defend himself. I wanted him to fight back, if only because it would help fuel the fire of wrath inside of me. I stabbed him in the hand he was trying to protect himself with. Pulling it free, I saw the opening to finish him. Reaching back so that I could pierce his heart with as much force as I had, someone grabbed me from behind. His scent identified him long before I saw his face—Merek. He pinned my arms to my side and dragged me away from Francisco, kicking and screaming.

"It was almost done! Let me finish him!" I yelled as loud as I could. I felt my sanity slipping as he continued to put distance between me and my objective. Silently, Merek place me outside of the cell and took the key from the panel that controlled the levers and returned to Francisco's cell, closing it with a loud crash behind him, locking himself in.

Merek went back to Francisco and kicked the hatchet free from his foot. Francisco let out a cry of pain in response. Towering over Francisco, Merek began to methodically smash his fists into Francisco's face one blow at a time. I watched with only the slightest remorse that if Merek killed him, Merek would reap my consequences. That's when I heard them, footsteps growing ever closer. Don came through the guard's observation area first followed by Justin, Colin, and a guard. They all began speaking at once, but I wasn't comprehending what was said. Don shook me and yelled in my face.

"Where is the key?" His words finally broke through my insanity.

"He has it," I replied, pointing to Merek.

The guard rushed away, going for a key, I was sure. Colin, Justin, and Don stood at the bars of the cell, yelling for Merek to stop. He didn't even acknowledge their presence. Francisco couldn't survive such a beating; his body was slumped on the cot as Merek continued to pummel him. The guard returned and placed the key into the panel, opening the cell. Immediately they tried to pull Merek away from Francisco's limp form. It took all three of their combined strengths to end the carnage. Others had come into the holding cell at this point, but I knew none of them. A medic came in with a syringe and plunged it into Merek's neck; he was subdued within seconds. They placed Merek onto a gurney and strapped him in. I started to follow in a daze. Don stopped me.

"What happened here?" he asked me.

"I planned to kill Francisco, but Merek stopped me," I told him honestly. Now that Francisco was dead, I had no reason to withhold truth. The medic was hovering over the body on the cot. I had no remorse for his death, but I also had no relief for my fury. I finally looked back at Don. He was stunned by my words, I could see.

"What did he do to you in the camp?" Don asked, blocking out my view of the body by shaking my shoulders earnestly. How do you put into words the utter shame I had endured? The horror that had become my life? I could form nothing tangible, so I said the first thing that would suffice without much explanation.

"I am with child. His child." I croaked out the foul-tasting words, shrugging my head in the direction of Francisco.

A myriad of emotions crossed his face—shock, pain, anger—and I wasn't sure, but something like disgust. I was unceremoniously pulled into a fierce hug. The tears that came I let fall, unchecked.

"Let's get you out of here," Don said above my head. He turned my body without letting me see Francisco and escorted us away from the scene. We walked past the guards, medic, and all else who had gathered. Once we were back into the main hallway, I saw the smoke from my earlier destruction and people rushing to its source. We went the opposite way at a slow pace.

"Why didn't you tell anyone?" Don finally broke the silence between us.

"Mother knew, the medic that examined me knew," I told him. "Where are we going?" I asked him.

"I am taking you somewhere to rest. I am not sure what lies ahead, and you look like you might keel over at any second," he said. The usual lightness to his voice was absent. We continued on without any words spoken among us. I noticed we passed the Militant Headquarters, and then we were in what I assumed was Don and Merek's shared chamber. It was very sparse with only two small beds. Don helped me lie down on what I knew to be Merek's from its scent—woodsy, fresh, and strong. It comforted me, and my last thoughts were of Merek's well-being before I fell into a deep sleep of emotional exhaustion.

STAGE 4:1

Mother was beside me when I woke, sitting in a chair at the foot of the bed, her head bowed and hand placed on my feet. I didn't stir, but she must have sensed a changed and looked up at me. Tears were on her beautiful face.

"Are you terribly disappointed?" I asked before she could speak.

"Of course not. You are in pain, hurting. How could I be anything but concerned for you?" she asked me softly. Her words were kind, which surprised me, because I thought she would be more upset than anyone else. I had killed a person that once meant something to her.

"Will they exile me, imprison me, or put me to death? What will happen to Merek?" I asked, not really caring what my fate was. I did what I had to do, although I felt confused that my pain and anger were still gripping my heart like a vice. My own penalty didn't matter, only that Merek didn't take the blame for what I intended to do, even if he finished the job.

"I don't think the punishment will be that severe. The damage to the atrium was confined to the arbor, and no one was hurt. I am not sure what they will do to Merek. He nearly killed Cisco," she told me with apprehension in her tone.

Francisco was alive! My stomach dropped with the new information. "He is a…alive?" I asked, choking on the question.

Mother looked at me as if she thought I already knew. "Yes, he is barely holding on, but he is alive," she told me carefully. My utter disappointment was only lessened by the fact that Merek's punishment wouldn't be for murder; that was my burden to bear, not his. I couldn't speak. I was too weary to consider trying to end Francisco again, and now everyone would know my shame anyway. I had failed.

"You are awake! Do you realize how worried we were?" Kasi asked as she entered the small chamber. Her presence filled the room to overflowing. She brought her delight for life everywhere she went. I felt agitation that she could be so happy while my life was falling apart more and more each day.

"I'd like to be left alone," I told them both, and I saw the pain I caused by my rejection. I avoided eye contact with Kasi. I hated to hurt her more than I already had, but I could no longer handle her light in my dark world. I looked away as they exited, silent tears flowing; it was better to be alone than face their questions and pity. My hand went to the slight swell in my abdomen. A child grew there—his child—and he lived. I wanted to scream at the injustice, but I knew my chance at revenge had passed, and I was left with only the consequences.

No matter what happened, Merek couldn't be the one to be punished for this. Getting out of the bed, I dressed quickly; someone had taken my dagger and hatchet. I wondered if they would have a guard at my door too. I walked quietly to the door, hoping I could leave without an escort. I cracked it open only enough to see and was surprised no one was there. Throwing my satchel over my shoulder, I rushed to the Militant Headquarters, hoping they would let me speak with Merek. I didn't have far to go before I encountered a small crowd that had gathered around the headquarters, all buzzing with the information about Merek, the fire, and Francisco.

Some of the Outlandish recognized me and stopped their idle chatter, but others went on and on about what Merek's fate might be. I too wondered about that. I saw Don standing at the entrance. He saw me and shook his head as if I shouldn't be there. I was past caring what he said. I had to know about Merek.

"You shouldn't be here," Don said, pulling me close so that no one else would hear. "Merek is taking all the blame. He says that he set the fire, which we know was you from the surveillance cameras. When Justin told him we saw you on the camera, he says he put you up to it and that you were forced," Don said, shaking his head sadly.

My heart was pounding to a loud rhythm that I could hardly hear Don over. "That's not true and you know it," I told Don hysterically.

"Everyone knows it, but we can't do anything about it," he said, defeated. "Merek asked me to keep you away. He doesn't want you hurt anymore," Don finished.

I wanted to scream that this wasn't how it was supposed to happen, but I knew that was pointless. Colin came through the doors and immediately saw me. His gaze softened as he headed purposefully toward us. Colin didn't say a word as he gently pulled me into his arms. I was surprised, because we never had much physical contact, but also the fact that his breathing was forced made me wonder what all he knew. I looked at Don over his shoulder, and he nodded in confirmation; Colin knew everything too.

"Why didn't you tell us?" Colin asked in a scratchy voice.

I didn't know how to answer a question that had more than one answer. *I didn't want you to look at me in pity and I couldn't let you stop me from trying to end Francisco's life.*

"I couldn't…" I didn't know what to say. I choked.

Colin looked at me with compassion and seemed to understand my reasoning, even if it was only half.

"I have to see Merek," I told them both.

"He doesn't want you to be here," Colin said calmly. "He wants you to stay away. We have this handled. Justin and the rest don't know what really happened, and Merek would like to keep it that way." Colin said the last part quietly so that only I could hear.

"Please, Colin, Merek can't take the punishment that is meant for me," I begged.

"What kind of friend would I be if I didn't honor his one request?" Colin asked me in response.

"What kind of friend would you be if you let him suffer for me?" I asked, hoping to break through to him.

"You didn't put Francisco into the medic's station. That was Merek. He is taking the punishment for his own deeds," Colin said.

"Besides, the atrium fire isn't that big of a deal. No one was hurt, and the arbor can be rebuilt," Don said, interrupting what I had been about to say.

"I have to do this," I told them, holding back tears.

They looked at each other before Colin nodded and led me into the headquarters. The entrance had a small desk that an enormous Outlandish woman sat at that looked like she could smash me into the earth, and I would never to be seen again. She motioned for us to proceed but watched me closely as I walked beside Colin, Don bringing up the rear. Two doors down, and we turned on the third to the right. Colin opened the door and ushered me in. There was only a table with a few chairs around it. Merek was sitting in one chair with elbows on the table, rubbing his temples. He looked up with the click of the shutting door.

"I asked you to keep her out of this," he said to Colin, annoyance in his voice.

"I tried. I really did," Colin said and then exited out of the room.

I was in the room where I wanted to be but at a loss for words. What do you say to the person you had all but been lying to who was now trying to save you from yourself?

"You can't do this," I said simply, no grandiose words coming to mind.

"Yes, I can," he returned without looking at me. I knew he had to be upset with me, I had lied, used people (mainly Gabby), and gone behind his back, but I hoped he wasn't angry for other reasons like the child growing inside of me against my will. Everything in me wanted to kneel down by his chair and beg him to forgive me, but I was terrified by the thought of his rejection, so I kept my distance.

"I knew what I was doing. I knew the punishment would be extreme, and I was prepared to take it," I told him from my position across the room.

"Why?" he asked me to bypass my statement. "Why didn't you tell me? Anyone in authority? We would have treated Francisco different. Being an informant wouldn't have been an option for him," he said, finally looking up at me. I saw pain there and confusion. I wanted to make it better but didn't know how.

"You would have stopped me," I told him honestly.

"I did stop you, and I would have killed him for you if they hadn't stopped me." He spoke the words easily as if taking Francisco's life didn't affect him in the least. "He deserves to die for what he did to you," Merek said without remorse. "I can speak with Justin. They will find a suitable punishment for such a man," he said, anger rising in his voice with each word. There wasn't any point in trying to hide the shame that soon would be visible to all, so I nodded in agreement.

"Only if you let me explain that it was my intention to kill him and it was me who set fire to the arbor in the atrium," I said with resolve.

"Fine, I agree," he said. The ease with which we had spoken together in the past was absent, and the loss was disheartening.

"How did you find me before I killed Francisco?" I asked him.

"I was worried about you when I heard the alarms go off for the fire. I came to the lab and saw the passageway entrance cracked open. When I opened it all the way, I thought you had to be down it somewhere, so I went after you. As I drew closer, I could hear you speaking to Francisco. I think I always suspected something horrible happened to you in that camp, but actually knowing it, hearing the suffering in your voice, I was blinded by my rage. I could think of nothing else but ending your agony." He paused, not looking at me. "What he did…I can't even fathom. After that, I had to destroy him." Merek said the rage I had hidden for months was now present in him. It put a weight upon my shoulders, hearing his words and knowing I could have lessened the pain by telling him from the start.

"While I was captured in the camp, all of my thoughts were of your well-fare. After so many days with no end in sight, I began to wonder if I would ever see you again, and then all I remember is being knocked unconscious and waking to your beautifully concerned face. I can't express the elation I felt. You were alive, and then you never left my side, and I thought we truly had a chance. But you were different, and I tried to understand, but you never let me in. In fact, you all but lied to me. Alex, I loved you, and you don't even trust me."

I realized in that moment I did love him too. His strength, his thoughtfulness, and his determination drew me in like a moth to the flame, and now I would surely be scorched alive. Funny how I realized my feelings for him now that there wasn't a chance for us.

"I was afraid. I could hardly look at myself in the mirror for the shame. I see the brand Francisco scorched my body with and I want to vomit. I look down on my growing womb and feel utter disgust. I know I didn't let you in, I know I was wrong to lie to you, and if you never want to speak with me again, I completely understand. I am broken, I feel rage all the time, and you deserve a whole person in your life, a person that isn't eaten up with fury," I said and noticed he flinched with my last comment. The words hung in the air for long moments before he finally spoke.

"Alex, I don't know what I want right now," he said, confusion clouding his voice. I felt as if my journey was a mirror of my mother's—fall in love, the male finds out you are carrying another male's child, and then rejection. I knew this would happen, but it didn't stop the pain I felt when it happened.

Someone opened the door, and I turned around at the sound; it was Justin and Colin.

"I need to speak with you," Justin said very formally, gesturing me toward the exit.

"Listen, no matter what she says, I am the one that put Francisco where he is and I am the one that can pay for that," Merek said, rising quickly from the chair to his imposing height. I looked at him sharply, wondering if he was going back on our earlier agreement. "No matter her intentions, I did the deed." He finished just as Justin shut the door between us. Colin stayed in the room with Merek as I followed Justin through the hallways to another small room that looked to be a meeting area.

"Tell me what is going on," Justin said simply.

My chest squeezed tight at the thought of sharing the things that happened, but I had to in order to get Merek free from condemnation. I didn't respond for a few tense moments, and Justin waited patiently, watching me intently.

"I am carrying Francisco's child against my will." I put it as simply as I could without giving away intimate details. He didn't seem shocked, and I suppose if anyone would know what my experience had been in the Seditionist camp, it would be Justin.

"As I suspected. Why didn't you come forward with this information before now?" he asked.

"Because I know you all do not have capital punishment here in the Republic, and I wanted him dead," I told him truthfully. "I was afraid you would stop me. I started the fire as a distraction and I am the one that stabbed him." I hoped he would reconsider Merek's involvement with my honesty.

"How did Merek become entangled with your plot?" he asked me.

"He came upon me in the act and overheard what had transpired between Francisco and myself. He was furious and didn't think. He just acted. I am the one who planned it all. He had nothing to do with that," I said earnestly.

"I understand why you felt the need to avenge yourself. However, we can't have people taking the regulations into their own hands. I will convey what happened to the Council of Elders, and they will determine both of your fates," he said and then seemed to consider his next words carefully. "I am truly sorry for what happened to you. I once failed your mother and naively placed her in an unforgivable situation. She somehow overcame it all. I can never make up to her what I did, but maybe I can help you," he said sincerely.

I didn't necessarily desire his help, but for Merek's sake, I would accept. "Please help Merek. I don't care what my fate is." I had nothing left, and nothing could help me.

STAGE 4:2

The next few days I spent without much to do. I stayed with Don and avoided everyone else. The Council was convening soon, and I hoped that they would look favorably upon Merek. I had not spoken to him since our conversation in the Militant Headquarters. Don kept me up-to-date on everything happening in the bunker, and he asked me constantly how I was faring. Don's questions didn't bother me; it was as if the way in which he asked wasn't out of pity or worry, more to know the answer and allow me to talk without judgment.

"How is today going?" he asked one morning as he brought me toast and tea; that's all that would stay in my stomach before 1100 hours.

"I couldn't sleep last night," I told him honestly, combing through my unruly hair with my fingers. The only peaceful sleep I had gotten since being captured was the night I slept in the atrium in Merek's arms, I recalled painfully.

"I know, I heard you," he replied, rubbing his eyes in exhaustion.

"I am sorry, I didn't mean to keep you up," I told him, knowing I wasn't a prisoner, so to speak, but I also knew that I was under the watch of both Don and Colin until after the Council met and decided my punishment.

"It's no problem, who needs sleep anyway?" he said, smiling sardonically.

"How is Merek?" I asked, knowing that Colin and Don went back and forth between Merek, and I keeping us both occupied and watched.

"He doesn't talk much, but Merek isn't really a big talker anyway, so who knows?" he said, shrugging his shoulders.

"You are just a well of information," I replied dryly.

"He is miserable, almost as miserable as you," he said truthfully. "He hardly eats, he doesn't talk to us, except to answer questions, and he looks more fierce than normal, which is saying a lot," Don finished.

"I hate this. I hate that I wandered off to bathe in the woods. I hate that I let Francisco capture me. I hate that Merek gave himself up to save me. I hate that I didn't fight Francisco to the death. I hate that he violated me. I hate that his child is within me. I hate that I didn't succeed in killing him. I hate that I hurt Merek in the unsuccessful attempt to end my pain. I hate that even when I thought that Francisco was dead, my pain wasn't lessened, but what I hate most of all is that I have so much hate inside me," I told him, feeling the defeat of everything upon me.

Don didn't say anything for a time and only drew me into a gentle hug of reassurance. For never having physical contact with others for the majority of my existence, I was amazed at how much peace it brought to me.

"I have been talking to your mother quite a bit lately. She is very worried about you and has some interesting ideas about hate and love and things. Has she told you about this Ruach HaKodesh?" Don finally asked into my hair.

Stepping back, I tensed at the mention of this ambiguous being that may or may not exist. "She has. I don't know what to think about it, though," I told him thoughtfully.

"I find it interesting, to say the least. Its origins must be from the religions of old, but it is so in contrast to them in the same sense. No judgment, forgive no matter the offense, love your enemies. It's actually quite insane if you really think about it. I mean, it goes against every natural instinct to put others above yourself," he said with a slight laugh. "And yet studies have shown over and over that those that are working in some sort of service to others, such as medics, teachers, caregivers, and anyone that gives their time and concern to others is perpetually happier than the rest of us. This psychology can't explain, but yet it is," he said in bewilderment.

Thoughts of my mother were conflicting and difficult to decipher. She understood exactly what I was going through right now, but her reaction had been so different from my own that I felt as if I couldn't confide in her, because she would want me to love this child, to forgive, and those weren't things I was capable of. I couldn't try to fathom Ruach HaKodesh and the validity of his existence. I wasn't even sure if it was a he.

"She spoke of this being with great confidence. Whether or not 'it' is real, she believes it with her entire heart," he said.

"I can't. The thought of forgiving Francisco for such a horror, letting him off for such an offense, is more than he deserves," I replied.

"You are absolutely right. He doesn't deserve anything, but what do you deserve?" he asked me gently.

"What do you mean?" I questioned, unsure.

"Plainly put, as long as you hold onto anger, Francisco will have a hold on you," he replied with quiet wisdom. "Case studies have shown that bitterness causes all kinds of emotional issues, and if not dealt with, it can literally lead to health issues such as hypertension. Although I am not sure about this 'being' your mother claims has helped her to forgive, I do not doubt the truth behind the message."

"I see her, her peace, her kindness, and knowing that what she has gone through was much like my own experience, I don't see how she could forgive and become who she is today. The path to peace eludes me. I have heard no still soft voice, no words of love and freedom," I said with despair.

"Maybe your path won't be led by a voice but instead by a choice," Don replied carefully. "I believe we have the power of conscious direction. Our lives aren't meant to be lived passively, allowing the wind to blow us wherever it wills, but instead, we must fight to become the person we desire to be no matter life's hardships. No matter the way the wind blows," he said, giving me pause.

I saw the truth and wisdom in his words and I wanted to choose to follow his guidance, but they seemed as impossible as Mother's Ruach HaKodesh. I nodded my understanding and sipped my tea, hoping to dissuade him from this line of conversation. It was growing ever more uncomfortable.

"When will the Council tell me my fate?" I asked, going to an entirely new subject.

"I am sure they will call you both to the meeting area and announce it this afternoon," Don said. We then spoke of lighthearted things, like Kasi and her many humorous mishaps. "Every single time I have seen her, she inquires about when she can see you. It is getting pretty old," he said, laughing good-naturedly. A comfortable silence fell between us, and we waited, and I couldn't help but wonder what today would hold for me and for Merek.

STAGE 4:3

Colin came to fetch us for the adjudication. Mother and Kasi were sitting in the front row. Both looked nervous. My eyes locked with Merek's. He seemed resolved and perhaps slightly concerned for me. My chest beat painfully with the knowledge that he was in this situation because of me. Colin led me to the table and empty chair next to Merek, and I sat down slowly. My hand hung between us, but soon I felt the warmth of his hand grasping my own. I didn't look at him for fear of my reaction in this public setting. I tried not to allow myself much joy that he desired my touch, because I knew it could be only a gesture of kindness.

"I have spoken on behalf of both of the accused. The Council has heard their recorded testimonies, looked over the surveillance, gone through all the evidence, and they now have come to their decision. Everyone please be seated and silent," Justin said to the small group that had gathered to watch the proceedings.

Out of the large group of what I surmised to be the Council of Elders, a short older gentleman stood as Justin took a seat beside Merek and Gabby.

"This adjudication is for the fire located in the atrium and beating of prisoner Francisco Fuerte. We have reviewed all things presented and heard many speak on the behalf of the accused. We have decided to be somewhat lenient, and the punishment will be as follows. Merek Wharrier, you will be on three years' probation without being able to advance in your standing in the Militant until further review. Alexandra, last name undecided, you will be put to community service for three years and be reassigned from the data lab to work under the tutelage of Colin Brody, seeking a cure, without advancement until further review. Gabby Masterson, you face probation for one year for aiding and abetting a crime.

"Under the circumstances and considering that the man beaten is a criminal and Seditionist along with the fact that the fire was confined to the arbor, we have been very merciful in this instance. However, if any attempts are made again to take the regulations into your own hands, the punishment will be severe."

The short man finished, and the Council dismissed us. I felt instant relief that Merek wouldn't suffer too much for my sake and total confusion that they would punish poor Gabby. Don roughly patted Merek's back in happy support. Colin drew me into a hug. From the corner of my eye, I saw Gabby rush away. She was rushing away from me.

"Justin really fought for you all," Colin said so that only I could hear. "I guess you are stuck with me now." He laughed. Mother was waiting for me as Colin released me. She looked unsure but hugged me anyway. Kasi was next, hugging me fiercely also, despite my earlier rejection of her. Then I was swept up into Don's arms, and he swung me around in excitement. I felt lightheaded when my feet finally touched the ground. I stumbled slightly into Merek and looked up at his unsure eyes. He reached for my hand and gave it a reassuring squeeze, but what I wanted most of all was for him look at me without doubt and distrust, and that would take time that I now had.

"What will happen to Francisco?" Merek asked Justin. I waited for the answer with bated breath.

"The Council has decided he will be our prisoner without any chance of release for his many crimes," Justin replied.

"Will he continue to be an informant?" Merek asked, anger in his voice.

"We plan to use him to whatever advantage we can against the Seditionist," Justin told us.

I wanted to rage against the light sentence, but I knew that my chance for revenge had passed, and in the short time I had believed Francisco dead, nothing had been any better.

"I think you're making a big mistake. He will betray us the second he gets a chance," Merek replied irritably.

"I am sure you are correct, but we will be careful to watch for any deception," Justin said considerately. Just like that Justin stopped the conversation and dismissed Merek's opinion, I could tell it did not sit well with him. Justin and Mother joined the Council, and Don was whisked away to speak with some attractive Outlandish female. Colin and Kasi were in deep conversation about who knows what, and I was left alone with Merek.

"I am truly sorry you were brought into my problem." I said the first thing that was on my mind.

He looked at me sharply. "You think I'm upset that I was brought into it?" he asked me tensely.

"I wish I could have spared you the heartache of finding out the way you did," I told him.

"I am not upset with you about being involved. I guess I just realized that you don't trust me as I did you," he said slowly.

"I couldn't bear for you to know," I told him honestly. "I thought that if I ended Francisco, it would change how broken I feel, it would stop the anger, and then I could take my punishment, knowing I exacted the revenge that saved me. But for the few hours I thought him dead, I felt the same. Nothing can restore me back to the person you once knew," I told him, defeated. I said what I needed to tell him and knew that any chance we had was gone, so I turned to give him the space he deserved. I briskly walked past Don and then Mother and finally reached the all but deserted hallway. I took several deep inhales trying to calm myself without much success. I had shed so many tears in the last few months that I promised myself I wouldn't let a single tear fall, even with the knowledge that something I had never thought to have my entire lifetime was something I acutely desired, something I longed for—another person's love. I felt a hand on my shoulder. I quickly turned to see Mother. She had a look of deep concern furrowing her brow.

"Let me help you, little bird?" she asked with desperate hope in her eyes. I knew I had lost Merek, and the thought of losing another person wasn't something I was willing to do. I nodded, and she embraced me without reservation. We walked in silence back to her chamber, and I was glad she didn't try to cheer me up or try to have idle chatter between us. The quiet was what I wanted in that moment; no words were needed, just her silent acceptance. We both went about readying ourselves for sleep, and I saw that Mother had an extra bed brought in for Kasi.

"She loves you dearly, you know?" Mother asked as she saw me looking at the new bed in our small chamber.

"She loves the person she knew before. I am not that girl anymore," I told Mother plainly.

"Do you think Kasi will love this new person less?" she asked in response.

"Nothing is what it was before. She can't ever really even know this me. I used to love her silliness and lighthearted nature, but now it is almost as if her happiness only highlights my misery," I confessed sadly. "I don't want to darken her with the person I am now," I finished lamely.

"I think she can handle it, and I know that you could use her light in your world right now," Mother replied carefully.

Maybe she was right, but it was so hard; I still hadn't even spoken to Kasi privately since the truth came out about my abuse. What must she think of me? I had spent weeks looking for revenge, thinking that would stop the constant pain and unruly anger inside. It hadn't quenched the flames. I felt like a ship without a rudder, no purpose, no direction. Mother had been through the same experience and somehow had come out a woman that desired to help all no matter who they were; it all seemed so impossible. She too had been pregnant with a child that wasn't conceived in love but forced upon her. Even if it was done through a science lab, the outcome was the same: an unplanned child.

"How did you love me?" I asked her. "How could you look at me every day, knowing you had no choice in my conception?" I added.

"I didn't even know what real love was until I experienced it from Ruach HaKodesh. When you were born, it only expanded, multiplied," she told me quickly. "Not long after you were born, they administered the injection, and I knew immediately that it didn't work. I tried to hide my love for you from everyone, and later, 92345 exposed my immunity to the injection. I was taken to the reformatory by the Sovereignty, and the parting was more difficult than I would have thought possible. I loved you so," she said sadly.

"This was done to me. I had no choice, and I don't think I am capable of loving the seed of such a man," I confessed.

"The child had no choice either," Mother said simply.

"I am sure someone in the bunker would want to take care of a child," I responded, knowing her point was valid.

"Yes, there are many who would take the child in," she told me gently.

I didn't feel as if she thought less of me for my confession, but I somehow did. Mother loved me, accepted me, raised me for five years, and was torn from my life without her consent; I couldn't even stand to see the swell that was my normally flat abdomen.

"Please rest, you need it so badly," she told me with concern.

I heeded her request and lay my head down on the pillow, and only a few minutes later, I was in a dark room and haunted by a small dementor, a child with eyes like Francisco's.

STAGE 4:4

I woke to find Kasi standing over my bed.

"You don't look very good," she told me. "Did you have terrors in the night?" she asked with worry in her voice.

"I always do," I told her honestly, but I realized that wasn't entirely true. I had slept peacefully in Merek's arms.

"I know you haven't wanted to talk about everything that has happened, but just know that I am always here for you and love you dearly," she told me, holding my hands tightly between hers. I didn't know what to say but nodded. Maybe, in time, we could once again be as close as we were before this all had changed me.

Kasi began filling me in on the progress they had made with the cure and all the rumors about the imminent battle with the Seditionist.

"Raymon has attacked a party of Outlandish that were tending the animals on the surface. Everyone has been ordered to stay below ground until they have made their plans for attack. If things get worse, I am sure we will be in complete lockdown," she informed me. "From all the preparations I see going on, I think the fight will be soon."

With all my thoughts going to revenge, I had totally missed the things going on around me. I never even noticed that the fight was coming this quickly or that Raymon had attacked the Outlandish. I felt that I had lost touch with reality. "I didn't even realize," I said. Looking around, I noticed that Mother had already left for the day. I wondered how long I had slept. "What is the time?" I asked.

"It's nearly the noon meal. You slept for quite a while," Kasi replied. "Why don't you put on your clothes, and we can get something to eat? I am famished," she said dramatically.

I nodded and dressed in my normal attire—pants with multiple pockets, sturdy button-up shirt, a belt that held my scabbard, hook for the hatchet, and lace-up boots. Once dressed, we ventured out, heading to the mess hall. Many of the Outlandish waved to Kasi as we passed, and I once again wondered how she so quickly made friends. She had only been in this bunker for a few weeks, and I had been much longer and didn't know anyone other than those I had come with, besides Gabby, of course. Gabby, I didn't know how I would face her. She had to know I had used her by now. I had hurt so many in the pursuit of revenge.

The mess hall wasn't far from Mother's chamber, and soon, we were seated with our food trays in front of us. The room was slightly empty with only a few other people eating the noon fare this early. We sat alone, and I began eating in silence, hoping the food wouldn't upset my now sensitive stomach. Between bites, Kasi would talk to me about the things she did for Justin.

"I make his schedule, organize his paperwork, and rewrite his notes. His handwriting is so hard to deciphered," she told me with a laugh.

Soon we were done eating. Kasi fluttered off to Justin's new makeshift office, and I headed out to find Colin, knowing he was in the main lab, working on the cure. Walking the hallways alone, I had some time to reflect on my journey thus far. I had been through devastation, tried to achieve retribution, failed, and now was faced with where to go from here. Merek was lost to me, I was carrying a monster's seed, and I didn't have much to live for. Part of me wanted to break free from the bunker and tempt death to take me whether death came in the form of the elements or the Seditionist; it made no difference as long as it did come.

The longer I thought about it, the more I realized that wasn't an option, though. I could still live this life. I may have lost at revenge and lost at love, but I had Mother, Kasi, Don, and even Colin. I had a goal to end the tyranny of the Sovereignty and defeat the carnage of the Seditionist, so I hastened my gait, and with a new purpose, I went in search of Colin. He was bent over a microscope, humming a soft tune.

"I am late, but I made it," I told him.

He jerked his head up and smiled. "Glad you made it," he replied. "We have had some interesting developments with the cure. After running multiple tests, CT scans, MRI, and bloodwork, the only thing unique that we found was her blood has the RH negative antigen protein, and before The Great Synthetic War, that blood type was only found in about 15 percent of the population. However, after the wars, that number was close to nonexistent. In fact, when a woman went to the sanatorium to become a carrier, they weren't chosen for that reason alone, essentially wiping out the blood type entirely. Their reasoning was because that blood type cannot accept the positive blood types, making a person with the RH antigen more unique and harder to deal with medically, so they didn't allow people to procreate that had RH negative antigen proteins," Colin finished excitedly. "I am not sure yet how this plays into your mother having an immunity to the injection, but so far, that is the only difference I find." He finished with an air of happy discovering.

"Could her being chosen for a carrier attribute to it?" I asked.

"I wondered that myself. How they overlooked her blood type, I am not sure. Perhaps it was human error or perhaps the scientist wanted to experiment with her blood type?" he mused.

"We should run tests on my blood," I told him, catching some of his excitement.

"I am glad you think so. I hated to ask," he said, smiling self-consciously.

So we began. I sat down in the chair beside him, and he took a sample of my blood. I felt somewhat light-headed but tried to think of other things like nature's beauty, mother's kindness, and Kasi's lust for life. Soon it was over, and I was writing down numbers Colin spouted off to me. We worked tirelessly together; no extra talk was necessary. Before I realized it, time had come for the evening fare.

"We had better close it up for the evening," Colin said, exhaustion in his voice.

"I suppose," I replied reluctantly. I had felt a purpose that was to heal and not harm today, and it felt good.

We walked to the mess hall together, both lost in our own thoughts, then I felt a flutter in my womb; the child had moved. It felt so strange that I abruptly stopped, and Colin looked at me with concern.

"What's wrong?" he asked, worry on his brow.

I almost blurted out what was happening, then I quickly made a random excuse. "Some nerve must be pinched, just felt strange for a second there," I told him with some honesty.

"Do you need to see a medic?" he asked, troubled.

"Oh, no, I'm sure I'll be fine. Maybe its hunger pangs. I haven't eaten much in the last few weeks," I told him. We continued to walk and were passing the Militant Headquarters when I saw him, Merek. He was there half-listening to an animated Don talking about who knows what. I tried to hurry past him without being seen, because I didn't know what to say after our last encounter when he saw me. We hadn't parted on the best terms, but we also hadn't parted on the worst of terms. Our eyes connected, and he left Don immediately. Don was still talking and then rolled his eyes and followed after Merek.

"You two should probably speak alone," Colin said from behind me.

"I am not sure there is anything to talk about," I replied with remorse.

"Merek isn't one to shy away from something just because it is complicated," Colin told me with a laugh.

"It is a bit past complicated," I said, hoping to make it to the mess hall without any confrontation from Merek. I kept my pace at a quick clip, but he caught up to me.

"Alex," Merek said from behind me.

I wanted to pretend not to hear him, but beside me, Colin stopped and looked back at Merek, so I had no choice.

"I'll go save us a table and get some food for you," Colin said, leaving me to face Merek alone.

My heart had started pounding. He didn't deserve the story my life had become, yet I didn't want to actually hear him reject me either.

"Can we talk?" Merek asked quietly.

"You don't have to explain anything. I don't even want to face the problems I have now, how can I ask you to?" I told him honestly.

"I still don't think you understand why I am upset, do you?" he asked, somewhat frustrated. "I thought we had experienced this thing, this tragedy that bonded us, so much so that it would never be broken, and then I came to realize you don't feel like I do. I told myself to stay away. If you truly wanted a relationship, you would have been honest with me, but here I am trying to fix it, because as much as I want to bask in my hurt pride, I can't stay away from you. I see you and I am drawn like a moth to a flame," he said, a slight desperation in his voice.

I was taken aback. He spoke the words I couldn't. I had been, and knew always would be, frightened by the excitement and desire I felt in his presence. There wasn't much distance between us, so I took the two small steps and wrapped my arms around him. It took more courage than I thought I possessed, but he pulled me into his arms with a fierce need. I saw Don over Merek's shoulder, shaking his head with a laugh as if he knew something that we didn't. We parted and, without any more words, headed to the mess hall together, met by Don.

"Shut up, Don," Merek told him before he could even speak.

"I wasn't going to say a word, not a single word," Don said with a large grin.

Colin had saved us a table with Mother, Gabby, Abia, and Kasi seated there. They greeted us as we sat, all chatting about me, and for a few moments, I remembered what my life was like before I so carelessly snuck away to bathe in a seductive pool.

STAGE 4:5

Once again, I became engrossed in an intense schedule—wake up before the rest of the world, run the lab with Colin making some headway with a cure, then lunch with everyone. Four more hours looking over more data and in microscopes, I skipped the evening fare to once again train with Merek, allowing us to be alone, and helping me to not feel helpless. With the Seditionist above trying to find a weakness to the bunker, war was imminent, and I planned to be ready.

Two weeks passed, and then Mother had talked me into checking on the baby with the medic. I couldn't think of it as anything else now that I constantly felt its movements. Today I would have a sonogram done and see the tiny life inside; it both repelled and intrigued me at the same time.

Merek had offered to go with me, but I couldn't put him through that. Mother had wanted to attend, but she was supposed to have more tests done for the cure. Finally, Kasi heard and insisted she accompany me.

"I am going. So stop arguing," she told me, her hands placed on her narrow hips. Off we headed to the medic station, past the atrium I hadn't been in since the night I set the arbor on fire and passed the entrance to the holding cell where Francisco had been held and nearly beaten to death.

"Are you frightened?" Kasi asked me out of nowhere.

"Of what?" I asked confused.

"Of having a child," she said incredulously.

"Not so much of having the child but more of where the child came from," I told her honestly. We hadn't spoken of the rape or the child much.

"I would be frightened. I have heard its horribly painful, and although I know that the Republic has some advance medical equipment, I don't think they have much for birthing mothers. I would be scared stiff," she said with an exaggerated chill down her spine.

"I am sure you are right. I just haven't thought about it, I guess," I replied. We had arrived at the medic station and were ushered into an empty room.

"Here, strip down and put on the gown," the medic told me.

I was having flashbacks to the last time I had to strip down in a medical facility much like this one; this experience was much worse. The medic left, giving me the privacy to change, and Kasi was inspecting the many pictures on the walls with intrigue. Once I was covered, I sat on the exam table and waited with anxiety crawling up my neck into my head, causing discomfort.

"How is the little mother today?" the overly cheery medic asked when coming in. No one had dared call me that. She didn't know the circumstances, I was sure, but the words still shook me to the core. I had not yet associated that title with myself. It was unnerving to think about.

"She has been training and working and hardly eating and doesn't get much sleep," Kasi told the medic, disapprovingly. The medic smiled as she continued taking my vitals, only half listening it seemed.

"I haven't been ill to my stomach anymore, though," I said, hoping to appease them both.

"Your blood pressure is slightly elevated, but other vitals seem good," the medic informed us. "Now let's take a look at the baby," she said with excitement. Again, she spoke as if this pregnancy was something to be joyful about, and I tried not to violently tell her to stop talking, and Kasi looked at me with pity. The sonogram machine was outdated and pieced together with parts that must have come from other medical equipment and devices. I watched the monitor with slight dread. I didn't want it to be real. Being distracted by the monitor, I almost didn't notice Kasi whisper something to the medic. From their facial expressions, I knew Kasi had informed her of my circumstances. I pretended not to notice and just kept watching the dark screen.

"Is that the baby?" Kasi asked loudly.

"Yes, it looks like it's a girl," the medic said, very reserved since she had the whispered exchange with Kasi. Francisco was right—a little girl. Somehow this new information made the little life inside me take flight—a baby girl, my child. I felt so confused by all the emotions going through my mind. I wanted to be excited, I wanted to loathe her, yet I couldn't really do either.

"You are approximately fourteen weeks along and should expect the child March 7, judging from her size," she told me cautiously. March 7 seemed so far away, yet much closer than was comfortable. What would I do? Give her up? I wish I didn't know her gender. I wish Francisco had been wrong, and I wish he hadn't shown so much excitement at the prospect of a child; it only made me not want her even more. Somehow, I did want her, though. I just didn't want the part of her that was Francisco.

"You can get dressed now, and if anything comes back abnormal on your tests, we will let you know," the medic said, pushing the sonogram machine out the exam room door. I began dressing myself behind a curtain as Kasi started talking.

"Well, at least you know when to expect her. Now you can prepare and make some decisions," Kasi said carefully. I hated that people were so afraid of upsetting me now that they knew my condition, but I didn't know how to stop it. I laced up my shoes and stood unseen behind the curtain, frustration building.

"Yes, I have a lot of things to consider," I replied. "This has all been impossible and horrible and dumb, but you have to stop," I told her, jerking the curtain back. The irritation in my voice surprised even me and my use of the word *dumb*.

"What?" she asked, taken aback.

I walked close to her and said, "Stop being fake and stop stopping yourself from blurting out the first thing that pops in that beautiful head of yours. Stop trying to keep me from real things, and stop tiptoeing around me." I used the slang from the primal times, hoping she would understand that I would rather have a real relationship with her than this fake thing it had become. "I didn't tell anyone for so long for two reasons. I didn't want anyone to stop my murder attempt." I could admit it for what it was now. "And I hated the thought of you all treating me differently. So *just stop*." I told her with as much force as I could without making her run screaming from the exam room. She looked at me for a few long tense moments before a smile spread across her wide mouth.

"You got it," she replied simply and opened the door for me to exit. I walked through the door lighter than I entered, and we parted ways, headed back to our respective posts, me to the lab, her to Justin's office.

I was nearly out of the medic station when I heard Mother's voice. It was coming from a patient's room. I drew closer, knowing she had tests done and wondering if they involved medical assistance. I stopped abruptly when I heard another voice, Francisco's.

"How is she?" he asked her.

"She is seeing about the baby's health today. I think she is doing better," Mother replied to him.

"She will keep the child then?" he asked.

"I don't know that she can keep the child. So much pain is associated with the conception," she replied without malice.

"Yes, yes, of course. I can never make up for what was done. I wish I could change things now that I see, now that I am no longer blind," he said, confusing me completely. Blind? His eyesight had seemed fine to me.

"You were living the life that you had been taught, the life your father had planned for you and, in the process, had hurt others, most tragically, and especially Alexandra. People believe life is only meant to be lived to find their own joy but don't realize that this is what creates pain in the world. Ruach HaKodesh tells us to humble ourselves, and we will be exalted to love others as we love ourselves. In order to find peace and purpose, we must seek his presence. All else is empty and like footprints in the sand," she told him gently.

"Your guidance has brought me to the awareness of his presence. I can never thank you enough for that, but how do I make up for the past things I have done? Before I even left the camp, I knew

I loved her for her strength, for her will to survive, her passion, her beauty. Now she is carrying my child and she wishes me dead," he finished in a voice barely above a whisper.

"You can never make up for these things. You can only change what you do from this time on," she replied sadly. I didn't forgive Francisco, but I was absolutely shocked by his words. He loved me?

"She will always hate me," he stated.

"I beseech Ruach HaKodesh that she will find it in her heart to forgive. Hating you will only cause her pain and bitterness," she said.

"She has every right to hate me," he replied.

"Perhaps in this world, but in the kingdom, she mustn't. If only she would find that freedom. My heart breaks for the pain you both have been through, but healing can come with true forgiveness." She spoke with hope. I peeked through the crack in the door and saw that mother was in the bed beside Francisco's. They must have been monitoring her after the tests. Francisco looked healed from his ordeal with Merek and was sitting upright in bed with his hand chained to the bed.

I was standing in the hallway, listening to their unsettling conversation, and everything in my body screamed out that I would forever detest Francisco! I had ample reason to want him dead, and yet mother spoke as if my feelings would hurt me, as if I had control over my anger, and prolonged hatred would endanger me. I stormed away, not wanting to hear any more of their thoughts and feeling completely confused by Francisco words of regret, remorse, and love. I bypassed the lab and headed straight to the training facility. I needed physical exertion to calm the storm raging inside.

Don was there with a small group of Outlandish I didn't recognize. He waved cheerfully when he spotted me. I nodded back and headed to the weight sets on the corner farthest from Don. I didn't want to hear his analysis of my problems right now. I lifted weights, ran, beat the punching bag with all the anger welling inside, and yet nothing changed. I couldn't find peace in this place. If anything, my frustrations seemed to grow. I was over trying to murder Francisco, but the thought of him proclaiming his love for me to Mother awakened an anger that wouldn't be dispelled with mere exertion.

"Alex, the bag is dead," I heard Merek say from behind me with a chuckle.

I stopped pounding my frustrations out as he placed a gentle hand on my back.

"I know, I just feel so confused and angry," I said through my clenched jaw.

"You found out about the baby?" he asked me. I could tell he was hesitant to mention the child, and I knew the feeling.

"It's not just that. Why does my mother spend so much time with Francisco?" I asked, allowing him to see the anger I had been concealing for the last few weeks, but I dared not tell him of Francisco's love for me. His entire demeanor changed with just the mention of Francisco. He was another subject we never mentioned.

"Your mother has some strange sense of responsibility to him. I don't try to pretend to understand it," he stated simply. "She believes she can 'change' him. People can't change. They are who they are," he finished cynically. I wasn't sure I agreed entirely, but I knew how he felt.

"They were talking in the medic's station as if I should forgive him, as if I was the one that caused this…this thing to happen." I couldn't help but look down at my protruding belly and cringe.

"This isn't your fault, and you have every right to hate him until he dies. If I could, I would end his existence for you." He repeated words he had said to me before. I knew he meant them. "Let's get out of here," he said, pulling me away from the bag that had taken the brunt of my frustrations.

I followed him through the hallways, not really paying attention to where we were headed. Suddenly, we came to a threshold that I didn't recognize, and Merek opened the door to an empty chamber. He turned on the soft lighting, and I noticed a table placed against the far wall set with delicate dinnerware and steaming food. He had planned an evening for us alone. It was so out of character for Merek that I look at him in astonishment.

"We are never alone, so I knew this chamber wasn't being used and thought it might be nice for us to eat together without Don and Kasi talking our ears off," he said with a small grin.

"Talking our ears off?" I asked.

"It's a primal saying, like they are the only ones that talk and a lot," he said, laughing at my lack of knowledge about the primal sayings. He pulled out a chair at the table and gestured for me to sit. It all felt so strange being completely alone with him. My worries of earlier were there but somehow didn't seem as important. I pushed them further from my mind and tried to enjoy his company. I sat down, and his strong fingers brushed my neck as he pushed my chair in gently. My skin tingled where our skin connected.

"It all smells so wonderful," I told him, trying to break the silence.

"Good, I got it from the mess hall, but Fred made it specially for us. It is a primal meal—steak, mashed potatoes, fresh rolls, and a salad."

I had never heard of most of those things, but my mouth watered from the aroma. He served me the food, and we ate in almost complete silence. I had never tasted anything so delicious. "Do you love it?" he asked when I had nearly cleaned the plate.

"Can't you tell?" I asked with a laugh.

"Good," he said.

I could tell he wanted to say more and wondered what it could possibly be.

"Alex, I know today was difficult for you, finding out the baby's gender, your mother and Francisco's strange relationship, and just everything that has gone wrong since we left the other bunker, but I want you to know something. I am here for you. Even if you decide to keep the child, I am here. I can't imagine my life without you." He had knelt beside my chair midsentence, and I couldn't help the swelling in my chest at his complete acceptance of me and all that I now brought with me. He lifted his calloused hand to my cheek and brushed a tear away that I didn't realize had fallen.

I carefully pressed my lips to his. I felt light. My heart fluttered as his arms slowly pulled me into an embrace. I was completely safe and loved. He was so tender. The kiss lingered on, and the very moment I felt his tenderness turn to passion, memories of another embrace rudely broke through my dream state, and it all became a nightmare. I pushed him away in panic and backed against the wall with ragged breaths.

"I can't, please," I said, holding back tears.

"I am so sorry. I would never force you or hurt you in any way. I didn't intend to frighten you," he said, holding his hands out in a gesture of peace.

"I know, I know, I just can't. I can't be that way with a man… yet. Maybe never," I told him, knowing that might change his mind about staying with me. Being with the Outlandish this long I knew the importance of intimacy within a relationship. He slowly walked to me and carefully held my hands in his.

"It doesn't matter, I am not going anywhere," he said, looking deep into my eyes. He sat down against a wall and tugged me down beside him. Now that I could think again, I remembered I was with Merek. I was safe, and he would never hurt me. I leaned against him and sighed.

"I am quite the mess, you know?" I told him in a joking manner.

"That only makes me love you more." He hadn't spoken of love since we were in the Militant Headquarters, and then he had said it only in the past tense.

"You love me?" I asked. *Love* was coming to be a common word for me but still slightly confusing.

"I know you aren't used to words like that, but yes, I love you," he stated confidently and pulled me closer in a warm hug.

"I think I love you too," I told him tentatively.

He kissed my brow and settled in against the wall in comfort. "So when shall we have the wedding? Will you wear my ring?" he asked with a lightness in his voice I hadn't heard for some time. I inspected the ring. It was simple but elegant with only three bands intertwined, almost like a braid. I knew I would treasure it always.

"Yes, but what is a wedding?" I asked, confused, but taking the ring he offered.

"It's a ritual for two people becoming united," he answered, laughing at me. "I can wait for you as long as you need, but you should know when we do have a wedding, it is going to be quite a celebration," he informed me.

I wasn't sure if it was a celebration or a ritual, so I just listened for him to continue explaining it all.

"It's an ancient ritual from the primal times. The female, which they call a bride, wears an only white gown. The male, called a groom, wears a fancy black suit or tux, and all their family and friends attend to cheer them on," he explained simply. We sat like that, entwined, Merek leaning back against an uncomfortable wall, me leaning against his comfortable chest, late into the evening, speaking of weddings, our favorite things, and life after the world was free of tyranny and destruction—our life, together.

He escorted me back to my chamber with only a chaste kiss on my brow, and I was walking on clouds, as they said in the primal times. It didn't seem to matter that Francisco proclaimed his love for me or that I would soon bear his child. Merek loved me, and for tonight, that was the only thing I wanted to think about.

STAGE 4:6

I woke up the next morning, only slightly less elevated than the night before. The baby was extremely active and not to be ignored. Mother had stayed in the medic's station overnight, and Kasi was still sleeping soundly as I left for the main lab.

"You are here bright and early," Colin said in greeting.

"Yes, well, I skipped training this morning to get some extra sleep and just headed straight here," I replied, not telling him the morning fare still upset my stomach and that I avoided it most days.

"I ran some more tests on the blood samples you gave me, and surprisingly, your blood has a weak resistance to the injection. Now mind you, it wouldn't be wise to try it out because it would probably only last for a few days and then take the full effect, but it seems that your body is creating a blockade, so to speak, against the chemicals in the injection," he said with excitement.

"I am creating an immunity to the injection?" I asked him.

"Yes, I believe it could have something to do with your blood type and the pregnancy. The combination of the two perhaps," he told me. "We will need to draw more samples, but we have a good start," he added enthusiastically.

I sat down and felt the pinprick of a needle as he drew more blood from my veins and tried not to faint. We began working in comfortable silence when Mother came rushing into the lab.

"Can I steal you away, Alex?" Mother asked me, somewhat distraught. No matter my confusion about her relationship with "Cisco," her love and kindness to all made it impossible to deny her any request.

"Yes, of course," I said, following her out of the lab. I rushed to keep up as we wove through the hallways, getting close to the main exit from the science bunker. We came to an abandoned corner to see Gabby. I still hadn't spoken to her since the incident or I should say since I used her.

"Gabby needs our help," Mother told me quietly, seemingly not wanting others to hear.

"Fred, he…he went out to gather herbs despite the semi-lockdown. He hasn't come back, and I am afraid the Seditionist have captured him or worse," Gabby said through tears.

"Why don't you tell the Militant?" I asked with concern.

"They will punish Fred for breaking the lockdown regulations. They might not even help because he broke regulations," she told us, near hysteria now.

I knew it was unwise to leave the bunker and risk capture myself, but I did owe Gabby for all I had put her through, making her an accomplice to my crimes with probation for an entire year.

"How long has he been gone?" I asked, recalling that Fred prepared my meal just last night.

"He went out late last night and never returned. I know where he normally gathers herbs. I thought we could leave through the tunnel near the mess hall undetected and try to find him," she said softly.

"We will need help. I can get Merek to come," I told her.

"*No!*" Gabby said panicked. "Merek will be obligated to report to the Militant. We must be the only ones who know about this," she said, leaving no room to question her.

"I will have to get supplies and weapons. That might take a while," I told her.

"I have already taken care of that. Fred has an extensive collection of weapons, and I got all the supplies we need. We're just waiting for your decision," Gabby said. I was surprised Fred the chef had a "collection of weapons," but it only helped us, so I didn't ask.

"We should leave before the noon meal then," I said with reservation. Gabby seemed off somehow, but then again, we hadn't spoken since before the adjudication.

"Fred's chamber is this door here. Help me gather the weapons, and we will head to the mess hall," she said with relief. She opened the door to our right with a key and led us into Fred's chamber. It was decorated strangely with blacks and reds, large swords hanging from the walls, and murals of delicate flowers that I had never seen before. "He studied ancient martial arts," Gabby informed us. I didn't know what that was, but from the strange markings on the wall, it wasn't from this land.

"Should we take the swords off the walls?" Mother asked Gabby.

"No, those are collector's items, not something we should use. The weapons are locked up in his bedroom, this way," she said, motioning us on. We followed into the side room, and Gabby went directly to a closet with a combination lock on the door. After a few tries, she swung it open to reveal guns ranging from small handguns to long-range rifles, knives, and an assortment of protective gear. Gabby pulled a large case from under the small bed and began filling it with the weapons.

"We need to hurry. The longer it takes us, the less likely we are to find him," I told them both. Soon we were heading back into the depths of the bunker toward the mess hall and its somewhat secret exit, carrying an overly large case, hoping no one would notice our strange behavior. The staff at the mess hall seemed too busy to notice us and, I am sure, were completely used to Gabby's presence, so soon we were in the tunnel that led to the ground above. Mother was carrying the case at this point.

Gabby quickly typed in the code to unlock the hatch door. It was no easy feat, and after Gabby and me both wrenched at the hatch, it finally swung open to a blinding light from the blue sky above. We all grabbed a side of the weapons case and lifted it out. Soon we had it open, and I was handing them gear and weapons and putting it into our smaller packs.

"We will carry as many weapons and ammo as we can and hide the case in those bushes over there," I told them.

"Fred usually picks herbs about two kilometers east of here," Gabby said through ragged breaths; she wasn't one for training, and the exertion was a little much.

"Let's head that way but be on the lookout. The Seditionist attacked the main entrance twice now since Cisco was captured," Mother said.

The leaves were turning the autumn colors, and we tried to avoid making too much noise as we passed through the fallen. I felt my heart begin to pound uncontrollably with the mere thought of being captured again, so I fought to suppress the fear and remembered I owed Gabby this. We walked along a dried creek bed for what felt like hours when we came upon an opening, and Gabby abruptly stopped.

"This is where Fred gets his herbs," she said very quietly.

"Look around and see if you see anything that would tell us where he could have gone," I said barely above a whisper. We all began looking at the ground, the bushes, and anything, really, hoping to find some indication he had been here. I looked up at Gabby and noticed she was even more upset than when we left. She reached inside her pack pulling out a 9mm handgun as she aimed it straight at Mother and then me. I knew something was terribly wrong.

"Gabby, what are you doing?" I asked, surprised I was able to form words past the utter shock stuck in my throat.

"They have Fred and wanted Cisco. I told them I couldn't get to him after your murder attempt, so they said to bring you both instead," Gabby said through tears.

I glanced at Mother, thinking her shock would reflect mine, but she looked almost at ease. A hostage, Fred was their captive, and Gabby was giving them the ransom.

"Gabby, there has to be another way," I begged her. I wasn't going back there. I would rather die here, free, than go back and live as a slave, tortured for my remaining existence. I edged closer to Gabby, knowing I had to get her weapon or die trying. The barrel of her 9mm was unsteady as I inched nearer. She noticed my movement and jerked the gun up to my head.

"*Not another step!*" Gabby yelled, the 9mm shaking even worse in her hand now.

"Calm down, Gabby, you know we would never hurt you," Mother said with a peace that seemed supernatural.

"I have to do what they say or they will kill Fred!" she said, only lowering her voice by a decibel. With Gabby's attention on Mother, I gauged the distance between myself and her; it was too far to leap with the shaking 9mm, knowing any sudden movements from me would cause Gabby to jerk her finger and blast me. I began running through all the training I had received in the last year and knew I had to get her calm in order to detain her.

"Gabby, we can help you rescue Fred without giving into their demands," I told her as evenly as I could.

Her gaze swung back to me, and there wasn't much kindness in her eyes. "You have caused me enough trouble, don't you think?" she asked bitterly.

I knew she was right, but I didn't want to be enslaved by the Seditionist for my betrayal either. "I never meant for you to get into any trouble," I told her lamely.

"I did, though, didn't I? Not only that, but now my brother is taken captive by the Seditionist, only because they can't get to Cisco or you! This is all your fault!" Her voice had risen once again to a high-pitched squeal that grated on my nerves more than I could explain.

"I am sorry. Truly, I am," I told her sincerely. "The true enemy here is the Seditionist, though, can't you see that?" I asked, hoping to help her see the truth.

"Gabby, causing more pain won't ease your own," Mother said softly. "Let us help you save your brother and all return to the bunker safely."

Gabby seemed to relent slightly with Mother's gently spoken words. It was then that I heard them and knew we had run out of time to negotiate. Without much thought, I leapt toward the 9mm Gabby held pointed at my feet and hoped I could overpower her quickly. The gun fired, and I felt the sting in my right side. She had shot me. I was more surprised she actually hit me than anything. I fell upon her with all my strength and felt the gun fire once more, missing me entirely. The struggle wasn't much once I had my hands on her. She fell to the ground, and I wrestled the 9mm from her weak grasp.

Gabby jumped up as if she was going to attack me, and I slammed the butt of the gun across her forehead. She wilted to the ground, unconscious. For a split second, I had guilt but then shoved it down with all the other unwanted emotions of late.

"Help me drag her into those bushes other there," I told Mother.

She immediately came, and we quickly hid Gabby where the Seditionist wouldn't see her and crouched down beside her for concealment. They had to have heard the gunfire and were scouting the area for trouble.

"They will find us, you know," Mother said rather reluctantly.

"Yes, I know. Perhaps we can take them by surprise, though," I replied hopefully.

"You are losing a lot of blood. You aren't up for a fight," she stated plainly. It was as if her words held some power, because the moment she said them, I felt the pain of the gunshot and a lightness to my head I hadn't up to that point. I saw them then, more men, then we could fight off, even with guns, and they had Fred right out in front as their hostage. Mother took one long look into my eyes and began to stand up. I tried to grab her arm, but she shook me off and made herself visible to them.

"Take me! Let the boy go," she said firmly.

Not one man verbally acknowledged her presence, but they parted down the middle for their leader, Raymon Fuerte. He smiled an evil grin when he saw mother. "Isa, I have missed you," he said, each word dripping with cruelty.

My head was swimming now. It took everything in me to stay conscious. I pressed my hand against the wound, hoping to stanch the flow of blood leaving my body. My heart was breaking in my chest with the knowledge that Mother would once again be his captive.

"Let the boy go, Raymon, I am a better bargaining chip than the cook there," Mother told him. Gabby would hate for her brother to be called a mere cook; he was a master chef, as she so liked to put it. "I will go peacefully, just release him," she finished with authority.

Raymon seemed to contemplate his options for a few tense moments before he made any decision, and then like a viper, he struck and had Mother captive once again.

"I will let this...cook go. But remember, Cook, you are my messenger, and I want Francisco back before the sun falls in five days. If I don't, I will torture Isa until her death and find you once again to do the same. *Now go!*" Raymon yelled at poor Fred as he scurried off to deliver the madman's threats. Raymon must have been smarter than I supposed. He knew that if he broke into the bunker, he and his men would be slaughtered. He had to draw the Republic out if he wanted to stand a chance against them. The Seditionist began to slowly file back the way they had come, Mother under the watchful and evil eye of Raymon.

Fear that Gabby would awaken drawing their attention to us or that I would lose complete consciousness weighed down on me, but more than anything, I couldn't fathom how Mother could willingly go back into slavery…to save us. Death sounded inviting compared to what she must now endure. I couldn't have given myself over freely to them no matter what was at stake.

The clearing in the forest was soon empty. I wondered how far Fred had gone. I needed his help to get back to the bunker in my current state. Gabby was too much to drag a few feet, much less two kilometers. I couldn't cry out, knowing the Seditionist might hear me. So I inspected Gabby's immobile body once again for any sign of awareness—none. Carefully, I stood to begin down the path Fred had taken. Only a few steps were made before I realized how incredibly weak I was. My vision blurred, and my body swayed as if to tumble. Before I knew what happened, my vision went completely black, and I was on the ground, staring up at a beautiful blue sky.

Helplessness like I had never known enveloped me. This was not where I wanted to die. I had to save Mother. She sacrificed herself for me. I couldn't let her suffer. A thought floated through my mind, more an impression really. Could Ruach HaKodesh help Mother? Although the being's existence was still under scrutiny in my mind, I didn't doubt that Mother believed him to have saved her before.

"If you are out there, and I am not sure that you are…in fact, I am probably wasting my energy, but if by some crazy marvel you are listening to me, please help me save Mother," I begged the heavens. Strangely enough, I felt a weight being lifted from my shoulders. No voice spoke to me, but I wanted to sleep in this peaceful place I was stranded, and I didn't even care that I might not wake up. My eyes closed, and a gentle darkness fell upon me, luring me into its comfort.

STAGE 4:7

My legs felt strange as if I was lighter than normal, as if the gravity in the atmosphere had changed in some way. I walked to a pool of water and sat down. All the colors of the forest were brighter, bolder, and there was cool breeze blowing through, making my skin tingle… something was off. This couldn't be the same forest I had lost Mother, the same forest where I had knocked Gabby unconscious, could it?

I looked at the pool beside me. Not a single ripple, a perfect reflection of the sky, completely still. The sky was a myriad of colors. Once, when I was very young, I saw pictures in a book on the primal times about kaleidoscopes. The sky now resembled that, only bigger and livelier; in fact, the colors seemed to dance across my vision. I was confused about where I could possibly be, but in the same heartbeat, I was at peace with this place. I looked back at the pool and reached out to touch the glass-like water. As I brushed my hand across the liquid, it was only disturbed for a moment before it went back to silky smooth.

"Do you like it here, Alexandra?" a voice asked me from behind.

Although I had thought myself completely alone in the colorful forest, the voice didn't frighten or upset me. I slowly turned around to face a tall man wearing a white robe, sandals, and carrying an ancient shepherds' staff. His dark skin seemed to glow, and his kind smile felt familiar somehow.

"Yes, I thought I was alone," I told him simply.

"You are never alone, Alex," he said with a grin.

"Who are you? How do you know my name?" I said slowly without much care if he answered or not.

"You called for me," he replied.

I had been so entangled by the peace of this place, I forgot about Mother. "You are Ruach HaKodesh?" I asked, perplexed.

"I have been called many things before, but yes, that is one of the names," he said, still smiling.

He was real. My mind felt blank. I could hardly fathom his existence. "Will you save my mother?" I asked him with as much intense emotion as this peaceful place would allow me.

"She is already saved, Alex," he replied not making any sense.

"No, no, she was captured by the Seditionist once again. Please help me save her," I begged.

"Man cannot kill the soul. Isa is abiding in me, and I in her. She has peace no matter the circumstance as long as she remembers what I freely give her," he told me, only causing more confusion.

"She will be tortured and beaten, perhaps killed. Don't you rescue your believers?" I asked him. "She sacrificed herself to save me. Please, you have to do something," I finished, wondering at the peace I felt despite the turmoil of the conversation.

"Isa doesn't fear those who can kill only her flesh. She knows her soul can never die in me. She is showing you my love. The greatest love a person can show is to lay down their life for a friend," he said.

"Your love doesn't seem to help her. She is going to die," I replied.

"She is laying down her life for you. Will you be saved?" he asked me.

"I don't need anything but my mother to be safe," I replied, confused by the entire conversation.

"Ah, but that's not true, is it? You desire healing from your wounds. You desire peace from your pain," he replied, holding out his hand.

My mind told me not to take his hand, but it seemed as if I had no control over myself. I reached out and grasped his hand, and instantly, I felt strange. His hand was strong and cool. I looked down and noticed a scar at his wrist. Looking back up to his face, he smiled kindly. That's when the humiliation, the pain, the suffering, and the unquenchable anger toward my captor, all the raging emotions seemed to pulse in my blood as he held my hand, and through the connection with this being I hadn't believed was real, I felt the emotions beat out from my veins into his, leaving me somewhat empty. "I can take your burdens, Alex. I can save you too," he told me gently. "Be a part of my family?" he asked.

Family. A primal word meaning blood relatives, which means he was asking me to become something that was simply impossible.

"How can I become part of your family? I cannot change what I already am," I answered, knowing biologically I had relatives, but Mother was my only family. I felt void without my pain as if a limb was missing, not as if I had been relived a burden.

"That's correct, you cannot change in your own power. Lasting change comes only through me," he replied simply. The words only confused me more, but then I remembered Mother's peace, and I needed that right now so badly. I could taste it, just out of my reach, but there tormenting me with its promises of relief. He was still gently holding my hand and brought my hand up to his lips. "Trust me, Alex, follow me," he said quietly. Follow him where, I wasn't sure, but the words held me in rapture, and I wanted more than anything to do the things he said. "I will take your burdens. You only have to give them up and follow me. You must wake now," he finished.

I woke to a harsh reality that it was all a dream, yet it didn't feel like any dream I had ever had before. It was so real, even though it was not. I had all my burdens back in this reality. They weighed me down and felt more cumbersome than before. I still felt weak. Placing my hands on my sides, I pushed myself with all my strength to a sitting position. The world seemed dull and dank compared to my experience with Ruach HaKodesh. Part of me wanted to go back to be with him in that place where peace was within my grasp and never see this place again. I forced those thoughts from my mind and lay back down from exhaustion. I could feel the blood pooling around me. I would die soon without help. I had to get up and stop the steady loss of blood.

I took off my outer shirt and tied it around my middle, pulling it as tight as my weakened state allowed, hoping to slow the blood from leaving me. I rested for only a moment so as not to pass out again, and then got up on my knees, then pulled myself up with the aid of a nearby tree to completely standing. I continued to hold onto the tree for support until my head stopped spinning. I looked around for a long stick to steady my steps, but everything around me was blurry, so I waited for it to clear.

I took a few unsteady steps, making it to the next tree, my vision would blur once again, and I'd take another few breaths, waiting for it to clear. I repeated this process for what seemed like forever, going from tree to tree when my vision blurred and wouldn't seem to focus. I waited even longer, feeling exposed and vulnerable. Once it cleared, I saw a figure coming toward me at a quick pace, I couldn't make out who it was, but from the direction they were coming, I was hoping they were Outlandish.

I didn't have the strength to hide much less run. I stumbled behind the tree I was clinging to and hoped they hadn't seen me. That was the best I could do at this point. With my back against the tree, I sank down to a sitting position. My breathing was ragged and uneven. I could see the bright red ooze of blood through my makeshift bandage.

"Alex!" I heard the voice yell and knew it was Merek.

The relief I felt was instantaneous. We could find Mother, and perhaps I wouldn't die just yet. I tried without much success to stand, so I gave up and yelled as loud as I could, which was pathetic, I'm sure.

"Merek, over here," I rasped out, hoping he heard me.

He continued to yell for me, so I knew he was unable to hear my weakened cry. I could feel myself losing the battle to stay conscious. I felt a rock at my fingertips and halfheartedly threw it in the direction of his voice. He must have noticed that, because he got quiet as if to investigate. I felt more than heard him draw near to me.

"Alex, what happened?" he asked, fear laced in his question.

I moved my hand away from my side to reveal the wound Gabby had so graciously given me, and I grated out, "Shot."

"You've been shot?"

So quick to catch on, I thought. I nodded yes.

"Can you put your arms around my neck?" He was pulling me into his arms now, and I forced my arms around his neck. The pain was growing now that I could give into it and didn't have to push past it to survive. Merek began jogging toward the bunker.

"*No.* Gabby," I said as loud as my strength would allow into his ear as my head rested on his shoulder.

"Gabby? She is out here too? Where?" he asked, slowing to a standstill.

I was disoriented but knew Gabby had to be back behind us somewhere.

"Back in that clearing. She is unconscious," I told him between breaths.

Merek placed me against a tree and took his transistor from his belt.

"Headquarters, this is Merek Wharrier requesting immediate aid to the southwest exit number 5.2, I have an injured party and another one still missing," he told the transistor operator.

"We will send medics and Militant immediately," the transistor squalled back.

"We will find her. How was she injured?" Merek asked.

I didn't want to have to explain what had transpired, but I also knew I had enough strength to give him the short version.

"Betrayed us…shot me…and I hit her, knocked her unconscious. They have Mother," I said haltingly, struggling myself to stay lucid.

Merek, without comment or expression, picked me up again and began jogging back to the bunker. Resting my head against his shoulder, I looked up into the blue sky as the clouds, tree branches, birds, and bugs passed over our heads carefree and untouched by any tragedy. Being held securely in Merek's arms gave me the freedom to analyze my "experience or dream." I wasn't ready to categorize it quite yet.

Ruach HaKodesh had told me I could be saved and needed to follow him. How or what it meant to follow was still unknown. The burdens he had relieved me of felt heavy and cumbersome now. They had returned the moment I awoke; the weight was almost suffocating. I felt a burning desire to hand over all my "burdens," as he so called them, but I didn't truly know how. It seemed impossible, all of it. Merek came to a stop outside of the hidden bunker hatch, and there were medics and Militant pouring out.

"Gabby is a few kilometers that way," he said, gesturing toward the clearing. Medics came with a stretcher and began placing me on it from Merek's arms. "She has been shot and is losing a lot of blood. She is with child also," Merek told them quietly.

"We will take care of her," a female medic replied, pulling my hand from the clasp I had on Merek's arm.

"Please don't leave me," I begged him selfishly, knowing Mother needed him more than I did. He nodded his head in agreement but didn't move with me as they began moving toward the bunker. He was speaking to the Militant group. I felt the all familiar emotion of fear rise up in me as the gap between us grew. I could feel myself being lowered down into the dark tunnel, and still Merek wasn't coming. I felt almost choked by the terror now. It was strange because I wanted him out there saving Mother, yet I couldn't be alone now. I couldn't face what could be my last moments on earth without him either. The light blinked out as they carried my prone body deeper into the tunnel, and I could no longer see Merek. I could no longer breathe.

"She isn't breathing! Stop!" a medic yelled.

They quickly put me down on the cold tunnel floor. I could feel the dampness through the fabric and my clothing, but I still couldn't breathe. They began pumping my chest. My mouth began to taste metallic. Blood.

"She must have a punctured lung. Quickly, we need to drain the blood before she suffocates," the medic said. I felt as if I was floating above, watching them work, not caring if the body below lived or died; but then I saw a panicked Merek come up beside the working medics.

"What's happened?" he yelled.

"The gunshot must have punctured her lung," the medic said somewhat calmly. "We don't have sterile equipment, but we have to ease the pressure or she will die," the medic said, looking through their small bags.

"Do you have a pen?" Merek asked quickly.

“Yes,” the medic said, handing it to him. Merek grabbed the pen, removing everything from its core, leaving only a hollow tube, took out his knife from his belt, and tore my shirt away from my ribs. He hesitated only for a few seconds, taking in my protruding belly, and then put a small incision between my ribs. The pain seemed separated from me somehow, or maybe this is how death felt as it took your life. I am not sure; I had never died before. I felt more, then saw him push the hollowed-out pen into my lung. The pain brought me back to reality.

The instant relief of oxygen reaching my lung was unexplainable. I couldn’t speak, so I could only thank him with my eyes. He seemed to know exactly how I felt, and we began down the tunnel to the bunker once again. The quietness of the tunnel lulled me into unconsciousness, and all was dark.

STAGE 4:8

Time was irrelevant to me. Light and dark intermingled, flashes of worried faces would come in view and disappear just as quickly. My body ached from some wound. I couldn't remember how I acquired it. My eyes opened once to see a medic carrying a small bloody bundle away from the table I was lying on. My brain would not accept what that could mean. Pain tore through my womb like none I had ever known. I wanted to go back to the peaceful place where I encountered Ruach HaKodesh, but no matter how much I willed myself to find that place, it was always on the fringes of my awareness.

Did death feel like this? Was my eternal soul destined to be in this nothingness? I had no fear here, but neither did I have joy nor any emotion at all. I was empty. The thought should have provoked hysteria, but instead, I only felt the tremendous gaping hole of nothingness.

It could have been a moment or days; time didn't seem to exist here. Then I heard summons from somewhere above me.

"Don't leave me," the all too familiar voice pleaded. Merek. He was speaking to me.

I felt reality flood over me with the recognition. I was lying in a bed in the medic station. My eyes fluttered open to see Merek's head resting against my leg, his hands clasped together, his knuckles white from the strain of his grasp. His distress was overwhelming. I reached out and touched his dark hair in comfort. He immediately turned his face into the palm of my hand. "You're awake," he stated obviously.

"Yes," I croaked out, my voice rusty from not being used. "How long was I sleeping?" I asked in confusion.

"Two days," he said, holding my hand gently. "You were shot, and the bullet punctured your lung. You lost a lot of blood. Alex, the baby…well, the baby didn't make it," he stuttered through.

How was I supposed to react? My muddled emotions were all over the place. I had just found out the baby was female and I had somewhat come to terms with her birth, and now…well, now she was gone. Tears unbidden came pouring down my face. I hated myself for that.

Merek looked uncomfortable and confused, which I shared that with him. I was confused by my reaction. Something broke inside, and the loss of that unwanted child left me feeling empty. I remembered every movement she made, every unwelcome thought of what she would look like, and secret thoughts of how I could love her despite her conception. I turned my face from Merek to hide the shameful tears that continued to flow.

"I am sorry, Alex. I know this is all so confusing and difficult," Merek said, trying to comfort me.

I took several steady breathes in and calmed my jumbled self. "Any news on Mother?" I asked, needing something good to happen.

"Well, yes, but you may not like it any more than I did," he said slowly.

"What is it?" I asked, fear replacing the grief I felt moments before.

"Francisco wants to help us rescue her. He doesn't want to return to the Seditionist camp," Merek said simply.

"What? Why?" I asked with a raised voice.

"He said that your mother saved him, and he must now save her. Last I heard, the Council of Elders haven't decided if they will trust him yet," Merek informed me carefully. "We should find out today, and if they decide to believe him, we will attack the camp in two days. If not, we will do a prisoner exchange at that time," he finished.

"Why don't we attack without Francisco's help?" I asked.

"The advantage is theirs unless we have better knowledge of where she is being held, the layout of the camp, and the location of

Raymon. We can't risk an attack and lose your mother. She is the only key to the cure."

I didn't tell him that I well may be the key also. I didn't want anyone to know she could be replaced. They had to do anything and everything to save her. I tried to push myself up in the bed and found myself weak. Merek jumped up and gently pressed my shoulders back down to rest in the bed. "Please, you aren't ready to leave here yet. The medic said it will be a few days before you can even get out of this bed," he told me with concern.

"I have to help. I can't just lie here and worry," I told him.

"If you go, you will only slow us down," Merek said with honesty. I wanted to beg Merek to allow me to go, but I could tell by his clipped words he wouldn't give in. I would find another way. "Colin, Kasi, and Don are outside waiting to see you. Can I let them in?" he asked.

I nodded my head in agreement, knowing I needed to speak with Colin alone about "the cure." Merek got up slowly as if he was stiff from sleeping there, which I am sure he had been.

My hands instinctively went to my stomach that was still protruding but had a soft feel to it without the child inside. I had no time to analyze my thoughts about the loss until Mother was safe, so I pushed it to the back of my mind and would deal with it later, maybe. Kasi burst through the door first, followed by Don with Colin and Merek pulling up the rear.

"I am so glad you're awake! I have been sick with worry!" Kasi said with excitement.

"She is not lying. I almost thought we would have to admit her into the medic's station soon if you didn't awake up," Don said, rolling his eyes in exaggeration.

"We knew you would be fine. Nothing seems to defeat you," Colin spoke from behind them. How wrong he was, but I didn't correct him.

"Have you heard anything about Mother's rescue?" I asked Colin pointedly.

Colin looked to Merek as if in permission, and I saw the slight nod from Merek, giving him consent to speak.

"The Council has decided to use Francisco," Colin stated simply.

I wanted to throw something or scream or maybe even break something. Didn't they realize Francisco could be leading them into a trap? He would betray them if he was given the chance. He would return to his old ways. "His intel was good when we saved Merek. They believe he cares deeply for your mother and doesn't want her to be tortured any more than we do. He will help us to save her and, if he proves his loyalty, perhaps even defeat the Seditionist," Colin finished. I am sure he saw the skepticism on my face.

"You have more faith in him than I ever will," I told him. I looked at Merek and knew that he felt the same.

"How are you feeling?" Kasi asked, trying not so subtly to change the conversation.

"I am fine," I told her, but I was definitely not. My head pounded, my side ached from the gunshot, and my insides screamed in agony where a child had once been. For the sake of Merek, Colin, and Don, I was absolutely "fine."

"Sure, you are," Don said, shaking his head.

I ignored his comment and reached for a glass of water at my bedside.

"Here, let me get that." Kasi came around, quickly pushing the men out of the way to hand it to me. "You should probably rest, Alex," Kasi said sternly.

"I will try," I told her, not committing.

"Kasi is right. Alex needs rest, and we all have a lot to get done before we rescue Isa," Colin said, being the responsible one that he always was. As they filed out of my room, each one hugged me and said they would be back soon, trying to raise my spirits. I was alone then, and a blanket of despair covered me from which there seemed no escape.

STAGE 4:9

Merek was busy planning Mother's rescue or he would have stopped me. Kasi was busy scurrying around for Justin or she would have noticed. Colin was in charge of the armory, so he wasn't around. Don was assisting Merek in all things Militant or he would have scolded me like a child, and I couldn't blame him. The medics were busy gathering the necessary supplies for the upcoming confrontation. I was left unattended, without prying eyes, and no one to tell me no.

I swung my feet over the side of the bed and pulled myself to a sitting position. I tried to ignore the pain radiating from deep within. My hand went to my abdomen. Anguish washed over me for the life lost, which I had claimed weeks before that I didn't want. I should feel relief, not this guilt pounding through my brain, and that only served to confuse me more.

I tried to recall the peace I had felt in Ruach HaKodesh's presence, but my mind could only feel the pain—Mother gone, Francisco being allowed to leave, and the child I didn't want dead. I felt to blame for all the problems I was facing, and I knew I couldn't lie in this bed while others fixed them. I stood up with a determination I wasn't aware I possessed. Waiting for the ground to stop spinning, I found my clothes and dressed as quickly as possible. My pack was leaning against the wall, filled with some provisions and first aid. I secured it to my back and pushed past my pain.

How I could rescue Mother without anyone stopping me seemed impossible, but I knew I had to try. I had no plan; honestly, I had no clue, but I knew if I could get to her, I could try something, anything.

Heading to the door, I slowly opened it to peer out and make sure no one was in my path. As the hallway was clear, I hurried to the mess hall, hoping none of the Outlandish I would pass knew I should still be in a medical bed. Once I was clear of the medic's station, I felt some relief, but that soon went away as Don came into sight up ahead. I knew if he spotted me, my mission was over, and I would be under guard until they rescued Mother without my interference.

I looked around, hoping to see a door or alcove so that I could hide from him. I spotted it. Behind me to my right was a door ajar that looked private. I stepped back amongst the crowd and slipped inside the door as Don came within ten feet of where I had just stood. I watched him pass by through a crack in the door.

"Alex?" the voice of my tormentor said from behind me… Francisco.

I turned around with dread and saw his face. It was still bruised from the beating Merek gave him but healing. My insides twisted in rage, and then an idea began to form at my great luck. I could save Mother and keep him in prison, a prison of my creating. His hands were bound to the table and his feet to the chair.

"You are going to help me save Mother," I told me without preamble. I took out my pocketknife and cut the zip ties at his feet, urging him to stand.

"I already told Justin I will do whatever is necessary to save Isa," he told me in confusion.

"Yes, but I must save her, and I won't let you escape. Justin might," I told him. I was about to fold the knife and place it back into my pant pocket when I debated cutting his throat and being done with him, but I knew I couldn't save Mother alone, so I put it away. He seemed to understand the dilemma I had gone through, and relief washed over his face as I returned the knife to its resting place.

"How do you plan to get us out of here without Justin's approval?" Francisco asked.

I ignored his question and gabbed his shirt collar, urging him to the exit. With his hands still bound, I pushed him unnecessarily hard, and he fell at the opening. As he was rising back to his feet, I peered through the door to see only a few Outlandish scurrying about in preparation for the upcoming battle, no doubt. All the confusion and preparation was to my advantage, and I slowly led Francisco into the hallway, headed to the mess hall exit. I hid my face behind Francisco and hoped all who saw him pass would just believe him being transported to a new area. My heart was pounding in my chest. If anyone I knew saw me, my chances at saving Mother were over.

It was a few hours before the noontime meal, so the mess hall was deserted, and the second we were out of view of the hallway sojourners, I rushed Francisco along to our escape. The tunnel didn't seem as long now that I was familiar with it, and Francisco didn't slow me down at all either. Soon the sun was shining down on us as I opened the hatch to the outside world. I immediately set out to find the case of weapons we had hidden in the bushes on my last journey out, hoping Merek or the others hadn't found it.

I pulled Francisco along with me and soon felt the smooth metal case under my hand amidst the bushes. My hand latched onto the handle, and I pulled it from its hiding place, thankful Gabby hadn't told anyone of its whereabouts. The weight of each weapon I strapped on was a burden I was glad to carry, the cool metal against my skin reassuring. We didn't have a lot of supplies, but the Seditionist camp was only a few days trek from the bunker. I knew we could survive long enough to make that. Francisco's mere presence was a thorn in my side, but I knew for Mother's sake, I would endure the constant agitation. It wouldn't last forever, and then I would have to decide his fate.

"You say that you care for my mother?" I asked him, breaking the silence.

"I do. She has saved me twice in this lifetime," he said.

"Then lead me to her. Your father plans to torture and kill her," I told him, which I am sure Justin already informed him of such things.

He nodded his head in answer and began heading north, which I knew was toward the Seditionist camp. I followed, having the handgun within easy reach if he decided he wasn't going to help me.

We walked for hours, and with each kilometer, my pain increased from my injuries. I needed to rest but didn't want to expose my growing weakness. We came upon a stream, and I made the excuse of needing to refill my water supply. Kneeling beside the stream, I brought out my water filtration canister and began filling it.

Francisco was watching me from his perch on a large rock. His stare disturbed me, and I attempted to refocus on my mission. "You are growing weak?" He posed it more as a question than a statement.

"That doesn't concern you," I replied briskly, anger rising that he could read me so well.

He opened his mouth as if to reply and changed his mind, remaining silent.

I drank my fill and begrudgingly passed it to Francisco. Once he had his fill, we ate from the meager provisions I brought in my pack. Without a word, we began again only having a few more hours of daylight before we needed to find somewhere safe to camp. I remembered Merek's rescue on horseback, and I knew my slow painful pace could be overtaken by either the Outlandish or the Seditionist. I was determined to make it without giving up Francisco, though, so I didn't dwell on the what ifs.

We walked on in silence. The wind blew through the trees, and birds sang from their branches, playing a pleasant song. Funny how it reminded me of my dream with Ruach HaKodesh. Peace seemed to flow where people weren't present to destroy it. I could feel my body growing ever weaker, and the sun sinking below the tree line gave me ample excuse to rest.

"We can stay here for the night," I told Francisco. The hill beside us formed a shield for our backs, the outcropping of rocks in the side of the hill a cover from any potential rain, and the thick tree line concealed us from anyone that could be traveling on the path only a few kilometers away. Gathering wood for the fire, Francisco didn't seem to mind the silence, and to me, the silence held both peace and words unspoken. I wanted to scream in his face but knew it wouldn't ease the anger that tormented me, so I remained silent. I needed him to be cooperative and docile so I would keep the rage bound inside for now.

Francisco gathered branches and leaves, and the slight overhang of rocks became a lean to for shelter in only a few minutes. I had set up a fire and was contemplating if I should find wild game for us to eat rather than deplete our already small supply of provisions.

"I am going to find something for us to eat. I will have to tie you while I am away," I said. My words seemed rough and coarse after such a long silence.

"I can make a few snares. The forest is teeming with rabbits. Perhaps we can catch more than one and have food for the next few days," he said.

I knew Francisco had much more experience than me in such matters. The Seditionist lived off the land, but I didn't want him to be so helpful. I wanted to find more and more reasons to despise him. On the other hand, I knew his idea held merit and nodded my head in agreement. He began to make the snares, and I gathered more wood so as not to feel useless.

Once Francisco was done building his snares, I followed him, not letting him leave my sight as he placed them strategically within easy walking distance of our camp. The sun was barely peeking through the trees on the distant horizon by the time we had finished preparing our camp, and all the snares were in place. After zip tying his hands and feet together, I sat down the opposite side of the fire from my tormentor and pulled out the remaining provisions, hoping Francisco's snares were successful and we could eat tomorrow. He seemed to be watching me, but every time I would look up to tell him to stop, he quickly looked elsewhere, so I never got the chance.

I passed him the remaining half of hard tack, and we ate once again in silence. My side was aching from the bullet wound, and my womb felt empty. I wondered if Francisco knew. He didn't seem upset, and I remembered how he had begged me not to hurt the child before. He couldn't possibly know yet.

"Are you well?" he asked quietly.

His question surprised me after so much silence. I must have looked the way I felt if he could see that I was frail. "I am fine," I stated testily.

“I can carry your pack tomorrow, if that would help,” he replied, undeterred by my angry voice.

“And find a weapon? I think not,” I said with a short laugh of unbelief.

“Women that can bear children are to be held in high esteem and helped at every turn,” he stated as if a quote from some book.

“I won’t be bearing any children anytime soon,” I said callously, knowing my words would devastate him.

His head jerked up from where he had been gazing into the fire.

“You took an innocent’s life?” he asked, voice unsteady.

“I took no one’s life. Gabby shot me trying to save her brother from *your father*. The child was lost,” I told him, trying to keep my own voice steady. I pulled my shirt up and revealed to him the now festering wound at my side. The firelight reflected off a tear that fell from his eye, or at least I think it was a tear. Was it grief for the child or something more?

I didn’t explain more of the incident, even though the stillness across the fire unnerved me. I wanted to know what he was thinking, and my desire for that knowledge confused me. “The child was just starting to move inside of me. She was starting to feel real to me. I would lie awake at night, wondering what she would look like, what she would be like. I was so furious at you, at her, and even my mother for asking me to consider her an innocent. But something was changing inside of me toward her, and then she was taken away.”

I poured out my feelings to this man that caused my pain. Literally, he was the reason my life was drowning in confusion and agony, and yet I knew he, more than Merek, Kasi, Don, or Colin, could understand my sorrow. It might have been the late hour combined with my exhaustion or the fact that I couldn’t make out his face in the darkness with only the firelight reflecting on his face every now and then, but for those few minutes, I put aside my fury at him and shared my strange heartache.

“I can never undo the pain I have caused you. I can give you a million reasons why I hurt you so fiercely. In my camp, that is how you take a woman to be your own. That is just the way things are, and many others, but those are all just empty excuses. I remember when Isa came to our camp, and I watched my father try to break her spirit. I knew then it was wrong, and yet I continued in the same way when I saw you and wanted only to possess you. Only two things place a woman in high esteem in our camp—unbreakable spirit and bringing forth life. You had both, so after I came to see that, I only wanted you more.

"I can beg at your feet for forgiveness, but I don't deserve your clemency, and the child dying is surely punishment for my wrongdoing. Once we have saved Isa, I pledge to do as you say no matter the cost to myself. I will spend the remaining life I have as your servant. If you tell me to go, I will go. If you tell me to stay, I will do so."

He pledged his life to me in penance for all his sins against me, and I was speechless. Thoughts ran rampant, but I couldn't form words. I didn't have the energy to sort through all the things I could say in response, so I remained silent.

"We don't have to talk about it anymore. I have to rest," I told him, cutting off the connection we had for those few tense moments. I lay on my side, believing sleep to be far from me with all the emotions that were running through my body, but despite my raging thoughts, my weary body gave in to sleep. My last thoughts were wondering how Francisco could sleep, bound as he was in the zip ties.

STAGE 5:0

The birds singing to raise the sun up woke me. My body ached, so I stretched as much as I could without angering the wound. Francisco was sitting up, poking the fire with his bound hands.

"If you will let me, I can place herbs from the forest on your wound to help you heal," he told me gently.

I stiffly got up and removed the zip ties from his hands and feet, knowing he must have had a sleepless night. I nodded in agreement and followed him back into the depths of the forest. We checked each snare, having caught three small rabbits. My stomach rumbled from its emptiness. The small portion the night before hadn't lasted long.

Francisco began gathering plants I wasn't familiar with, and once he was done, we headed back to our makeshift camp. The fire had burned down to coals while we had been away, so I added wood as he prepared the rabbits for roasting. I knew time was running short on the hostage situation. Not to mention Merek would be tracking us by now and would probably catch up any moment if we weren't careful and quick. I didn't allow myself to dwell on Merek. He may never forgive me for this last betrayal.

"Can you lift up your shirt?" Francisco asked cautiously, looking uncomfortable and ill at ease. He had the poultice ready for my side. I knew he intended to apply it for me, but the thought repulsed me, and I could tell he suspected that. "Just put this on the wound and wrap it tightly so that it doesn't come off," he said quickly, placing the mixture on the ground in front of me on a large leaf. He backed away, showing me he wouldn't crowd me or threaten me. His entire demeanor was changed from our time in his tent. I wanted to ignore it and hold on to my fury, but it was getting harder and harder to do so.

"Thank you," I replied softly. The roasting meat caused my rumbling stomach to clench in hunger and my mouth to slightly water. I was ravenous. Doing as Francisco instructed, I finished wrapping up my side, and soon the first rabbit was ready for us to eat. He offered me the first choice, and I could have nearly eaten the entire thing alone, except I knew he had to be just as hungry as me. So having control, I passed him the rest. Soon we were done eating and had packed up the extra meat for our journey. It was well before 0900 as we headed off.

Somewhere between the late-night talk, our shared meal, and his consideration for my desire for distance from him, we had reached a treaty of sorts. We had only a short distance to reach the Seditionist fort, so I knew we needed to plan how we would rescue my mother.

"What would be the best way to go about this?" I asked Francisco after some hours of walking.

Francisco seemed to consider my question for a long moment before he answered me. "We have the element of surprise and the fact that Padre believes that I want to rejoin him and his war. We could go in the front, but it would take you trusting me?" He posed the last part as a question.

"What reassurances do I have that you won't betray me?" I asked him suspiciously.

"I have nothing except my word. I am pledged to you. Upon my life, I will only do as you bid. I am no longer my own," he said sincerely.

The choices were slim. We could try to find where she was and hope to slip inside without their knowledge or we could try to fight our way in, but that would be futile. Truly, the only good option was to pretend Francisco had escaped and brought me along as his captive once again.

"I agree we have few choices, and that would be the best. Just know this. I don't know if I trust you yet. However, if you help me save my mother, I release you from this self-inflicted servitude." I spoke the words and surprised myself with the promise, but I knew I would do whatever I could to save Mother.

He stopped walking and turned back to me. "I don't deserve release and will never stop protecting you from others who may seek to hurt you as I have done so horribly," he said, refusing my release. "I will help you save Isa because she has saved me, and I must now save her," he finished. And no more was spoken about it.

We continued walking, and I knew the moment of truth was before us. We were almost within sight of the fort. Soon the scouts would spot us, and I could possibly be a captive right along with Mother if Francisco decided to betray us.

"I will have to bind your hands to make this believable," he said tentatively. I thrust out my hands, knowing it could be my demise but hoping he would stay true to his word. He bound my hands with zip ties and took the pack and all my weapons but a small knife he hid under my pant leg. Starting back on our way, my heart was pounding with uncertainty, and soon we were discovered by a tall Seditionist that was overly excited to see Francisco, especially with a captive.

"Cisco! I knew they couldn't keep you long. What do you have here? A little morsel from those peace-loving fools?" the large man asked, nodding his head in my direction.

"This is the woman that I had before. She displays my mark," Francisco said, jerking me forward and showing the distorted mark above my breast. He looked it over, realizing in that moment I had tried to remove it myself; regret lay in his eyes. The man didn't notice Francisco's expression and slapped him on the back in congratulations. Not only had he escaped, but he brought back a woman as a trophy.

As we ventured into the camp, more and more men accompanied us so that by the time we reached the entrance, it was a parade of men laughing at the "peace-loving fools" that couldn't keep Francisco captured, even underground. I cringed at their crude words and hoped to get a glimpse of Mother but only saw frightened women cower back into their tiny tents away from the large crowd of men. Being in the camp brought back memories of my previous time spent here. I felt the fear creeping up my spine and hoped our stay would be brief. I vaguely recalled the camp layout, so I assumed the men were leading us to the center where Raymon's dwelling was located. Surely, Mother would be there.

"Francisco! My son! It is good to have you back!" I heard Raymon's low gravelly voice before I spotted him at the entrance to a large tent. As the flap of his tent swung shut, I thought I caught sight of Mother's favorite blue shirt, but it may have been wishful thinking. The minute Raymon realized that Francisco had brought me back with him, a scowl came across his face. "You bring this witch back?" he asked angrily. The rift that had begun to form between father and son was because of me, and Raymon wasn't happy I was present.

"She is mine, and I keep what is mine," Francisco replied firmly. The words were frightening, but I knew he had to convince his father that I was a captive once more. I writhed against the restraints and men holding me in place, proving I wasn't happy about being once again under their control.

"To escape an underground fortress would be difficult, but add a hostage to that, and it would become near impossible," Raymon said with suspicion.

Panic was clawing up my throat. If he didn't believe us, he might put us both to death; or worse, I would become someone else's woman, and who knew what he would do to Francisco for such a betrayal?

"She naively thought I would help her rescue Isa. She doesn't know how deep my loyalty to you runs." His words rang so close to the truth, I wondered who he was lying to—me or his father.

Raymon laughed an evil guffaw and slapped his son on the shoulder as if in felicitation. "Let us feast! My son has returned!" he yelled to the crowd gathered about us. They all let out a loud cheer and began heading toward the feasting tent, dragging me along. I was shoved down roughly onto the ground beside a table way at the back. I looked up to see Francisco flinch as I hit my head on a table with the fall. He came to my side and shoved the men aside.

"I will not lose sight of her again. She stays with me," he said, pushing me toward the head table, not nearly as rough as the other men. His gentleness reassured me slightly that he was wasn't fooling me but instead these men around us.

Once at the head table, he pushed me down into a chair beside his own. He leaned forward for only a moment and whispered, "We will find her at dusk once they have their fill of grog." He immediately went back to laughing and carrying on with those around him, ignoring me completely. The men were served by women that worked quickly to avoided being slapped for their sluggishness. The men's cups never quite reached empty before the women would fill them up once again with grog.

I watched Francisco closely and began to notice he wasn't drinking the grog but instead secretly pouring into the dirt at his feet. I wondered if his father would notice and grow more suspicious. The more grog consumed, the louder the men became, and Francisco was putting on a nice show of it himself. Dusk had fallen, and the men began to fall asleep where they sat. Some wandered off to their tents, and finally, Raymon got up, heading to his own dwelling.

Francisco stood me up, stumbling around as if he had drank every drop that was poured for him. Soon we were back to his old tent where so many horrible memories lay for me. I couldn't help the few tears that fell, but I quickly wiped them away before Francisco saw.

"I heard Padre's right-hand man say that Isa was in his tent," Francisco told me the moment the flap closed on the tent.

"Where is it located?" I asked him, hoping we could leave this horrible place sooner rather than later.

"Only a short distance. We have to wait until everyone is sleeping before we try anything," Francisco replied. "How long do you think we have before Merek catches up to us?" he asked carefully.

"They have horses and vehicles. I am sure they are out there deciding what to do," I told him. I hoped they wouldn't attack before we could save Mother, because if they attacked now, they would put us all at risk.

"Will they punish you for this?" Francisco asked, releasing my hands from the zip ties. My hands ached from the ties, and my wound was worse.

"If they didn't banish me for trying to kill you, surely they won't for us saving Mother," I replied with a short laugh, not worried about my punishment from the Council but more how Merek would react.

"You should probably change the bandage," Francisco indicted toward my wound. I nodded my head in agreement and began to undo the bandage. The smell of the poultice was strong, and my head felt light from the sight of my own wound. Francisco handed me the fresh poultice mixture but didn't make an effort to help me. In this place, at this time with so many memories running through my mind, I was glad he gave me my space. With great awkwardness, I reapplied the poultice and replaced the bandage. Francisco turned his back, giving me some privacy. Strange.

"When can we find Mother?" I asked Francisco's back.

"Not long, and everyone except the guards will be asleep for the evening," he replied without turning around.

"Passed out drunk you mean?" I said to state the obvious.

He turned around at that with a rakish grin. "All the better for us," he replied with a light laugh.

We both began to restlessly roam the tent, beating out a path in the dirt floor where we kept going to look out and see if the fires where dim, indicating that all was clear and we could find Mother. It felt like an eternity before Francisco finally motioned for us to head out. I grabbed my pack, and Francisco put two handguns into the waist of his pants. I knew guards would be roaming about but hoped we could get by without an encounter. Following Francisco, I wasn't aware of where we were headed, but he seemed to, so I kept pace and kept quiet. It wasn't long before all the winding through the tents came to a halt, and we were standing before the tent I presumed was where he believed Mother to be.

Francisco pulled out a knife and began to carefully cut along the seam. Peeking in, he signaled me closer. "I think she is in there," he said, barely above a whisper.

I looked through the small opening and saw a woman's back. She looked to be chained to the center pole of the tent as I had once been. I couldn't make out if it was Mother, but most women in the camp weren't chained, so it was rather likely to be Mother.

"It must be her," I said just as quietly.

Francisco nodded and made his small opening man size so that we could slip in behind and hopefully go unnoticed by the inebriated guard. Every noise Francisco made as he cut through the thick fabric caused my heart to skip. It seemed so loud in the still of the night.

We could see where the guard's pallet was by the front entrance, and Francisco motioned to be silent and pointed out his sleeping form, not quite on the pallet, snoring as only a man can that has overindulged. Francisco went through the opening, and then I followed, but as we drew closer to the chained woman, something seemed wrong. I was within five feet of her when I was certain it wasn't mother. Francisco kept walking, so I quickly reached out to stop him, but it was too late. The woman saw us and began jerking on her chain that apparently had bells attached. She was frantic to get away from us. Soon we were surrounded by guards and Raymon.

"Ah mi hijo, I hoped you hadn't betrayed me, but I needed to know," Raymon said, shaking his head. "Angel here thinks you are the devil inside Cisco's body. She can't scream anymore without her tongue, so we added the bells to know if you had arrived." Raymon said it all with an air of detachment as if Francisco wasn't his own son. We walked right into his trap, and neither one of us had known.

"I can no longer live the way you live, Padre," Francisco informed him.

"Yes, Cisco, even as a boy you were weak, but I thought I had broken you of such weakness. Then this thing." As he spat the words, he pointed his hand at me. "This thing came along, and I saw the weakness once again. You started out to conquer her, but she conquered you." Raymon seemed finished with his speech, and Francisco made no effort to confirm nor deny his father's claims.

"What are we to do with them?" a man asked at Raymon's right.

"We will let the strongest man claim this woman, and Francisco will watch. Perhaps that will break him of the hold she has on him."

Francisco had been calm and silent until those words, and then he erupted as if to kill them all. I had never seen him with so much rage; it was frightening. The guard closest to Francisco was immediately knocked from his feet. The other guards hesitated for only a moment and then charged to overpower him. The confusion gave me the opportunity to draw my weapon, and I began shooting the guards. One, two, three guards fell, and then Francisco was at my side.

"*Run!*" he said, grabbing my free hand and pulling me toward the opening we had come through before. Above the chaos, I heard her Mother yelling in pain. We stopped in our tracks.

"Don't be so naïve, Cisco, I brought my leverage. Drop your weapons or I'll kill her in front of you," Raymon said, waving a guard forward, Mother being dragged behind. We dropped our weapons. From the looks of her, she had already been beaten. She was crying out in pain. The shackles weren't around her wrists but attached to hooks that went through her wrist directly below her palm. There was minimal blood, so they must have purposely avoided the arteries. My throat closed up at the sight of her; defeat lay in her eyes.

"Isa," Francisco choked out her name. "Take me, Father, punish me as you will, but let them go. I beg you," he spoke with such earnest. I hoped Raymon would listen. A man came from outside the tent and whispered to Raymon.

"It would seem we are under attack from the underground fools. I don't have time to negotiate. Kill them all and be done with it," Raymon said and headed out of the tent in a rush, leaving only two guards to finish us off. Mother stumbled to the ground. The guard raised his rifle aiming at Francisco. As I saw the guard squeezing the trigger, I pushed Francisco from harm and saw Mother leap in front of the rifle, tearing the hooks from her skin. The echo of the gun rang in my ears as I watched, in slow motion, Mother drop to the dirt floor, limp, and heard more, then saw Francisco grab the weapons we had given up earlier and shoot both the guards without remorse. I rushed to Mother's prone body but knew before I reached her, the wound was fatal. She was bleeding from her wrist profusely, and now a gunshot to her chest.

"Mother!" I cried, cradling her head gently. "Please, please." I don't know who I was pleading with, but I couldn't stand another loss.

"Find freedom, Alex. Find love," she said haltingly.

Francisco was at her other side now, holding her hand to his lips, tears pouring out. "I will avenge you, Isa," he vowed.

"No, no, Cisco, you must forgive. You must," she said weakly.

She had saved us both. I couldn't fathom the pain she was in. I couldn't understand the sacrifice she had made, and my heart was not broken into pieces but blown up into tiny particles of dust. I would never heal. I saw the life leave her eyes. I heard her last breath with a finality that rang through my entire being. Francisco angrily wiped the tears from his eyes and reached across Mother's lifeless body pulling me to standing.

"We must go before someone realizes we aren't dead," he told me as I followed him without the will to protest. I stared at the empty body until I could no longer see it, and my mind, soul, and heart felt as dead as my mother lay behind me, out of sight.

STAGE 5:1

It was all a blur, but I found myself hidden in a tent I had never seen before with a group of women who had prepared me, perhaps saved me from the cleansing so many months before. Francisco was at the entrance of the tent, and the women were scurrying around, draping my head with the traditional clothing they were wearing.

"We can get you out this way," the tallest woman said quietly, pointing to the back of the tent.

"Alex, you need to get back to Merek," Francisco said from his outlook at the entrance. "They will help you," he finished, nodded toward the women.

"What are you doing?" I asked once I could find my voice.

"I will make sure you make it out of camp and no one follows you," he replied.

This man who had been my complete enemy somehow wasn't anymore. He cried over our lost child, wept over my mother, he had pledged his life to me in penitence, he had kept his word to help me rescue Mother, even if it wasn't the outcome I had desired. I couldn't leave him here to become another sacrifice for me.

"I will not leave you," I said firmly.

"You can be rid of me this way," he replied with raised eyebrows.

"I will not owe you. You will live," I told him firmly.

He nodded his head and came toward me. "We need to circle around the back to try to find your people," he said.

"I don't know how much they will want to see me right now." I realized in that moment I had failed as I had been afraid about what they would do. The result: Mother was dead.

"Then we need to leave this place behind until we decide what to do," Francisco replied without addressing our complete failure. "I cannot fight my own people. They are only a few that are truly loyal to mi Padre once he is gone. The rest will be free." An idea seemed to dawn in Francisco's mind, but he didn't share.

"What is it?" I asked him.

"Nothing, nothing."

I knew it wasn't nothing but didn't pursue the question. I just wanted to be far from this place. Francisco explained his plan of escape. All six of us would cover ourselves in robes as the women were and leave the camp unnoticed. With all the confusion, the plan seemed simple. Francisco draped a robe over his head and stood amongst us as we headed out the back. The men we saw didn't look our way twice, and soon we were past the rear guard that wasn't concerned if a group of crazy women left the camp or not. Once we had reached a safe distance and cover of trees, Francisco threw off the robes and began to roam back and forth restlessly.

"I have to go back," he finally said after many moments of silence.

"Why? What good can it do?" I asked, surprised he wanted to go back to that wretched place.

"There will be much bloodshed of innocent people. Padre will never surrender, and many will die," he replied haltingly.

"What can you do?" I asked him. The women were paying close attention, but none spoke.

"I am not sure, but I have to try," Francisco said. Somehow, I knew he was lying to me, but I had no reason for knowing it. If he had intended to betray me, his chance had passed. This was something else. "Will you allow me to go?" he asked. I realized he took his servitude to me seriously.

"I hold no authority over you. Do as you like," I replied, uncomfortable with his plea. He wasn't sacrificing himself for me. This was for his people, so I would owe him nothing.

He grabbed my pack from the ground where I had placed it and took out more ammo for his weapon and looked up at me hesitantly. Before I knew what was happening, he pulled me into an embrace and whispered softly, "If I don't come back, I hope one day you can forgive me for the wrong I have done you." I could barely make out what he said. It was so quiet. The words came out desperate and broken. My wall of anger toward him took another crack. He kissed my hands as if in reverence and swiftly turned back to the camp where he hoped to save his people from his father's pride.

I watched him head back until I could no longer see him. I didn't mourn him leaving. I just felt strange being left with these women that I didn't know and who hardly spoke. They were in a tight bunch, whispering amongst themselves when I turned back around. I wanted to ask what they were talking about so vehemently, but I refrained. Instead, I sat down and tried to sort out what in the world I should do next. My options were limited.

Waiting for the battle to be over seemed cowardly, and that wasn't really an option. Fighting from this side as Francisco was doing seemed like suicide. The only choice I had left was to skirt around the camp and try to reconnect with Merek and the rest while trying not to be killed.

"I am going to find my people," I told the women slowly, not sure if they spoke my own tongue. They all shook their heads quickly as if I had lost my mind.

"You must not leave. They will find you and kill you," the leader of the group of women said with concern.

"I can't stay here while my friends are fighting for my mother." Just speaking of her brought instant tears to my eyes.

"You will do your friends no good dead," she replied with finality. In the last few months, I had risked my life so many times that now it mattered even less. No child, no mother, Merek may never forgive me, and now this confusing chink in my armor toward Francisco—I didn't have a very bright future before me.

"Would you have me do nothing?" I asked her in anger.

"You are in pain because of your mother's death. I would advise you to think clearly before making any rash decisions." She was right but had only skimmed the surface of my pain.

We stopped talking, he and I could hear the battle waging on at the camp. An explosion rang out, shaking the ground we stood on. I turned around to only see the smoke rising above the distant camp. I could stand it no longer. Picking up my pack with the remaining weapons, I started off in that direction. People were dying, and I could no longer stand around and wait for it to be over. I heard the women yelling after me, trying to dissuade me, but I ignored them and kept going.

The walk back seemed much shorter than the adrenaline run we had leaving, but soon I was at the back gate and saw the destruction that the Republic had done. Tents were ablaze and the fortress walls destroyed in many places. The dead and wounded lay throughout without anyone to tend them. I hated these people, but the sight of their destruction wasn't easy to swallow. I crept through the camp, coming nearer and nearer to the center where I heard the battle. Carefully coming around a tent, I stumbled over a child's lifeless body. Coming face-to-face with the dead eyes, the oxygen left my lungs, and I scrambled away as fast as I could.

Leaning against a post, I caught my breath before moving on. In the distance, I saw a group of Seditionist hunkered down below the platform I had once stood on to be "cleansed." They were under fire from somewhere at the front of the camp. Raymon was amongst them. This seemed the last stronghold left. I had once tried and failed to exact my own revenge upon Francisco. Looking at Raymon, I knew I couldn't fail this time.

It only took a few seconds to realize I could sneak up closer to end his miserable life and perhaps the battle itself. I knew they hadn't spotted me yet, so I quickly crouched down and went along the backside of the platform. The closer each step brought me, the harder my heart pounded in my chest. Within three meters, I could hear only the racing of my heart. With the raising of my handgun, I must have alerted Raymon of my presence, because he turned and stared at me with death in his eyes.

I froze. He smiled his cruel smile and raised his own weapon; we stood that way for a stilled moment in time, and everything seemed in slow motion as I squeezed the trigger. At that same instant, my body was pushed from the line of fire by Francisco as he flew through the air from the above platform. Several things seemed to happen at once. Francisco threw a knife toward Raymon, Raymon's shot made impact with Francisco, making him go limp, my bullet found the right shoulder of Raymon, and the knife found its target protruding from Raymon's left eye. When I hit the ground, time returned to its normal speed.

I jumped up and ran to Francisco's prone body. I didn't know whether I hoped he was alive or dead, but I had to know. Blood seemed to be everywhere. I knelt beside his head, placed my hand on his neck to find a faint pulse; he was alive. Strange relief poured through my body; he didn't die to save me.

Soon the Republic was upon the remaining Seditionist. They quickly surrendered without their leader to push them on. Don was among the conquering Republic. He saw me beside Francisco and ran over to us.

"Alex, are you okay?" he asked, worry in his eyes. He ignored Francisco's body.

"Yes, yes, I am fine," I told him.

"Now that we have established your safety, can I kill you?" he asked me, only slightly joking, I was sure.

"I had to, Don," I replied.

"Had to do it alone? Had to scare the life out of us? Had to release Francisco? Had to betray us?" Each question he fired at me stung. My plan didn't make much sense when I thought back, but I couldn't have stayed in that bed and hoped Mother was safe. Now instead, I had a hand in her death. "Did you save your mother?" The last question destroyed me. I couldn't reply, but my tears told him the entire story. Don pulled me into a warm embrace, and I hoped Merek would be as forgiving.

STAGE 5:2

The Republic Militant soon began taking prisoners and carrying away the wounded. I tried to busy myself with giving water to those remaining injured while they waited for the medics to tend to their wounds. Francisco had regained consciousness and was sitting up against the side of the platform. I had stopped the flow of blood from his wound and left him there some time ago. Still no sight of Merek.

Don had informed me that Merek had led the attack and was now rounding up the most loyal to Raymon. No one had dared to move Raymon's body, so there it lay, only a few meters from Francisco, and he couldn't seem to look anywhere else; not that he had much to look at. He was now once again shackled and a prisoner of the Republic.

My body was weak from my wounds now that I knew the battle was over, and the only thing I was left to feel was the wreckage of my life. I couldn't think of Mother or my lost child, even if she had been unwanted. I pushed the pain far from my mind and continued to help where I could. Working tireless across the camp, I could see Colin, Don, and Kasi. I wasn't sure if they saw me and ignored me or if they were so busy, they hadn't seen me yet. I chose not to dwell on how they must have felt with my newest betrayal.

The sun was setting in the distance, casting a strange light on the camp which made the carnage even more pronounced and horrifying. I stood up slowly, trying to avoid the dizziness that seemed to be my constant companion as of late. I heard commotion behind me but didn't turn to look or I would have seen Merek's imposing figure jump from his horse and draw me up into a bear embrace.

"You're alive," he said with great relief. I turned as well as I could in his arms and saw his happy face, knowing he had already forgiven me for taking matters into my own hands once again. I opened my mouth to beg for his forgiveness, and he stopped me with an ardent kiss. A kiss that took words, thoughts, and breath away to be replaced solely with his presence. He didn't seem to care that others had stopped to stare at us. He kissed me with all the passion he had been holding in for the last few months, or at least that's what it felt like.

My head felt light, my stomach turned upside down, and I myself forgot where and what went on around us. It was only us in that moment, and I was overwhelmed by the kiss that seemed to convey his unfailing acceptance and love for me. Tears of joy seeped from under my shut eyelids. I still had Merek. He still loved me.

STAGE 5:3

We returned to the bunker later that night, Merek never leaving my side nor asking for explanation about my actions. He seemed to know that I felt I had no choice but to try to save Mother. He didn't ask about her either. Everyone knew she was gone and everyone seemed scared of a future without her to save us from the injection.

"There might be another way," I told Merek out of the blue as we walked toward Colin's lab to find more disinfectant for the medics.

"Another way for what?" he asked confused.

"To find the cure," I told him simply.

"How?" he asked interested now.

"Colin said that Mother's blood type was RH negative. Mine is also RH negative," I told him quietly.

"So you aren't susceptible to the injection either?" he asked, excited.

"Colin did a few tests, and my blood wasn't quite as resistant as Mother's, but she wasn't injected until after she had me. Colin thinks it has something to do with both the blood type and pregnancy," I informed him.

"So now that you have been pregnant, maybe yours will be as hers was?" His question reminded me of her death, her sacrifice, and it pained me.

"Yes, that could be," I replied, ignoring my twinge.

We opened the doors to the lab. Colin was there with Don and Kasi too. Kasi seemed to come to attention with our entrance and took a few steps toward me, stopping just before she reached me.

"Are you okay?" she asked me, somewhat reserved. I ignored her question and pulled her into a hug.

"I'm sorry," I said, knowing she was hurt by my betrayal.

"It's okay. I was just so worried about you," she replied cautiously.

Colin nodded his head but didn't voice his displeasure or his concern.

"Can we use my blood to finish the cure?" I asked him.

"I think we can," he replied, excitement evident in his voice. Don took the disinfectant back to the medic station, and Merek and Kasi busied themselves looking anywhere but at Colin taking my blood, lots of blood so we could finish his work. I was extremely lightheaded but knew I hadn't saved Mother, but I could perhaps save others. We worked late into that night, Kasi and Merek asleep on the benches in the backroom. I found a strength I didn't know I had running numbers, computing calculations, and helping Colin in any way I could. A new determination to help end the tyranny of the Establishment now that we had conquered one cruel tyrant came alive in me, and I had a new purpose.

STAGE 5:4

The next morning, I woke up from my desk, back aching and wounds hurting more than they had the day before. Merek, Kasi, Don, and Colin were around a table, eating the morning fare.

"Sleeping Beauty awakes," Don said, standing and giving a dramatic bow.

"Sleeping who?" I asked, puzzled by his reference.

"Never mind," he replied, rolling his eyes.

"Come, eat something, the food never tasted so good. Fred is back in the kitchen now that Justin believes him to be loyal to the Republic," Kasi told me.

I could smell the food, and my stomach grumbled with hunger, so I went to sit and eat. It truly was wonderful, and we didn't speak much while we ate the delicious food.

"We have to head to the meeting area today. They will be hosting a commemoratory service for the fallen," Merek told our small group, giving me a careful look. I didn't really want to attend this event but knew I needed the closure it would provide.

"Alex and I must freshen up and will meet you all there," Kasi told the men, taking charge of me. I didn't mind, knowing I couldn't face this alone. Heading back to the dwelling I had shared with Mother was difficult. The smells, her clothing in the closet, her empty bed—it was all so hollow without her loving presence. I didn't even realize the tears were falling until Kasi wiped them from my eyes with a linen cloth from her pocket.

"She was the kindest soul I ever met," Kasi said, her own tears falling. "With all that she went through, she still seemed to pour out love on others without reservation. I couldn't understand it. My own surrogate never seemed to care for me. If I had a true mother, I would have wanted her to be just like yours." She held Mother's shirt close to her face, breathing in her scent.

"Mother attributed her loving kindness to her friend, Ruach HaKodesh," I said offhandedly.

"Yes, she spoke of him once to me. The being sounds surreal, and yet, wouldn't it be wonderful if he were true?" she asked me.

I recalled the dream I had of him in the tranquil forest. "I dreamed of him when I was shot," I told her.

"Really? How interesting. What was it like in this dream?" she asked with true Kasi enthusiasm.

"It was so real, yet not," I said, not knowing how to put words to the experience. "He said Mother was already saved and that I should follow him. It was all very cryptic and confusing," I confessed to her.

"Follow him? Where?" she asked, perplexed.

"That's the thing, I don't know where. He just said, 'Trust me, I will take your burdens,' and then 'Follow me,'" I told her.

She looked as confused as I felt. "It doesn't make much sense, does it?" she said, stating the obvious.

"I have never felt peace like I did in that forest, though," I explained. "It was as if I couldn't even remember my problems. I had to remind myself that Mother was captured and that I hated Francisco and the Seditionist and Gabby." I hesitated about mentioning Gabby. But it was true. I was angry with her for giving Mother up to the Seditionist.

"Gabby is still on house arrest. I don't think Justin knows how he will punish her. I mean, the Seditionist had Fred, and she didn't know what else to do," Kasi told me carefully.

"I know she felt she had no choice. I have done just as much, if not more. I wonder, though, if it hadn't been for me and Gabby, would Mother still be alive?" I replied grievously.

"You can't think like that! You're borrowing all sorts of trouble that way. You believed with all your heart that breaking Francisco free and trying to save Isa on your own was the only way. The outcome could have been the same had you stayed in the hospital bed. You'll never know, so you might as well not take that blame," she said vehemently.

"In the end, Mother threw herself in front of Francisco to save him. She took a bullet meant for him. I don't know how to feel about that," I said honestly.

"Well, I wish he would have died in her stead. He ruined your life and started this entire mess to begin with." I could almost see the smoke coming from her ears. She was so angry.

"He begged for my forgiveness, you know. In fact, he pledged his life to me in servitude for the wrong he did me," I confided in her.

Kasi was speechless, which didn't happen often.

So I continued, "I am still so disgusted by him and what he did, but somehow, I believe he has changed. He protected me through the camp, he was willing to betray his entire way of life, he was determined to save Mother, and he even killed his own father to save my life. I don't know how I feel about him, but he isn't the same man that captured me." My voice caught at the mention of our attempt to save Mother.

Kasi seemed to be considering my musings but didn't address them directly. "You have been through so very much in the last few months. I can't even imagine what you are going through, and now all this confusion. I wish I knew for sure he had changed, and I know that Justin is considering an alliance with him in order to convert the remaining Seditionist to our next mission against the Establishment, but… it's hard for me to trust him after all that has transpired," Kasi said in a rare moment of mature wisdom.

"I don't know either," I replied with all the perplexity I felt. "We'd better hurry," I said, even though I dreaded the idea of listening to others as they spoke of the fallen. We finished freshening up in silence. I put on a fitting dark dress mother had made me while I had been in the medic station after I returned from imprisonment. I felt uncomfortable wearing dresses now that I had worn my combat clothing for so long; the many hidden places for weapons comforted me. I couldn't help but hide a knife in my lace-up boots. Kasi looked beautiful as always in a bright dress with frills all about. It seemed to make the sunshine she held within evident for the world.

I took a deep breath, and we headed to the meeting area for the commemoratory service.

"Here we go," Kasi said, reaching for my hand in comfort. She held my hand on the disappointingly short walk to the meeting hall. All the residents of the bunker where present, including Francisco. He didn't look well; our eyes connected across the crowd. Merek came to my side and pulled me close to his side. I saw Francisco quickly look away.

"How are you?" Merek whispered in my ear. His hand was on my lower back as we sat amongst our people, Don, Colin, Kasi, and even Sabra.

"I don't know," I replied honestly.

Soon, Justin stood before us all and began speaking.

"Today is a bitter day for the Republic. Today we will remember those that have made the ultimate sacrifice. Today we will celebrate their lives and accomplishments through the years."

I drowned out the words once he started in on each individual person that had perished trying to save Mother's life and end the tyranny of the Seditionist. I didn't want to hear about the fathers, mothers, sons, and daughters that wouldn't be returning to the families. I couldn't handle the pain that I felt, knowing it was somewhat my doing, and my insides ached. I had lost a mother and a daughter. The reality of that seemed to hit me like a brick wall, and I wept. Merek looked at me with worried eyes, pulling me close once again. His presence, his scent, his beating heart gave me comfort, and I cried the cleansing tears into his shoulder.

"Let it out, Alex," he said for my ears only. Somehow, I knew he didn't see me as weak for crying but knew it was a sign of my total trust in him that he was my comforter. It seemed like an eternity before I heard him mention Mother's name.

"Isa was one of the most loving, giving, kind, and wise women I have ever known," Justin said, tears running down the corners of his eyes. "She once forgave me, even though I deserved her hatred. She sacrificed her well-being for her daughter and her life for someone we all thought of as the enemy."

My eyes cut to Francisco. Tears wet his face also.

"Her love for people seemed paranormal, selfless, and unconditional. I can't fathom how she did it, but I couldn't deny its power to change people around her. It was like she was a light in a dark place, sunshine through the rain clouds." He choked up, and Colin walked up to take over, patting Justin's back in comfort as he returned to his seat. I realized then just how much Justin loved Mother, and I felt pity for him.

"I couldn't agree more with Justin's words, but I also wanted to add how much she allowed us to put her through in order to find a cure," Colin told the crowd, referring to the many procedures and pain Mother had endured to aid in finding the cure. "In fact, as of today, I can say with confidence after many trials and error, we have found a cure."

Colin spoke the words the entire crowd wasn't expecting in the least. Even I, who had been in the lab only a few hours ago, was shocked by the news. "It was brought to my attention that the blood of RH negative carriers experiences a small but important change in the makeup of their blood after the birth of an RH positive child. Isa's body attacked the injection when it was administered after the birth of that child, which was made from RH positive blood. What this means for us is that if we can isolate the antigens in Alex's blood, Isa's first child, that is also RH negative. We can make it into a serum that can be injected to counteract the injections."

Colin said the words quickly and confidently. I was shocked to my core. Mother had another child and didn't tell me about him or her? Merek looked at me in question, I shook my head in response. Why didn't she tell me? Where was this child now? I wondered. The crowd was cheering and clapping. The applause was so loud, I could no longer hear myself think, and I halfheartedly clapped along. The commemoratory service was over, and I felt as if a rug had been pulled from under me.

"This is great news!" Don said exuberantly.

"Yes, but a bit of a shock. Why are we just finding this out now?" Kasi asked no one in particular.

"He stayed in the lab after we all left, right up to the start of the commemoratory service. Maybe he found out then?" Don said in his defense.

"*No,* a shock that Isa had another child and only told Colin," Kasi said, rolling her eyes at Don.

"Oh, that. Yes, I suppose so," Don replied awkwardly. We all went silent after that, each one in their own thoughts. I had no words, but somehow, deep inside, I knew there was a reason she kept it from me. A good reason.

STAGE 5:5

As we left the meeting area, I didn't see Colin to find out anything else about my newly discovered brother or sister. Kasi said she had to aid Justin in some assistant work. Merek was called into the Militant Headquarters for some mysterious reason, and Don had stomach pain, saying he needed the toilet. So I was left alone and decided to venture to the atrium for some peace and quiet.

I longed to leave the bunker and feel the wind through my hair and see all the beauty around me, but that wasn't an option. The Outlandish rushed through the hallways. They seemed to have a renewed sense of purpose, and all were scurrying off to perform some unknown task. I knew I could find Colin in the lab, and I am sure he could at the very least explain to me why Mother shared that news with him and not me. But in all honesty, I wasn't up to the task.

Entering the atrium, I saw that it was mostly deserted with only a few children playing in the artificial grass on the path to my left. I went right and found a quiet spot near the goldfish pond. I had a million thoughts running through my head, but I cleared them all out and focused on Mother. I recalled her in her entirety, her kindness, her grace, her unconditional love, and wondered what would cause her to keep such a secret from me. I discarded that part of her from my mind, just determined to find my sibling all on my own. Instead, I focused on her life.

Those thoughts brought me to the one she claimed saved her life, Ruach HaKodesh. Then and there, I decided I had two goals. I had to find out about my sibling, and even more importantly, I had to find Ruach HaKodesh; not in a dream, but his presence here—proof that mother wasn't believing in something that truly didn't exist.

"Alex," I heard Francisco say from behind me. I turned and saw he was standing on the path that ran along the small goldfish pond. I looked him over in a different light. His smirk from the first time I met him was gone. He held himself differently, humbled. He was still as strong and handsome as the day he found me. I now looked at his many tattoos and wondered what each one meant, but I kept my thoughts to myself, not wanting to open that door of intimacy. He was unaccompanied by guards or even a tracking device that I could see. Justin must have made a deal with him.

"I see you are free to roam about the bunker now," I stated, unsure how I felt about it.

"Yes, Justin saw that I could play the role of ally and unite the remaining Seditionist with the Republic. I am not going back on my pledge to you. I am at your disposal. If you would rather I leave and take my remaining people with me, you will never be subjected to my presence again. However, if you can put your animosity aside, I believe our separate groups of people could change the world as it is, united against the Establishment." Francisco finished his speech. I could tell by the way he said it all so automatically that it was very practiced. I remained silent for a few moments to ponder my emotions. If I put my feelings aside, we could very likely defeat the Establishment and change the course of the known world.

"I think our people would be better united. Stay and unite them, Francisco," I replied without the usual harsh tone. Mother had touched Francisco's heart; it seemed he was changed in a profound way.

"I will not rest until the cure is administered to all the residents of the Establishment. For Isa. For you?" He posed the last part as a question, and I wasn't sure what he was asking.

"For me?" I asked.

"Yes, for your sibling," he replied.

"Do you know anything about my sibling? Did Isa ever speak of it to you?" I asked, my curiosity raised.

"She didn't, but I am sure she had good reason," Francisco said with reassurance.

"I am sure you are right," I told him, only lying slightly. He turned to continue walking through the atrium but hesitated.

"Will you be united with Merek?" he asked me, completely changing the subject and raising my anger in the process.

"That is none of your concern," I said haughtily. How dare he think he was entitled to such information.

"He is a good man. Isa would be happy for you," he said very quietly. His gentle response stilled my anger.

"We haven't decided," I replied, not really knowing what my future held.

Francisco didn't say anything right away. He just had a sober look on his face.

"You will, I am sure of it," Francisco said, not looking happy about it.

I nodded my head but didn't know what to say. Francisco didn't seem to have anything more to say either.

"Thank you for helping me, saving my life, and trying to save Mother's. You could have easily betrayed me in the camp," I said, not sure where the words had come from but knowing I had to say them.

"I have sworn to protect you, that was part of it," he replied, without actually saying, "You're welcome." We seemed to have nothing left to say to one another. So much fury, sadness, and tragedy was shared between us, yet without it, we had no connection.

"I am going to tell Justin I will align my remaining people with the Republic to aid in administering the cure," he informed me.

"Yes, that will be good," I replied as if he was a stranger.

"You are safe in this bunker below the ground. You have no need of a protector. I will venture from here to unite us. However, I may not see you again. I pray one day you will forgive me for all that has happened." He rushed through the words as if he was trying to get them all out without me stopping him. When he finished, he turned without giving me time to respond, but then I realized he didn't want a response, only to say the words once again.

After he was out of eyesight, I sat there with my own thoughts, innocence lost, child lost, mother lost—I couldn't afford to lose anyone else. All those around me seemed to care so much. I had never felt this in the Establishment, except from Mother and Kasi. Colin, Don, Merek, and even Justin seemed to desire good for me, to empathize for me, to love me.

Merek's beautiful face came to mind then, and I thought what a strange thing love is. On one hand, Mother's love was so very sacrificial, giving, unending, and caring. Merek's, on the other hand, was wild, heady, intoxicating, and fearless. Recalling all he had done, all he had made me feel, all he had sacrificed, and all he had forgiven, I knew that if ever I understood romantic love, it was through his actions. I couldn't wait for this life to be "normal" before I pledged my life to Merek. I knew he was still probably at the Militant Headquarters, but I had to tell him. I had to ask.

STAGE 5:6

I hurried through the hallways as all the Outlandish were, because I had an urgency to see Merek as if this was my only chance, and I needed to declare my feelings for him. I passed by my dwelling, passed the labs, passed the meeting hall, and soon I was at his doorstep, hoping he was there. I raised my hand to knock and hesitated only for a moment before I rapped three times at the thick door. Immediately, I remembered that Don was sick and probably sleeping, but it was too late. The door swung wide to Merek with trimmed hair, and he was clean shaven. He looked so young and clean-cut, I was taken aback.

"Alex, I was about to go find you," he said, smiling bashfully.

"You shaved and cut your hair?" I asked, dumbfounded.

"Yeah, I didn't have much of a choice. You seem out of breath, what's up?" he asked, using primal slang.

"I need to speak with you," I replied, quickly so as not to lose my nerve.

"Don is asleep, but you can come in," he said, ushering me into their small Militant dwelling.

"I know that today is probably not the best day to say this and I know we have spoken of it in the past, but I can't wait any longer. I love you. I need you. I don't want to ever be separated from your side. I want to spend the rest of my life with you," I blurted out.

At first, he looked shocked, and then overjoyed, and then apprehensive. Silence rang loud in the small room. I waited for him to say something, anything, but he seemed to be contemplating his next words. I waited with bated breath.

"If you won't marry the girl, I will," Don rasped out from his sickbed a few feet away.

"Oh, shut up, Don, no one will be marrying her but me. It's not that. It's that I have new orders," Merek said angrily. My heart pounded in my chest, not knowing what orders could be holding him back from us being united. "I was informed today I will be joining the efforts to infiltrate the Sovereignty and find out ways to mass distribute the cure. I could be gone for days, weeks, or even months," he told me carefully, looking brokenhearted.

"Marry her in secret before you go, you idiot, and Justin might let her go with you," Don said with annoyance.

"And if he doesn't?" Merek asked, growing angrier with Don's input.

"You will at least have a few nights together as man and wife," Don said as if he solved all the world's problems.

I had remained silent through the entire exchange, but inside, I wanted to beg Merek to not leave me behind and to take me wherever he went. My pride was screaming to keep my mouth shut, but after all I had lost, remaining silent wasn't an option.

"I can't lose you too," I told him, tears welling in my eyes.

"Then it's settled. We will be united tonight," he informed me confidently.

I heard Don's chuckle and saw Merek's face break out in a wide grin.

"I guess it is," I said, laughing and drawing him into a kiss.

"Can't that wait till tonight too. I don't want to throw up all over this bed. I just washed it," Don said as we continued to hold one another.

We ignored him, and I felt as if nothing could destroy my overflowing joy.

STAGE 5:7

All that it would take for us to be united was a little bribery to one agreeing council member and signing our names to document. Even though Don was still ill, he said he wouldn't miss this for the world, so he went ahead and made inquiries to see if any council member would be agreeable to the union. No party was planned, no white dress, no tux as Merek had once told me of, but there were no two people that loved each other more. The joy I saw every day in Mother I felt in this moment. I would be Merek's lifelong partner, never to be separated, together forever.

A loud knock came at the door to my dwelling, and I quickly opened it to Justin's grim face.

"May I come in?" he asked gravely. I stepped aside, indicating my consent, and he walked past me with determination. "I heard what you and Merek have planned," he said, looking displeased.

"Yes, we plan to be united tonight," I replied not sure why he looked so upset.

"I am not sure that's such a good idea," he said, slightly shaking his head.

"Why not?" I asked, feeling my guard go up at his words of disagreement.

"I need you for an unsanctioned assignment, and if you are united, you will be assigned with Merek and won't be able to do what I need," he said.

"What kind of unsanctioned assignment?" I asked suspiciously.

Justin didn't answer but went to the door and waved someone in. It was Colin.

"Tell her what you told me," Justin said to Colin angrily.

"All I told you was Isa said her son would be eleven years old right now," Colin said, seemingly as confused as I was. *A brother. I have a brother*, I marveled.

"That may mean nothing to you both, but I found Isa again about twelve years ago. She was released from the reformatory and tried to escape the Establishment with a nomad group. I had joined the Republic by that time and was fighting for the cure. She didn't share with us that she was immune until the very end. I fell in love with her again, madly. I remembered how I had hurt her before and tried to stay away, but something in me was drawn to her like a moth to a flame. Her joy, her peace, her love overwhelmed me, and I couldn't get enough, so we wed," Justin confessed, tears running down his face.

"You see, I failed her twice. We had only been united for six days before she was once again captured by the Sovereignty and placed back into the reformatory." He took a deep breath to steady himself. He wasn't making much sense. "You see, her son had to have been my son," Justin finally explained.

The air seemed to be sucked from my lungs. I couldn't believe it. Mother had been united with Justin. They had a child together. I had a brother. Colin looked as stunned as I was, but he found words somehow.

"Why didn't you tell anyone?" Colin asked, perplexed.

"It all started after Colin had found out which Reformatory she was in. That was when he saved you and Kasi from the attack on the Establishment. I watched her from afar after Merek brought her back to me. Every time, she had forgiven me, but after so many years of her being captured, I never thought she could love me again, so I stayed away. I dared not ask for her to love me again, only for her forgiveness, which she lavished on me. Some knew about our union. I guess I didn't know what to say. I found myself still loving her even after all this time, but I knew we had more important things to do than find love for an old fool like me, so I asked her to go with you all to this bunker to find the cure. I couldn't stay away from her long, though," Justin replied.

"Why didn't Isa tell anyone?" Colin asked.

I still hadn't found my voice.

"She never explained it much to me, only that she needed time before we told others," he said, dejected.

"When I found out about the male child, Isa told me not to tell anyone, because it would put the child in danger. I kept my word until this day, but it is all so confusing," Colin told us.

"Alex, we share a purpose. Will you help me find my son? Your brother?" Justin asked with timid hope.

I could not gather myself. I didn't know what to say. Why was the child in danger? So many unanswered questions, but I knew it wasn't really a choice. I had to find my brother to honor Isa, to love him as she loved me.

"Yes, of course, I will," I replied with a firm nod.

"We must be careful whom we share this information with. Isa didn't want anyone to know, so there has to be danger for the child if his identity is found out," Colin said to us both.

"You can marry if you wish, but in order to find your brother, you won't be able to go with Merek when he leaves. Your journey is elsewhere," Justin said delicately. I figured that to be the case, but the words were still hard to hear. I wasn't sure what I should do.

"I will have to speak with Merek," I replied reluctantly, dreading the conversation ahead.

"Thank you," Justin said, hope shining in his eyes. "I can't trust anyone else with his safety."

I realized the trust he put in me was only because of the shared connection we now had, but it didn't matter. I had to find my brother. I had to keep him from danger.

"What will you tell Merek?" Colin asked.

"I am not sure, but I have to trust him with this. There can't be secrets between us," I replied, wishing I knew what the best route was. As if I had conjured him up, Merek walked through the door, followed by Kasi and Don. He seemed surprised to see Justin.

"What's going on?" he asked, voicing his confusion. He looked to me for answers.

"We need to talk. In private," I said, trusting Kasi and Don but knowing that Justin may not. Kasi and Don both looked hurt that I needed them to leave, but they followed Colin and Justin out, leaving me alone with Merek to decide our future.

"I have a brother," I said, not really knowing where to start the conversation.

"That's wonderful! Does Colin know how to find him?" he asked.

"No, no. That's what I need to speak with you about. Justin wants to send me into the Establishment to find him," I replied being as straightforward as I could.

"So he doesn't want us to wed and interfere with his mission for you?" Merek said, knowing full well the true reason for Justin's visit.

"He thinks it would be difficult for us to be separated if we unite," I replied, letting him decide.

"What do you want, Alex?" he asked me.

I paused for a few moments trying to fully grasp how I felt. I loved him, I knew the thought of being separated from him was almost unbearable, but I couldn't ask him to abandon his Militant career to follow me on an unsanctioned mission.

"I have never experienced this kind of connection with anyone. I can feel your presence from across any room. The very sight of you makes my stomach clench. I can't explain the current of electricity that courses through me with your touch, nor the desire to be held through the dark nights when the nightmares hit. And above all else, I feel your acceptance of me as a confirmation of how much you love me too. I could never ask you to give up the standing you have within the Militant to follow me on this unsanctioned mission. I know it has already taken hits for my sake.

"On the other hand, I need to, I can't not find my brother. He may be in danger. I never knew how much the word *family* could mean until I met you and reconnected with Isa. I cannot abandon my brother now, even if he doesn't know about me yet. We are family." I poured out my thoughts to him, hoping he would understand, hoping he would follow me to the ends of the earth, but scared out of my wits he wouldn't.

"Alex, I tried to sacrifice my very life for you. I attempted to murder a man for you. I chased you when you left me behind to rescue Isa. Alex, I grew to love the child within you because it was part of you. I too mourned her passing as confusing as that sounds. How can you not know that I would follow you into the very depths of a smoldering pit of fire if it only meant a few more moments to hold you close?"

With each word he spoke, my heart ached that much more for the man I saw before me. He took my hands in his own and looked into my eyes with promise. "We will unite and find your brother together," he finished with certainty.

STAGE 5:8

Kasi was running around our dwelling, preparing me for my wedding the next morning. "You have to be gorgeous. Wear this. Oh, let me add color to your lips." On and on she went, scurrying around as quickly as she could.

I indulged her every whim, knowing she was enjoying it far more than I. The only thing that mattered to me was my life after this night, my future with Merek. The closer the ceremony came, the more nervous I was. Now that Justin was informed that Merek would assist me in finding his son, my brother, he was all for our union, so Merek decided a celebration was in order. And the entire bunker was coming to the event first thing in the morning. I was excited to be united, but the thought of the crowd frightened me.

"You can't see Merek before the ceremony. It's bad luck," Kasi was saying.

"What is luck?" I asked, coming back to reality with confusion.

"Oh, don't you read any books? Luck is something people believed in the primal times. They believed if you did certain things, it would curse your future, so to speak," she said, flustered. I laughed behind my hand, not wanting to enrage her further. She continued to gather things together, preparing for the morning, definitely more nervous than I was, but I aided her in whatever way she asked, which honestly wasn't much. I eventually was prone on the edge of my bed, growing weary just from watching her.

"It's growing late. Shouldn't I sleep some tonight?" I asked her.

"Yes, you need your beauty rest," she replied.

"My what? Oh, never mind, could you stop so we both can rest?" I asked, adding a yawn to reinforce my point.

"Yes, fine, but we are getting up bright and early to get you prepared," she said sternly.

"Yes, yes, whatever you say," I said as my eyes closed in exhaustion.

STAGE 5:9

I could see her on the edge of the serene forest—Mother, walking beside him, Ruach HaKodesh. I longed to run into her arms, but somehow, that didn't seem appropriate. It was almost as if time and urgency didn't exist in this place. I walked to them and felt my heart swell with her beaming bright beautiful face.

"Mother," I breathed the word.

She smiled and, without saying anything, drew me into her embrace.

"Mother," I said again, stepping back to take in the sight of her, tears running unchecked down my face.

Ruach HaKodesh wiped them away and smiled a knowing smile. "I told you she was saved," he told me confidently.

"Are you safe? Are you well? They shot you. How can this be?" I asked with puzzlement.

"Alex, I am healed. I never feared those that can only kill the body," she said with a smile. It felt as if she was speaking in riddle as Ruach HaKodesh always did.

"What do you mean, Mother?" I asked.

"You must follow him, Alex. He will give you the peace you desire," she replied.

"I miss you, Mother," I told her.

"Seek him, and you shall find what you are looking for," she said, spreading her hands out to Ruach HaKodesh.

"Where can I find him, Mother?" I asked desperately. "He only seems to be here in this place."

"You look for him in time long passed. He is woven throughout all things, past, present, and future," she replied.

"I never heard mention of him until we met again," I told her, not knowing where to look.

"You will find him in the sacred writings," she said with joy.

"Where are these sacred writings?" I asked.

"You will find them when you are most in need," she said vaguely.

"When is that, Mother?" I asked, completely lost.

"You must wake up now, Alex," Ruach HaKodesh said, delicately closing my eyes with his fingers.

* * * * *

"Alex, *wake up!*" I was shaken awake by Kasi. "There is an attack on the bunker," she yelled worriedly. It only took a split second for the confusion to pass, and I bolted up from my bed.

"We have to find Merek and the others!" I replied, pulling on my clothing to the sounds of explosions much too close for comfort. We grabbed our packs and opened the door to look out on smoke and destruction at our doorstep. I saw sunlight, real sunlight streaming through an enormous hole in the ceiling of the bunker between our dwelling and the Militant Headquarters.

"It looks like they are targeting the Militant Headquarters," Kasi yelled over the roaring of warfare. I had no choice but to head right into the danger set before us. Merek, Don, and Colin were there, and we had to find them. The Outlandish were running the opposite direction, and it was then I noticed another group of people, Unity officers from the Sovereignty—they had found us!

They were streaming into a hole from above, killing all in their path. My legs were carrying me toward the height of battle when I felt someone from behind grab me around the waist.

"You can't go there. They will kill you." I recognized Francisco's voice and fought against him with all my strength.

"I have to find Merek," I screamed.

"He would not desire you kill yourself for something so futile," Francisco yelled back in response.

I saw Kasi from the corner of my eye, looking frightened and uncertain what to do. Francisco threw me over his shoulder and began running in the wrong direction. I kicked and screamed and punched and tried to get away, but his hold didn't budge. Soon we were in the mess hall, greeted by a group of Outlandish. Don, Colin, Fred, and Gabby were among them. Don came running when he saw us.

"I was just at your dwelling trying to find you," he said as soon as he reached me, and Francisco put me down. Kasi was beside me, not making eye contact.

"I was taken away by this miscreant," I replied with anger. Francisco seemed unfazed by my wrath.

"You were about to forfeit your life," he said calmly.

"Where is Merek?" I asked Don, ignoring Francisco completely.

Colin and Fred had joined us at this point, all looking defeated.

"I am not sure, but I think…I think they took him," Don said hesitantly.

"They took him?" I asked hysterically.

"They were grabbing the leaders. They took Justin, and I saw Merek trying to fight them off, and then there was an explosion, and then I ran to find you. Alex, I am not sure where he is," Don said.

"We have to get out of here," Francisco interjected. "Now," he said with authority.

"I can't leave without knowing!" I replied desperately.

"He is right, Alex. We need to get to the other bunker and warn them. We will do Merek no good dead," Colin said, trying to calm me.

I knew he was right, but it felt like betrayal to leave without knowing. I nodded agreement but felt crushed inside. Colin directed everyone to the exit I had once ventured to save Fred, and with the power gone from the attack, the hallways were dark and frightening indeed. The hatch to the surface seemed intact, and the men had it slightly open to survey the terrain before we left the safety of the hallway.

"It seems the Unity officers are focusing on the Militant Headquarters and haven't gotten this far south. Let's exit into the brush quickly and silently," Colin instructed. We all did as directed and were soon surrounded in a covering of trees and rocks.

"Follow me. There is a way station not far from here that can aid us in getting to the other bunker," Colin whispered, motioning us on with his hands.

I ran silently beside Don and Kasi. We took up the rear of the small group while Francisco and Colin led us. Each step was more difficult than the step before knowing Merek could be back there in need. Logic said it was complete folly to return, so I tried to think of regrouping and saving him another way.

We ran for what seemed like hours before we were at the way station Colin had spoken of. It was nothing more than a hole in the ground surrounded by a corral with horses, buggies, and one motorized jeep. A group of people were there I assumed to be former Seditionist.

"We can't stay long. They will be sure to find this place soon," Colin told the group. The men that lived at the way station, the keepers, had seen the smoke and began preparing their own supplies to head out to a safe bunker. They were happy to join our group and venture to what we hoped was safety.

"How did they know where we were?" Gabby asked no one in particular. We all seemed at a loss until I saw Francisco shake his head in annoyance.

"I had been trying to convert my people to your ways when I was informed some had made alliances with the Sovereignty," he said, disgusted. "This is the doing of my people. They are out for revenge after mi Padre's death," he finished, somewhat defeated.

"Actually, that may be good news then," Colin said after a short silence.

"How can that be good?" Francisco asked.

"They don't know the locations of our other bunkers then. We have a safe place to go that neither group knows of," he replied, hopeful. Francisco and Colin began speaking quietly together, making plans, both gesturing toward the south and the former Seditionist and toward our small group before they seemed to come to an agreement.

"We all," Colin said, including the Seditionist very clearly, "are going to the bunker. I expect you all to help one another and us get there long before the Unity officers begin to fan out and discover even this place." He finished his short speech, leaving no room for objection.

With renewed determination, we gathered the few supplies from the way station, saddled horses, loaded the buggies, and quickly headed off in the direction of the bunker where it all started. I pulled myself onto a saddle and rode behind the group slowly. I was reluctant to put distance between myself and Merek.

Cresting a hill, I looked back on the smoke and destruction. I stopped the horse and faced the sight. My hopes and dreams seemed to be burning right along with the Militant Headquarters. The peace I had yesterday seemed as if it never was. The peaceful forest where Mother and Ruach HaKodesh dwelled seemed a vague memory. "Seek him," Mother had said.

Once more, my peace was snatched from me by the wars of man. I heard the horses approaching but didn't acknowledge their arrival. All I could do was stare at what felt like my last hope burning down to nothing.

"I will help you find him," Francisco vowed from my side.

"And so will I," Colin said in agreement.

"You know you can't leave me behind ever *again*," Kasi spoke up from behind.

"Who would I annoy if we don't find him?" Don said in jest.

"Merek was my best customer," Fred said from the buggy he was riding in with Gabby.

"I owe my very life to you and Merek. We will find him," Gabby said with determination.

In my heart, I knew he stilled lived. He had to, so I didn't let fear come knocking. I would find him and my brother and Ruach HaKodesh. I would find peace.

The end. For now.

ABOUT THE AUTHOR

Coming from a family of seven children, Ashley McCoury learned to use her imagination at a very young age and never quite got over it. Ashley's large immediate and extended family play an important role in her life, and through her family's many ups and downs, she saw how important those connections are to mankind's well-being as a whole.

Having many different roles in life—wife, mother, real estate agent, business owner, and now writer—has given Ashley perspective on the world that not many see. With her deep love of reading and adventure, Ashley was an aspiring author from a young age.

Ashley lives outside of the city limits in West Texas. She has three pretty awesome kids and a wonderful husband who keeps her laughing.

CPSIA information can be obtained
at www.ICGtesting.com
Printed in the USA
BVHW051318020822
643615BV00021B/30

9 781646 708406